M

ROYAL BLOOD

ROYAL BLOOD

RHYS BOWEN

THORNDIKE
CHIVERS

This Large Print edition is published by Thorndike Press, Waterville, Maine, USA and by AudioGO Ltd, Bath, England.

Thorndike Press, a part of Gale, Cengage Learning.

A Royal Spyness Mystery.
The Edgar® name is a registered service mark of the Mystery Writers of America, Inc.

LIBRARY OF CONGRESS CATALOGING-IN-PUBLICATION DATA

Bowen, Rhys.
  Royal blood / by Rhys Bowen.
    p. cm. — (Thorndike Press large print core)
  "A Royal spyness mystery."
  ISBN-13: 978-1-4104-3324-4
  ISBN-10: 1-4104-3324-2
  1. Vampires—Fiction. 2. Aristocracy (Social class)—Fiction. 3. Transylvania (Romania)—Fiction. 4. Weddings—Fiction. 5. Large type books. I. Title.
  PR6052.O848R679 2011
  823'.914—dc22
                                2010038784

BRITISH LIBRARY CATALOGUING-IN-PUBLICATION DATA AVAILABLE

Published in 2011 in the U.S. by arrangement with The Berkley Publishing Group, a member of Penguin Group (USA) Inc.
Published in 2011 in the U.K. by arrangement with The Berkley Publishing Group, a division of Penguin Group (USA) Inc.

U.K. Hardcover: 978 1 408 49397 7 (Chivers Large Print)
U.K. Softcover: 978 1 408 49398 4 (Camden Large Print)

Printed in the United States of America
1 2 3 4 5 6 7 15 14 13 12 11

This book is dedicated to my
sister-in-law Mary Vyvan,
who always makes us so welcome in her
lovely Cornish manor house
where Lady Georgiana would feel
completely at home.

ACKNOWLEDGMENTS

Thanks as always to my brilliant team at Berkley: my editor, Jackie Cantor, and publicist, Megan Swartz; to my agents Meg Ruley and Christina Hogrebe and to my at-home advisors and editors Clare, Jane and John.

CHAPTER 1

Rannoch House
Belgrave Square
London W.1.
Tuesday, November 8, 1932
Fog for days. Trapped alone in London house.
Shall go mad soon.

November in London is utterly bloody. Yes, I know a lady is not supposed to use such language but I can think of no other way to describe the damp, bone-chilling pea-souper fog that had descended upon Belgrave Square for the past week. Our London home, Rannoch House, is not exactly warm and jolly at the best of times, but at least it's bearable when the family is in residence, servants abound, and fires are burning merrily in all the fireplaces. But with just me in the house and not a servant in sight, there was simply no way of keeping warm. I don't want you to think that I am a weak and delicate sort of person who usually feels the cold. In fact at home at Castle Rannoch in Scotland I'm as hearty as the best of them. I go out for long rides on frosty mornings; I am used to sleeping with the windows open at all times. But this London cold was different from anything I had experienced. It cut one to the very bone. I was tempted to stay in bed all day.

Not that there was much reason for me to get out of bed at the moment, and it was only Nanny's strict upbringing that did not allow bed rest for anything less than double pneumonia that made me get up in the mornings, put on three layers of jumpers and rush down to the comparative warmth of the kitchen.

This particular morning I was huddled in the kitchen, sipping a cup of tea, when I heard the sound of the morning post dropping onto the doormat in the upstairs hall. Since hardly anyone knew I was in London, this was a big event. I raced upstairs and retrieved not one but two letters from the front doormat. Two letters, how exciting, I thought, and then I recognized my sister-in-law's spidery handwriting on one of them. Oh, crikey, what on earth did she want? Fig wasn't the sort of person who wrote letters when not necessary. She begrudged wasting the postage stamp.

The second letter made my heart lurch even more. It bore the royal coat of arms and came from Buckingham Palace. I didn't even wait to reach the warmth of the kitchen. I tore it open instantly. It was from Her Majesty the queen's personal secretary.

Dear Lady Georgiana,
Her Majesty Queen Mary asks me to convey her warmest wishes and hopes you might be free to join her at the palace for luncheon on Thursday, November 8th. She requests that perhaps you could come a little early, say around eleven forty-five, as she has a matter of some importance she wishes to discuss with you.

"Oh, golly," I muttered. I'd have to get out of the habit of such girlish expletives. I might even have to acquire some four-letter words for strictly personal use. You'd think that an invitation to Buckingham Palace for luncheon with the queen would be an honor. Actually it happened all too frequently for my liking. You see, King George is my second cousin and since I'd been living in London Queen Mary had come up with a succession of little tasks for me. Well, not-so-little tasks, actually. Things like spy-

11

ing on the Prince of Wales's new American lady friend. And a few months ago she foisted a visiting German princess and her retinue on me — rather awkward when I had no servants and no money for food. But of course one does not say no to the queen.

You might also wonder why someone related to the royals came to be living alone with no servants and no money for food. The sad truth is that our branch of the family is quite penniless. My father gambled away most of his fortune and lost the rest in the great crash of '29. My brother, Binky, the current duke, lives on the family estate in Scotland. I suppose I could live with him, but his dear wife, Fig, had made it clear that I wasn't really wanted there.

I looked at Fig's letter and sighed. What on earth could she want? It was too cold to stand in the front hall any longer. I carried it down to the kitchen and took up my position near the stove before opening it.

Dear Georgiana,
I hope you are well and that the London weather is more clement than the current gales we are experiencing. This is to advise you of our plans. We have decided to come down to the London house for the winter this year. Binky is still weak

after being confined to bed for so long after his accident, and Podge has had one nasty cold after another, so I think a little warmth and culture are in order. We plan to arrive at Rannoch House within the next week or so. Binky has told me of your housekeeping prowess, so I see no need to pay for the additional expense of sending servants on ahead when I know you'll do a splendid job of getting the house ready for us. I can count on you, Georgiana, can't I? And when we arrive, Binky thinks we should hold a couple of parties for you, even though I did remind him that consider-able amounts were already spent on your season. He is anxious to see you properly settled and I agree it would be one less worry for the whole family at this trying time. I hope you will do your part, Georgiana, and not snub the young men we produce for you as you did poor Prince Siegfried, who really seemed a most well-mannered young man and may even inherit a kingdom someday. May I remind you that you are not get-ting any younger. By the time a woman reaches twenty-four, which you are ap-proaching, she is considered to be on

13

the shelf, remember. Her bloom has faded.

So please have the place ready for us when we arrive. We shall only be bringing the minimum number of servants with us as travel is so expensive these days. Your brother asks me to convey his warmest sentiments.

Your devoted sister-in-law,
Hilda Rannoch

I was surprised she hadn't also put "(Duchess of)." Yes, Hilda was her given name, although everyone else called her Fig. Frankly if I'd been called Hilda I'd have thought that even Fig was preferable. The image of Fig arriving in the near future galvanized me into action. I had to find something to do with myself so that I would not be stuck in the house being lectured about what a burden I was to the family.

A job would be a terrific idea, but I had pretty much given up all hope of that. Some of those unemployed men standing on street corners held all kinds of degrees and qualifications. My education at a frightfully posh finishing school in Switzerland had only equipped me to walk around with a book on my head, speak good French and know where to seat a bishop at a dinner party. I had been trained for marriage, nothing else. Besides, most forms of employment would be frowned upon for someone in my position. It would be letting down the family firm to be seen behind the counter in Woolworths or pulling a pint at a local pub.

An invitation to somewhere far away — that's what I needed. Preferably an invitation to Timbuktu or at least a villa on the Mediterranean. That would also get me out of any of the queen's little suggestions for me. "I'm so sorry, ma'am. I'd love to spy on Mrs. Simpson for you, but I'm expected in Monte Carlo at the end of the week."

There was only one person in London I could run to in such dire circumstances — my old school chum Belinda Warburton-Stoke. Belinda is one of those people who always manage to fall on their feet — or rather flat on her back, in her case. She was always being invited to house parties and to cruises on yachts — because she's awfully naughty and sexy, you see, unlike me, who hasn't had a chance to be either naughty or sexy.

I'd paid a visit to Belinda's little mews cottage in Knightsbridge when I returned to London from Castle Rannoch in Scotland a couple of weeks ago, only to find the place shut up and no sign of Belinda. I supposed that she had gone to Italy with her latest beau, a gorgeous Italian count, who was unfortunately engaged to someone else. There was a possibility that she had returned, and the situation was urgent enough to warrant my venturing out into the worst sort of fog. If anyone knew how to rescue me from an impending Fig, it would be Belinda. So I wrapped myself in layers of scarves and stepped out into the pea-souper. Goodness but it was unearthly out there. All sounds were muffled and the air was permeated with the smoke of thousands of coal fires, leaving a disgusting metallic taste in my mouth. The houses around Belgrave Square had been swallowed up into the murk and I could just make out the railings around the gardens in the middle. Nobody else seemed to be out as I made my way carefully around the square.

I almost gave up several times, telling myself that bright young things like Belinda wouldn't possibly be in London in weather like this and I was wasting my time. But I kept going doggedly onward. We Rannochs are known for not giving up, whatever the odds. So I thought of Robert Bruce Rannoch, continuing to scale the Heights of Abraham in Quebec after being shot several times and arriving at the top with more holes in him than a colander, managing to kill five of the enemy before he died. Not a cheerful story, I suppose. Most stories of my gallant ancestors end with the ancestor in question expiring.

It took me a while to realize I was hopelessly lost. Belinda's mews was only a few streets away from me and I had been walking for ages. I knew I'd had to move cautiously, one small step at a time, with my hand touching the railings in front of houses for security, but I must have gone wrong somewhere.

Don't panic, I said to myself. Eventually I would come to a place I recognized and I'd be all right. The problem was that there was nobody else about and it was impossible to read the street signs. They too had vanished into the murk above my head. I had no choice but to keep going. Surely I'd eventually come to Knightsbridge and Harrods. I'd see lights in shop windows. Harrods wouldn't close for a little thing like fog. There would be enough people in London who had to have their foie gras and their truffles no matter what the weather. But Harrods never appeared. At last I came to what seemed to be some gardens. I couldn't decide what they would be. Surely I couldn't have crossed Knightsbridge and found myself beside Hyde Park?

I began to feel horribly uneasy. That's when I noticed the footsteps behind me — slow, steady footsteps, keeping exact pace with mine. I turned but couldn't see anyone. Don't be so silly, I said to myself. The footsteps could only be a strange echo produced by the fog. I started walking again, stopped suddenly and heard the footsteps continue another couple of beats before they too stopped. I started walking faster and faster, my mind conjuring the sort of things that happened in the fog in Sherlock Holmes stories. I stumbled down some kind of curb, kept going and suddenly felt a great yawning openness ahead of me before I bumped into some kind of hard barrier.

Where the devil was I? I felt the barrier again, trying to picture it. It was rough, cold stone. Was there a wall around the Serpentine in Hyde Park? I felt a cold dampness rising to meet me and smelled an unpleasant rotting vegetation sort of smell. And a lapping sound. I leaned forward trying to identify the sound I could hear below me, wondering if I should climb over the wall to escape from whomever was following me. Then suddenly I nearly jumped out of my skin as a hand grabbed my shoulder from behind.

CHAPTER 2

"I wouldn't do that, miss," a deep Cockney voice said.

"Do what?" I spun around and could just make out the shape of a policeman's helmet.

"I know what you was going to do," he said. "You were about to jump into the river, weren't you? I was following you. I saw you about to climb over the balustrade. You were going to end it all."

I was still digesting the information that I had somehow walked all the way to the Thames, in quite the wrong direction, and it took a minute for the penny to drop. "End it all? Absolutely not, Constable."

He put his hand on my shoulder again, gently this time. "Come on, love. You can tell me the truth. Why else would you be out on a day like this and trying to climb into the river? Don't feel so bad. I see it all the time these days, my dear. This depression has got everyone down, but I'm here to

20

tell you that life is still worth living, no matter what. Come back to the station with me and I'll make you a nice cup of tea."

I didn't know whether to laugh or be indignant. The latter won out. "Look here, Officer," I said, "I was only trying to make my way to my friend's house and I must have taken a wrong turn. I had no idea I was anywhere near the river."

"If you say so, miss," he said.

I was tempted to tell him that it was "my lady" and not "miss," but I was feeling so uncomfortable now that I just wanted to get away. "If you could just direct me back in the direction of Knightsbridge," I said. "Or Belgravia. I came from Belgrave Square."

"Blimey, then you are out of your way. You're by Chelsea Bridge." He took my arm and escorted me back across the Embankment, then up what he identified as Sloane Street to Sloane Square. I refused his renewed offer of a cup of tea at the police station and told him I'd be all right now I knew which street I was on.

"If I was you, I'd go straight home," he said. "This is no weather to be out in. Talk to your friend on the old blow piece."

Of course he was right, but I only used the telephone in emergencies, as Fig objected to paying the bill and I had no money to do so. I realized it would have been more sensible today, but actually it was human company I craved. It's awfully lonely camping out in a big house without even my maid to talk to and I'm the sort of person who likes company. So I set out from Sloane Square and eventually made my way to Belinda's mews without further incident, only to find it was as I suspected and she wasn't home.

I tried to retrace my steps to Belgrave Square, really wishing I'd taken the policeman's advice and gone straight home. Then through the fog I heard a noise I recognized — a train whistle. So some trains were still running in spite of the fog, and Victoria Station was straight ahead of me. If I found the station I'd be able to orient myself easily enough. Suddenly I came upon a line of people, mostly men, standing dejectedly, scarves over their mouths, hands thrust into their pockets. I couldn't imagine what they were doing until I smelled the boiled cabbage odor and realized that they were lining up for the soup kitchen at the station.

That was when I had a brilliant idea. I could volunteer to help out at the soup kitchen. If I volunteered there the family would approve, in fact the queen herself had suggested that I do some charity work, and at least I'd get one square meal a day until Binky and Fig arrived. I hadn't been able to afford decent food for ages. In fact there was a horrid empty sick feeling in my stomach at this moment. I started to walk past the line to try to find somebody in charge when a hand shot out and grabbed me.

" 'Ere, where do you think you're going?" a big, burly man demanded. "Trying to cut in, weren't you? You go to the end and take your turn like the rest of us."

"But I was only going to speak to the people who run the kitchen," I said. "I was going to volunteer here."

"Garn — I've heard every excuse in the book. Go on, to the back of the queue."

I turned away, mortified, and was about to slink off home when the man behind him stepped out. "Look at her, Harry. She's all skin and bone and anyone can see she's a lady, fallen on hard times. You come in front of me, ducks. You look like you're about to pass out if you don't get a good meal soon."

I was about to decline this kind offer but I caught a whiff of that soup. You can tell how hungry I was when boiled cabbage actually smelled good to me. What harm could there be in sampling the wares before I offered my services? I gave the man a grateful smile and slipped into the line. We inched closer and closer and finally into the station itself. It had an unnaturally deserted air, but I heard the hiss of escaping steam from an engine and a disembodied voice announced the departure of the boat train to Dover, awaking in me a wistful longing. To be on the boat train to Dover and the Continent. Wouldn't that be ripping?

But my journey terminated a few yards ahead at an oilcloth-covered table to one side of the platforms. I was handed a plate and a spoon. A hunk of bread was dumped onto the plate and then I moved on to one of the great pots full of stew. I could see pieces of meat and carrot floating in a rich brown gravy. I watched the ladle come up and over my plate, then it froze there, in midair.

I looked up in annoyance and found myself staring into Darcy O'Mara's alarming eyes. His dark, curly hair was even more unruly than usual and he was wearing a large royal blue fisherman's sweater that went perfectly with the blue of his eyes. In short he looked as gorgeous as ever. I started to smile.

"Georgie!" He could not have sounded more shocked if I'd been standing there with no clothes on. Actually, knowing Darcy, he might have enjoyed seeing me standing in Victoria Station naked.

I felt myself going beet red and tried to be breezy. "What-ho, Darcy. Long time no see."

"Georgie, what were you thinking of?" He snatched the plate away from me as if it were red-hot.

"It's not how it looks, Darcy." I attempted a laugh that didn't come off well. "I came down here to see if I could help out at the soup kitchen and one of the men in line thought I was coming for food and insisted I take his place. He was being so kind I didn't like to disillusion him."

While I was talking I was conscious of mutterings in the line behind me. Good smells were obviously reaching them too. "Get a move on, then," said an angry voice. Darcy took off the large blue apron he had been wearing. "Take over for me, Wilson, will you?" he called to a fellow helper. "I have to get this young lady out of here before she faints."

And he almost leaped over the table to grab me, taking my arm and firmly steering me away.

"What are you doing?" I demanded, conscious of all those eyes staring at me.

"Getting you out of here before someone

recognizes you, of course," he hissed in my ear.

"I don't know what you're making such a big fuss about," I said. "If you hadn't reacted in that way nobody would have noticed me. And I really was coming to offer my services, you know."

"You may well have been, but it is not unknown for gentlemen of the press to prowl the big London stations in the hope of snapping a celebrity," he said in that gravelly voice with just the trace of an Irish brogue, while he still propelled me along at a rapid pace. "It's not hard to recognize you, my lady. I did so myself in a London tea shop, remember? And can you imagine what a field day they'd have with that? Member of the royal family among the down-and-outs? 'From Buckingham Palace to Beggar'? Think of the embarrassment it would cause your royal relatives."

"I don't see why I should worry about what they think," I said. "They don't pay to feed me."

We had emerged from the soot of the station through a side door. He let go of my arm and stared hard at me. "You really wanted that disgusting slop they call soup?"

"If you must know, yes, I really did. Since my last attempt at a career last summer —

a career you cut short, by the way — I haven't earned any money and, the last time I heard, one needs money to buy food."

His expression changed and softened. "My poor, dear girl. Why didn't you let someone know? Why didn't you tell me?"

"Darcy, I never know where to find you. Besides, you seem to be broke yourself most of the time."

"But unlike you I know how to survive," he said. "I am currently minding a friend's house in Kensington. He has an exceptionally good wine cellar and has left half his staff in residence, so I don't do badly for myself. Are you still all alone at Rannoch House, then?"

"All alone," I said. Now that the shock of seeing him in such upsetting circumstances had worn off, and he was looking at me tenderly, I felt as if I might cry.

He steered me to the edge of the curb and found a taxi sitting there.

"Do you think you could manage to find Belgrave Square?" he asked.

"I could give it a ruddy good try, mate," the taxi driver replied, obviously only too glad to earn a fare. "At least we won't have to worry about traffic jams, will we?"

Darcy bundled me inside and we took off.

"Poor little Lady Georgie." He raised his

hand to my cheek and stroked it gently, un-nerving me even more. "You really aren't equipped to survive in the big world, are you?"

"I'm trying to," I said. "It's not easy."

"The last I heard of you, you were with your brother at Castle Rannoch," he said, "which I agree is not the jolliest place in the world but at least you get three square meals a day there. What in God's name made you leave and come down here at this time of year?"

"One word: Fig. She reverted to her usual nasty self and kept dropping hints about too many mouths to feed and having to go without her Fortnum's jam."

"It's your ancestral home, not hers," he said. "Surely your brother is grateful for what you've done for them, isn't he? Their son would be dead and so might Binky be, had it not been for you."

"You know Binky. He's a likeable enough chap, but he's too easygoing. Fig walks all over him. And he's been laid up with that horrid infection in his ankle; it has left him really weak. So all in all it seemed more sensible to bolt. I hoped I'd be able to find some kind of work."

"There is no work to be had," he said. "Nobody is making money, apart from the

28

bookies at the racecourses and the gambling clubs. Not that they make money out of me." He gave me a smug grin. "I won fifty quid at the steeplechases at Newmarket last week. I might not know much but I do know my horses. If my father hadn't sold the racing stable, I'd be home in Ireland running it right now. As it is, I'm a rolling stone like you."

"But you do work secretly, don't you, Darcy?" I said.

"Whatever gave you that idea?" He shot me a challenging smile.

"You disappear for weeks at a time and don't tell me where you're going."

"I might have a hot little piece on the side in Casablanca or Jamaica," he said.

"Darcy, you're incorrigible." I slapped his hand. He made a grab at mine and held it firmly.

"There are certain things one does not discuss in taxicabs," he said.

"I think this is Belgrave Square." The taxi driver pushed open the glass partition. "Which house?"

"In the middle on the far side," Darcy said.

We came to a halt outside Rannoch House. Darcy got out and came around to open the door for me. "Look, there's little point in going out anywhere tonight in this fog," he said. "It will be impossible to get a cab to drive us anywhere after dark. But it's supposed to ease up a little tomorrow. So I'll pick you up at seven."

"Where are we going?"

"To have a good meal, of course," he said. "Posh frock."

"We're not gate-crashing someone's wedding, are we?" I asked, because we had done that the first time we went anywhere together.

"Of course not." He held my hand as I started up the steps to the front door. "Society of Chartered Accountants dinner this time." Then he looked at my face and laughed. "Pulling your leg, old thing."

CHAPTER 3

Rannoch House
Wednesday, November 9
Fog has lifted. Dinner with Darcy tonight.
Hooray.

I spent the day working on getting the house ready for impending doom. I took off dust sheets, swept carpets and made beds. I left laying the fires for another day. I didn't want my hair to be full of coal dust when I went out with Darcy. You see how frightfully domestic I had become. I kept darting over to the window to make sure the fog wasn't creeping in again, but a stiff breeze had sprung up and by the time I started to get ready for my date with Darcy, it had started to rain.

Having been home to Scotland, my posh frocks had been cleaned and pressed by my maid. I chose bottle green velvet and even attempted to tame my hair into sleek waves. Then I decided to go the whole hog and attacked my face with lipstick, rouge and mascara. I topped it with a beaver stole that was one of my mother's castoffs and was actually looking quite civilized by seven. Then of course I worried that Darcy wouldn't show up, but he was there on the dot, with a taxi waiting. We sped along Pall Mall, around Trafalgar Square and into the jumble of lanes behind Charing Cross Road.

"Where are we going?" I asked cautiously, as this part of the city seemed poorly lit and not too savory.

"My dear, I am taking you to my lair to have my way with you," Darcy said in a mock villain voice. "Actually we're going to Rules."

"Rules?"

"Surely you must have eaten at Rules — oldest restaurant in London. Good solid British food."

The taxi pulled up outside an unprepossessing leaded-glass window. We went inside and a delightful warmth met us. The walls were rich wooden paneling, the tablecloths starched and white, and the cutlery gleamed. A maitre d' in tails met us at the door.

"Mr. O'Mara, sir. How delightful to see you again," he said, whisking us through the restaurant to a table in a far corner. "And how is his lordship?"

"As well as can be expected, Banks," Darcy said. "You heard that we had to sell the house and the racing stable to Americans and my father now lives in the lodge."

"I did hear something of the kind, sir. These are hard times. Nothing makes sense anymore. Except Rules. Nothing changes here, sir. And I believe this must be the old Duke of Rannoch's daughter. It's an honor to have you here, my lady. Your late father was a frequent visitor. He is much missed."

He pulled out a chair for me while Darcy slid onto a red leather bench.

"Everyone who is part of London history has eaten here." Darcy indicated the walls, lined with caricatures, signatures, and theatrical programs. And indeed I could make out the names of Charles Dickens, Benjamin Disraeli, John Galsworthy, even Nell Gwyn, I believe.

Darcy studied the menu while I was gazing around the walls, trying to see if my mother or father had made it into the array of signed photographs.

"I think tonight we start with a dozen Whitstable oysters each," he said. "Then for soup it has to be the potato leek. You do it so well. Then some smoked haddock and of course the pheasant."

"An admirable choice, sir," the waiter said, "and may I suggest a very fine claret to go with the pheasant? And perhaps a bottle of champagne to accompany the oysters?"

"Why not?" Darcy said. "Sounds perfect to me."

"Darcy," I hissed as he went away, "this is going to cost a fortune."

"I told you, I won fifty pounds on the gee-gees last week," he said.

"But you shouldn't spend it all at once."

"Why not?" He laughed. "What else is money for?"

"You should keep some for when you're hard up."

"Nonsense. Something always turns up. Carpe diem, young Georgie."

"I didn't study Latin," I said. "Only French and useless things like piano and etiquette."

"It means seize the day. Don't ever put off anything you want to do because you're worried about tomorrow. It's my motto. I live by it. You should too."

"I wish I could," I said. "You seem to fall on your feet, but it's not that easy for a girl like me who has no sensible education. I'm already considered a hopeless case — twenty-two and on the shelf."

I suppose I hoped he'd say something about marrying him someday, but instead he said, "Oh, I expect a likely princeling will show up in good time."

"Darcy! I've already turned down Prince Siegfried, much to the annoyance of the family. They're all equally bad. And they are being assassinated with remarkable frequency."

"Well, wouldn't you want to assassinate Siegfried?" he asked with a laugh. "I know I would. My fingers are itching for his throat each time I see him. But some of the Bulgarians are okay. I was at school with Nicholas and he's the heir to the throne. He was a damned good scrum half on the rugby team."

"And to a man, that makes him good husband material?"

"Of course."

The champagne bottle opened with a satisfying pop and our glasses were filled. Darcy raised his to me. "Here's to life," he said. "May it be filled with fun and adventure."

My glass clinked against his. "To life," I whispered.

I am not a big drinker. After the third glass of champagne I was feeling decidedly carefree. The soup somehow came and went. So did the smoked haddock. A bottle of claret was opened to go with the pheasant, which appeared swimming in rich red-brown gravy with tiny pearl onions and mushrooms around it. I found myself deciding that I'd been stupid, trying to earn my own living. Life was for having fun and adventure. No more gloom and doom.

I finished every morsel on my plate, then worked my way through the bread and butter pudding and a glass of port. I was feeling content with the world as the taxi whisked us back to Rannoch House. Darcy escorted me up the steps and helped me put the key in the door when I was having trouble locating the lock. At the back of my brain a whisper was saying that I was probably just a little drunk while another whisper added that I probably shouldn't be letting Darcy come into the house late at night when I was all alone.

"Holy Mother of God, but it's cold and bleak in here," Darcy said as we closed the front door behind us. "Is there nowhere warm in this confounded place?"

"Only the bedroom," I said. "I try to keep a fire going in there."

"The bedroom. Good idea," he said and steered me toward the staircase. We ascended together, his arm around my waist.

I wasn't conscious of taking the steps. I was half floating, intoxicated with the wine and his closeness.

The last embers of a fire still glowed in the bedroom fireplace and it felt comfortably warm after the frigidity of the rest of the house.

"Ah, that's better," Darcy said.

I saw the bed before me and flung myself down on it. "Ah, my bed. Bliss," I said.

Darcy stood looking down at me with amusement. "I must say, that wine certainly has done wonders for your inhibitions."

"As you very well knew it would," I said, wagging a finger at him. "I know your evil intentions, Mr. O'Mara. Don't think I can't see through them."

"And yet I haven't noticed your telling me to go."

"You just said that the purpose of life was to have fun and adventure," I said, kicking off one shoe so violently that it flew across the room. "And you're right. I've been miserable and boring for too long. Twenty-two years old and a boring virgin. What is the point of that?"

"No point at all," Darcy said softly, removing his overcoat and draping it over the back of a chair. His jacket followed and then he loosened his tie.

"Don't leave me all alone here, Darcy," I said in what I hoped was a seductive voice.

"I've never been known to turn down an invitation like that," Darcy said. He sat to take off his shoes, then he perched on the edge of the bed. "You'll make that lovely dress all rumpled. Let me help you off with it, my lady." He lifted me into a sitting position, which was no longer easy, as my limbs didn't seem to want to obey me and I have to confess that the room was swinging around just a little. I felt his hands down my back as he undid the hooks on my dress. I felt it swishing over my head and then the cold air on the silk of my underslip.

"I'm cold." I shivered. "Come and keep me warm."

"To hear is to obey," he said and took me into his arms. I turned my face toward him and his lips found mine. The kiss was so intense and demanding that I found it hard to breathe. His tongue was exploring my mouth and I was floating on a pink cloud of ecstasy.

This is bliss, I said to myself. This is what I've been waiting for.

I was off on that pink cloud, flying over fields with Darcy beside me until I realized that his lips were no longer on mine and I was feeling cold again. I opened my eyes.

38

Darcy was sitting up on the side of the bed, putting on his shoes.

"What's the matter?" I asked blearily. "Don't you want me anymore, Darcy? You've been trying to get me into bed since we met and now here we are in a big empty house and you're going?"

"You fell asleep," he said. "And you're plastered."

"I confess to being just teeny bit tipsy, but wasn't that what you were planning?"

"That was my idea when I came up with the oysters and the champagne, but I find I've got a moral streak I didn't know I had, when it comes to you." He laughed almost bitterly. "When I make love to you for the first time, my sweet Georgie, I want you to be awake and fully aware of what you're doing. I don't want you to fall asleep in the middle of things, and I don't want you to think that I took advantage of you."

"I wouldn't think that," I said. I sat up. "Why is everything going round and round suddenly?"

"Come on," he said. "Let me get you into bed. Alone, I mean. I'll stop by in the morning. You'll probably have a devil of a headache."

He helped me out of my slip. "My, but you've got a lovely body," he said. "I must want my head examined."

Suddenly he froze. "What was that?"

"What?"

"It sounded like the front door shutting. Nobody else is here at the moment, are they?"

"No, I'm all alone." I sat up, listening. I thought I could make out the sound of footsteps and voices down below.

"I'm going to see what's going on," Darcy said. He went out onto the landing, while I reached for my dressing gown on the hook behind the door. It wasn't easy to stand up at this stage and I had to hold on to the door to steady myself. Then I heard the words that sobered me up instantly.

"Binky, Fig, you're back."

CHAPTER 4

Rannoch House
November 9 and 10

I staggered out onto the landing, conscious that the floor kept rising up to meet me and that the stairs were floating out into infinity. I clutched the banister as I made my way down the first flight. In the hallway at the bottom of the second flight, standing on the checkered black-and-white marble, were two blobs in fur coats with pink things on top. Gradually they swam into focus as two horrified faces with mouths open.

"Good God, O'Mara, what are you doing here?" Binky demanded.

"I should think that even for someone with your limited imagination it's pretty clear what he was doing here," Fig said in an outraged voice as she stared up at me. "How dare you, Georgiana. You have betrayed our trust. We graciously offer the use of our house and you turn it into a den of

— den of — what's it a den of, Binky?"

"Lions?" Binky said.

Fig sighed and rolled her eyes. "Utterly hopeless," she muttered.

"Iniquity?" Darcy suggested. He seemed to be the only person not in the least put out by this. I was still making my way unsteadily down the stairs and didn't trust myself to let go of the banister. I didn't trust my voice, either.

"Precisely," Fig snapped. "A den of iniquity, Georgiana. Thank heavens we didn't bring little Podge with us to witness this. It might have scarred him for life."

"To know that normal people might want to have sex occasionally?" Darcy asked.

Fig put her hand to her throat at the mention of the word "sex." "Say, something, Binky," Fig said, pushing him forward. "Speak to your sister."

"What-ho, Georgie," he said. "Good to see you again."

"No, you idiot, I meant speak to her." Fig was almost dancing around in anger by now. "Tell her that her behavior is simply not on. It's not the way a Rannoch behaves. She's turning into her mother, after all we've done for her and all that money we've spent on her education."

"Now look here," Darcy said, but she

leaped at him.

"You look here, Mr. O'Mara." Fig took a menacing step toward him, but Darcy stood his ground bravely. "I suppose you're to blame for this. Georgie has had a sheltered upbringing. She is inexperienced in the ways of the world and certainly lacking in judgment to allow you into the house when she is all alone. I think you had better leave us before I say any more, although I fear the damage is already done. Prince Siegfried would certainly not want her now."

For some reason I found this very funny. I sank onto the stair and started giggling uncontrollably.

"Don't worry, I'm going," Darcy said. "But I'd like to remind you that Georgie is over twenty-one and it's up to her what she does."

"Not in our house," Fig said.

"It's the home of the Rannochs, isn't it? And she's been a Rannoch a bally sight longer than you have."

"But it now belongs to the current duke and that is my husband," Fig said in her most frosty "I'm a duchess and you're not" voice. "Georgiana is living here on our grace and favor."

"With no heat and no servants. I don't consider that much of a favor, Your Grace,"

43

Darcy said. "Especially when your dear husband, the duke, might have been lying six feet under by now in the family plot, and your little son beside him, had it not been for Georgie. It seems to me you owe her more than a little thanks."

"Well, of course we're grateful for everything," Binky said. "Most grateful."

"Of course we are. It's her morals we're concerned about," Fig added quickly, "and the reputation of Rannoch House. Strange men going in and out at all hours will be noticed in Belgrave Square."

The choice of words made me start giggling again. Fig looked up the stairs and focused on me. I had just realized that my robe was not quite tied and I had nothing on underneath it. I tried to pull it around me to save what was left of my dignity.

"Georgiana, are you drunk?" Fig demanded.

"Just a little," I confessed and clamped my lips together so that I didn't giggle again.

"The champagne went to her head, I'm afraid," Darcy said, "which is why I brought her home and I thought it wise to put her to bed in case she fell and hurt herself, since she has no maid to help her. So if you want to know the sordid details of what happened, I put her to bed, she promptly fell asleep and I was just leaving."

"Oh," Fig said, the wind taken out of her sails. "I wish I could believe you, Mr. O'Mara."

"Believe what you like," Darcy said. He looked up at me. "So I bid you good night, Georgie," he said and blew me a kiss up the stairs. "See you soon. Take care and don't let her boss you around. Remember you have royal blood. She doesn't."

He gave me a wink, patted Binky on the shoulder and let himself out.

"Well, really," Fig said, breaking a long silence.

"It's bally cold in here," Binky said. "I don't suppose there's a fire ready for us in our bedroom, is there?"

"No, there isn't." I had rallied enough from my drunken stupor to be coherent, and more than a little angry. "You said you were planning to come in the next week or so, not the next day or so. And why is it that you are traveling without servants?"

"We're just on a flying visit this time, because Binky has secured an appointment with a Harley Street specialist for his ankle," Fig said, "and I also wish to consult with a London doctor, so we thought we could save the expense of bringing servants, since Binky told me what a whiz you had turned out to be around the house. Obviously he was exaggerating as usual."

I stood up, still a little uncertainly. My bare feet were freezing on the stairs. "I don't think that my father would expect me to act as a chambermaid in the family home," I said. "I'm going back to bed."

With that I turned and made my way back up the stairs. It would have been a grand exit had I not tripped over my dressing gown cord and gone sprawling across the first landing, revealing, I rather suspect, a hint of bare bottom to the world.

"Whoops," I said. I righted myself and hauled myself up the second flight. Then I climbed into bed and curled into a tight little ball. I had no hot water bottles to place around me but I wasn't going downstairs again for anything. And it did give me a certain sense of satisfaction knowing that Fig was about to climb into an equally icy bed.

I opened my eyes to cold gray light, then promptly closed them again. Darcy was right. I did have a hangover. My head was throbbing like billy-o. I wondered what time it was. Half past ten, according to the little alarm clock on my chest of drawers. Then the full details of the previous night came

46

back to me. Oh, Lord, that meant that Binky and Fig were in the house and by now they would have discovered that I had nothing to eat in the kitchen. I scrambled into a jumper and skirt and made my way downstairs, almost as shakily as the night before.

I was about to push open the baize door that led down to the kitchen and servants' quarters when I heard voices coming from my right. Binky and Fig were apparently in the morning room.

"It's all right for you," I heard Fig's voice with teeth chattering just a little. "You can go to your club where you'll be comfortable enough, but what about me? I can't stay here."

"It's only for two more nights, old thing," Binky said. "And it is important that you see that doctor, isn't it?"

"I suppose so, but being as cold as this isn't doing me any good. We'll just have to check into a hotel and never mind the expense. Surely we can still afford Claridge's for a couple of nights."

"You'll feel better after a spot of breakfast," Binky said. "It's about time Georgie woke up, isn't it?"

At that point I poked my head around the door. Both Binky and Fig looked haggard and grumpy, sitting wrapped in their fur coats. They also looked rather unkempt without a maid and a valet to dress them.

The atmosphere as Fig spotted me was frigid in more ways than one, but Binky managed a smile. "Ah, you're up at last, Georgie. I say, it's bally freezing in here, isn't it? I don't suppose there's any chance of a fire?"

"Later, maybe," I said. "It takes a lot of work to light a fire, you know. A lot of scrabbling in the coal hole. Perhaps you'd care to help me."

Fig shuddered as if I'd said a rude word, but Binky went on, "Then maybe you'd be good enough to cook us a spot of breakfast. That will warm us up nicely, won't it, Fig?"

"I was just about to make some tea and toast," I said.

"How about a couple of eggs?" Binky asked hopefully.

"No eggs, I'm afraid."

"Bacon? Sausage? Kidneys?"

"Toast," I said. "One cannot buy food without money, Binky."

"But, I mean to say . . . ," he sputtered. "Dash it all, Georgie, you haven't actually been reduced to living on tea and toast, have you?"

"Where do you think the money might have come from, dear brother? I have no

48

job. I have no inheritance. I have no family support. When Fig says she has no money, she means she can no longer afford Fortnum's jam. I mean I can't afford any jam. That's the difference."

"Well, I'm blowed," Binky said. "Then why the deuce don't you come back and live at Castle Rannoch? At least we have enough to eat up there, don't we, Fig?"

"Your wife made it quite clear that I was one mouth too many," I said. "Besides, I don't want to be a burden. I want to make my own way in the world. I want a life of my own. It's just that it's so horribly hard at the moment."

"You should have married Prince Siegfried," Fig said. "That's what girls of your station are supposed to do. That is what your royal relatives wanted you to do. Most girls would have given their right arm to become a princess."

"Prince Siegfried is a loathsome toad," I said. "I intend to marry for love."

"Ridiculous notion," Fig snapped. "And if you're thinking of your Mr. O'Mara, then you can think again." Fig was now warming to her subject. "I happen to know that he doesn't have a penny. The family is destitute. Why, they've even had to sell the family seat. There's no way he's ever going to be able to support a wife — if he ever intends to settle down, that is. So you're wasting your time in that direction." When I didn't answer her she went on, "It's all about duty, Georgiana. One knows one's duty and one does it, isn't that right, Binky?"

"Quite right, old thing," Binky said distractedly.

Fig gave him such a frosty stare that it's a wonder he didn't turn into an instant icicle. "Although some of us are lucky enough to find love and happiness once we are married, isn't that so, Binky?"

Binky was staring out of the window at the fog creeping in again across Belgrave Square. "How about that cup of tea, Georgie?"

"You'd better come down to the kitchen to drink it," I said. "It's warmer down there."

They followed me like children behind the Pied Piper. I lit the gas stove and put the kettle on while they watched me as if I were a conjurer doing a spectacular magic trick. Then I put the last of the bread onto the grill to make toast. Binky watched me and sighed. "For God's sake, Fig, call Fortnum's and ask them to deliver a hamper. Tell them it's an emergency."

"If you give me some money, I'll be happy

to stock up the kitchen again for you — and more economically than a hamper from Fortnum's."

"Could you, Georgie? You're a lifesaver. An absolute bally lifesaver."

Fig glared. "I thought we agreed on a hotel, Binky."

"We'll dine out, my dear. How about that? I know that Georgie knows how to cook a splendid breakfast if we provide her with the ingredients to do so. The girl's a bally genius."

They sipped tea and ate toast in silence. I tried to get down my own tea and toast although every crunch of toast sounded like cymbals going off in my head. I was just wondering when Belinda might be home and how much better it would be to sleep on her uncomfortable modern sofa when the doorbell rang.

"Who can that be at this hour?" Fig said, staring at me as if she thought it was my next lover come to call. "Georgiana had better go. It wouldn't be seemly for you or I to be seen answering our own front door. Word does get around so quickly."

I went, as curious as she was to know who was at the door. I was half hoping it would be Darcy, coming to rescue me, although I suspected he wasn't the sort to be up and

51

around before noon. Instead, the first thing I noticed was a Daimler motorcar parked outside and a young man in chauffeur's uniform standing outside the door.

"I have come for Lady Georgiana," he said, not guessing for a moment that I was anything other than a servant. "From the palace."

That's when I noticed the royal standard the Daimler was flying. Oh, golly. Thursday. Luncheon with the queen. With my brain pickled with alcohol I had completely forgotten.

"I'll inform her," I muttered. I closed the front door and was about to rush up the stairs in flat panic when Fig's head emerged from the top of the kitchen stairs.

"Who was it?" she asked.

"The queen's chauffeur," I said. "I'm supposed to go to the palace for luncheon today." I implied that luncheon with Her Majesty was a normal occurrence for me. It always annoyed the heck out of Fig that I was related to the royals and she was only a by-marriage. "I'd better go up and change, I suppose. I shouldn't keep her chauffeur waiting."

"Luncheon at the palace?" she demanded, scowling at me. "No wonder you don't bother to keep any food in the house if you are always dining in high places. Did you hear that, Binky?" Fig called down the stairs. "The queen has sent a car for her. She's going to lunch at the palace. She's going to get a decent lunch. You're the duke. Why aren't we invited?"

"Probably because the queen wants to talk to Georgiana," Binky said, "and besides, how would she know we are here?"

Fig was still glaring as if I'd arranged this little tête-à-tête just to spite her. I must say it gave me enormous pleasure.

CHAPTER 5

Buckingham Palace
Thursday, November 10

In spite of a head that felt as if it were splitting down the middle and eyes that didn't want to focus, I managed to bathe and make myself look respectable in fifteen minutes flat. Then I was sitting in the backseat of the royal Daimler being whisked toward the palace. It wasn't really a great distance from Belgrave Square down Constitution Hill and I had walked it on previous occasions. However, today I was most grateful for the car because the fog had turned again to a nasty November rain. One does not meet the queen looking like a drowned rat.

As I looked out through rain-streaked windows at the bleak world beyond I had time to wonder about the implications of this summons and I began to worry. The queen of England was a busy woman. She was always out opening hospitals, touring schools and entertaining visiting ambassadors. So if she made time to bring a young cousin to lunch, it had to be something important.

I don't know why I always expect a visit to Buckingham Palace to signal doom. Because it so often did, I suppose. I remembered the visiting princess foisted on me by my royal kin. I remembered the instruction to spy on the Prince of Wales's unsuitable woman, Mrs. Simpson. My heart was beating rather fast by the time the car drove between the wrought-iron gates of the palace, received a salute from the guards on duty and crossed the parade ground, under the arch to the inner courtyard.

A footman leaped out to open the car door for me.

"Good morning, my lady. This way, please," he said and led the way up the steps at a good pace. I followed, being extra careful as my legs have been known to disobey me in moments of extreme stress.

You'd have thought that someone who was second cousin to King George V would find a visit to Buckingham Palace to be old hat, but I have to admit that I was always overawed as I walked up those grand staircases and along the hallways lined with statues and mirrors. In truth I felt like a child who has stumbled into a fairy tale by mistake. I had been brought up in a castle myself, but Castle Rannoch could not have been more different. It was dour stone, spare and cold, its walls hung with shields and banners from past battles. This was royalty at its grandest, designed to impress foreigners and those of lesser rank.

I was taken up the grand staircase this time, not whisked along back corridors. We came out in the area between the music and throne rooms where receptions are held. I wondered if this was to be a formal occasion until the footman kept going all the way to the end of the hall. He opened a closed door for me, leading to the family's private apartments. I found I was holding my breath until I couldn't hold it any longer when finally a door was opened and I was shown into a pleasant, ordinary sitting room. This lacked the grandeur of the state rooms and was where the royal couple relaxed on the rare occasions they weren't working. At least it probably meant that I wasn't going to have to face strangers at luncheon, which was a relief.

"Lady Georgiana, ma'am," the footman said, then he bowed and backed out of the royal presence. I hadn't noticed the queen at first because she was standing at the window, gazing out at the gardens. She turned to me and extended a hand.

"Georgiana, my dear. How good of you to come at such short notice."

As if one refused a queen. They no longer chopped off heads but one obeyed nonetheless.

"It's very good to see you, ma'am," I said, crossing the room to take her hand, curtsy and kiss her cheek — a maneuver that required exquisite timing, which I hadn't yet mastered and always resulted in a bumped nose.

She looked back at the window. "The gardens look so bleak at this time of year, don't they? And what horrible weather we've been having. First fog and now rain. The king has been in a bad humor about being cooped up for so long. His doctor forbade him to go out during the fog, you know. With his delicate lungs he couldn't be exposed to the soot in the air."

"I quite agree, ma'am. I went out in the fog earlier this week and it was beastly. Nothing like the mist in the country. It was like breathing liquid soot."

She nodded and, still holding my hand, she led me across the room to a sofa. "Your brother — he has recovered from his accident?"

"Almost, ma'am. At least he's up and walking again but he has come to London to see a specialist."

"A disgusting thing to have happened," she said. "And the same person apparently shot at my granddaughter. It was your quick wits that saved her."

"And the princess's own cool head," I said. "She's a splendid little rider, isn't she?"

The queen beamed. Nothing pleased her more than talking about her granddaughters.

"I expect you wonder why I asked you to come to luncheon today, Georgiana," the queen said. I held my breath again. Doom will strike any moment, I thought. But she seemed jovial enough. "How about a glass of sherry?"

Usually I find sherry delightful, but the mere thought of alcohol made my stomach lurch. "Not for me, thank you, ma'am."

"Very wise in the middle of the day," the queen said. "I like to keep a clear head myself." Oh, Lord, if she knew how unclear my head felt at the moment.

"Why don't we go through and eat, then," she said. "It's so much easier to discuss things over food, don't you agree?"

Personally I thought it was absolutely the opposite. I have never found it easy to make conversation and eat at the same time. I always seem to have a mouthful at the wrong moment or drop my fork when under stress. The queen rang a little bell and a maid appeared from nowhere.

"Lady Georgiana and I are ready for our luncheon," the queen said. "Come along, my dear. We need good nourishing food in weather like this."

We went next door to a family dining room. No hundred-foot-long tables here, but a small table, set for two. I took my place as indicated, and the first course was brought in. It was my nemesis — half a grapefruit in a tall cut glass. I always seem to get the half in which the segments are imperfectly cut. I looked at it with horror, took a deep breath and picked up my spoon.

"Ah, grapefruit," the queen said, smiling at me. "So refreshing during the winter months, don't you think?" And she spooned out a perfectly cut segment. Hope arose that this time the kitchen staff had done their job. I dug into the grapefruit. It slipped sideways in the glass, almost shooting out onto the tablecloth. I retrieved it at the last moment and had to use a surreptitious finger to balance it as I dug again. The first piece came free without too much effort. No such luck with the second. I held on to that grapefruit, dug and tugged. This time two segments were joined together. I attempted to separate them and juice squirted straight up into my eye. It stung and I waited until the queen was busy before dabbing at my eye with my napkin. At least I hadn't squirted grapefruit juice at HM.

It was with incredible relief that I finished the grapefruit and the shell was whisked away. A thick brown soup followed, then the main course. It was steak and kidney pie, usually one of my favorites. With it was cauliflower in a white sauce and tiny roast potatoes. I could feel my mouth watering. Two good meals in two days. But the first mouthful revealed that this course was not going to be easy, either. I've always had a problem with chewing and swallowing large chunks of meat. It simply won't go down.

"Georgiana, I have a special favor to ask of you," the queen said, looking up from her own plate. "The king wanted this to be done formally, but I managed to persuade him that a private chat would be more appropriate. I did not want to put you in a spot, should you wish to say no."

Of course my mind was now racing. They'd found another prince for me. Or even worse, Siegfried had officially asked for my hand, one royal family to another, and turning him down would create an international incident. I sat frozen, my fork poised halfway between my plate and my mouth.

"There is to be a royal wedding later this month. You have no doubt got wind of it," the queen continued.

"No." It came out as a squeak.

"Princess Maria Theresa of Romania is to marry Prince Nicholas of Bulgaria. He is the heir to the throne, as I expect you know."

I gave a half nod as if the royal families of Europe always discussed their wedding plans with me. Thank God it was someone else's wedding we were talking about. I brought my fork to my mouth and started chewing.

"Naturally our family should be represented," the queen went on. "We are, after all, related to both sides. He is from the same Saxe-Coburg-Gotha line as your great-grandmother Queen Victoria, and she, of course, is one of the Hohenzollern-Sigmaringens. If it were in the summer, we should have been delighted to attend; however, there is no question of the king himself traveling abroad at this bitter time of year."

I nodded, having found a particularly chewy piece of meat in my mouth.

"So His Majesty and I have decided to ask you to represent us."

"Me?" I managed to squeak, my mouth still full of that large chunk of meat. I was now in a tricky situation in more ways than one. There was no way I could swallow it. There was no way I could spit it out. I tried a sip of water to wash it down but it wouldn't go. So I had to resort to the old school trick — a pretended cough, napkin to my mouth and the meat expelled into the napkin.

"I'm sorry," I said, collecting myself. "You want me to represent the family at a royal wedding? But I'm only a cousin's child. Won't the royal families in question see this as a slight that you only send someone like me? Surely one of your sons would be more appropriate, or your daughter, the Princess Royal."

"In other circumstances I would have agreed with you but it so happens that the Princess Maria Theresa has particularly requested that you be one of her bridal attendants."

I just stopped myself from squeaking "Me?" for a second time.

"I gather you two were such good chums at school."

At school? My brain was racing again. I

62

once knew a Princess Maria Theresa at school? I was friendly with her? I went through a quick list of my friends. No princesses appeared on it.

But I could hardly call a foreign princess, apparently related to us, a liar. I smiled wanly. Then suddenly an image swam into focus — a large, chubby girl with a round moon face trailing after Belinda and me and Belinda saying, "Matty, stop following us around, do. Georgie and I want to be alone for once." Matty — it had to be she. I had never realized that it was short for Maria Theresa. Nor that she was a princess. She had been a rather pathetic, annoying little thing (well, not so little, but a year behind us).

"Ah, yes," I said, smiling now. "Dear Matty. How kind of her to invite me. This is indeed an honor, ma'am."

I was now feeling decidedly pleased with myself. I had been asked to attend a royal wedding — to be in a royal bridal party. Certainly a lot better than freezing and starving at Rannoch House. Then the ramifications hit me. The cost of the ticket. The clothing I would need . . . the queen never seemed to take money into consideration.

"I suppose I'll have to have a frock made for the wedding before I leave?" I asked.

"I believe not," the queen said. "The suggestion was that you travel to Romania ahead of time so that the dresses can all be fitted by the princess's personal dressmaker. I gather she has excellent taste and is bringing in a couturiere from Paris."

Had I got it wrong? Matty, who always looked like a sack of potatoes in her uniform, was bringing in a couturiere from Paris?

"I will have my secretary make all the travel arrangements for you and your maid," the queen continued. "You'll be traveling on official royal passports so there will be no unnecessary formalities. And I will also arrange for a chaperon. It would not do to have you making such a long journey alone."

Now I was digesting one word from that sentence. Maid. You and your maid, she had said. Ah, now that was going to be a slight problem. The queen had no idea that anyone of my status survived without a maid. I opened my mouth to say this, then found myself saying instead, "I'm afraid there might be a problem about finding a maid willing to travel with me. My Scottish maid won't even come to London."

The queen nodded. "Yes, I appreciate that could be a problem. English and Scottish girls are so insular, aren't they? Don't give her a choice, Georgiana. Never give servants a choice. It goes to their heads. If your current maid wishes to retain her position with you, she should be willing to follow you to the ends of the earth. I know that my maid would." She dug into the cauliflower. "Be firm. You'll need to learn how to deal with servants before you run a great household, you know. Give them an inch and they'll walk all over you. Now, come along. Eat up before it gets cold."

CHAPTER 6

Mainly at Belinda Warburton-Stoke's mews cottage
Thursday, November 10

The car was waiting in the courtyard to take me back me to Rannoch House. It would have been a triumphant return but for one small fact. In one week I had to come up with a maid who wouldn't mind a trip to Romania without being paid. I didn't think there would be many young women in London who would be lining up for that job.

Fig appeared in the front hall as I let myself in.

"You've been gone a long while," she said. "I hope Her Majesty gave you a good meal?"

"Yes, thank you." I chose not to mention the near disaster with the grapefruit and the steak. And the fact that blancmange had been served for pudding and another of my strange phobias is about swallowing blancmange, and jelly — in fact, anything squishy.

"A formal occasion, was it? Lots of people there?" she asked, trying to sound casual while dying of curiosity.

"No, just the queen and I in her private dining room." Oh, I did enjoy saying that. I knew that Fig had never been invited to the private dining room and never had a tête-à-tête with the queen.

"Good gracious," she said. "What did she want?"

"Does a relative need something to invite one to a meal?" I asked. Then I added, "If you really must know, she wants me to represent the royal family at the wedding of Princess Maria Theresa in Romania."

Fig turned an interesting shade of puce. "You? She wants *you* to represent the royal family? At a royal wedding? What is she thinking of?"

"Why, don't you think I'll know how to behave? Do you think I'll drop my aitches or slurp my soup?"

"But you're not even part of the direct line," she blurted out.

"Actually I am. Albeit thirty-fourth," I said.

"And Binky is thirty-second and at least he's a duke."

"Ah, but Binky wouldn't look quite right

67

in a bridesmaid's dress, holding a bouquet," I said. "You see, the princess particularly asked for me to be one of her bridal attendants."

Fig's eyes opened even wider. "You? Why on earth did she ask for you?"

"Because we were great friends at school," I said, not batting an eyelid as I said it. "You see, that horribly expensive education that you gripe about did have its advantages after all."

"Binky!" Fig shouted in a way no lady should. "Binky, Georgiana has been asked to represent the family at a royal wedding, in Romania."

Binky appeared from the library, still wearing his overcoat and muffler. "What's this?"

"She's been asked to represent the royal family, at a wedding," Fig repeated. "Did you ever hear of such a thing?"

"I expect they didn't want to send any of the direct heirs for fear of assassination," Binky said easily. "They're always assassinating each other in that part of the world."

It was clear that Fig liked this answer. I was being sent because I was expendable, not because I was worthy. It did put a different complexion on things. "And when is

68

this wedding?" she asked.

"I'm to leave next week."

"Next week. That doesn't give you much time, does it? What about clothes? Are you expected to have some kind of dress made to be part of this bridal procession?"

"No. Luckily the princess is having us all dressed by her couturiere, from Paris. That's why I have to go early."

"What about your tiara? It's still in the vault in Scotland. Will we have to have it sent down to you?"

"I'm not sure whether tiaras will be worn. I'll have to ask the queen's secretary."

"And what about travel? Who is paying for all this?"

"The queen's secretary is taking care of everything. All I have to come up with is a maid."

Fig looked from me to Binky and back again. "How are you going to do that?"

"At this moment I have no idea. I don't suppose any of the servants at Castle Rannoch would like a jaunt to Romania?"

Fig laughed. "My dear girl, it's hard enough to persuade the servants at Castle Rannoch to come down to London, which they perceive as a dangerous and sinful place. If you remember, your maid Maggie wouldn't do so. Her mother wouldn't allow it."

I shrugged. "Then I'll just have to see if I can borrow a lady's maid from someone in London. Failing that, I'll have to hire one from an agency."

"How can you hire one? You have no money," she said.

"Precisely. But I have to come up with a maid somehow, don't I? I may have to sell some of the family jewels. Perhaps you can send down a diamond or two with the tiara." I was just joking but Fig shot me a daggers look.

"Don't be ridiculous. The family jewels have to stay in the family. You know that."

"Then what do you suggest?" I demanded. "I can't refuse to go. It would be an ultimate insult to Princess Maria Theresa and Her Majesty."

Fig looked at Binky again. "I can't think of anyone we know who might be willing to lend her a maid for such an exotic adventure, can you, Binky?"

"Don't know much about maids, old bean. Sorry," he said. "You women better sort it out. Georgie has to go, that's clear, so if necessary we'll have to come up with the money."

"You want us to come up with the

money?" Fig demanded, her voice rising. "How are we going to do that? Sell the family jewels, as Georgiana suggests? Deny little Podge a tutor? It's too much, Binky. She's over twenty-one, isn't she? She's not our responsibility anymore."

Binky went over and put a hand on her shoulder. "Don't upset yourself, my dear. You know the doctor said you should try to remain calm and think peaceful thoughts."

"How can I think peaceful thoughts when we won't even have the money to pay doctors' bills or for the clinic?" Her voice was rising dangerously.

And without warning she did something I had never seen Fig, nor anyone in my immediate circle, do before. She burst into tears and rushed upstairs. Ladies are brought up never to show emotion, even in the direst of circumstances.

I stared after her openmouthed. I realized that a doctor's visit for Fig had been mentioned, but it hadn't occurred to me until now that it might be a psychiatrist. Was her permanent bad temper due to something darker, like insanity in the family? How delicious. Too good to miss.

"She's a little upset today," Binky said in embarrassment. "Not at her best."

"Fig went to a doctor for her nerves?" I asked.

"Not exactly," he said.

He looked up the stairs after her, weighed up if the wrath of God might fall, then leaned confidentially close. "If you want to know, Georgie, Fig is expecting again. A second little Rannoch. Isn't that good news?"

It was amazing news. That they had done it successfully once, to produce an heir, was mind-boggling enough. That they had done it a second time took some getting used to. I tried to picture anybody actually making love to Fig from choice. But then I suppose it is cold in bed in Scotland. That had to be the explanation.

"Congratulations," I said. "You'll have the heir and the spare."

"That was one of the reasons for deciding to spend the winter in London this year," Binky said. "Fig hasn't been having an easy time of it and the doctor recommends feet up and nothing to upset her. And she's got a bit of a thing about our lack of money, I'm afraid. I feel like an awful failure, if you want to know the truth."

I felt sorry for Binky. "It's not your fault that Father shot himself and saddled you with crippling death duties on the estate."

72

"I know, but I should be able to do more. I'm not the brightest sort of chap and unfortunately I'm not equipped for any kind of work, apart from mooching around the estate and that sort of thing."

I put my hand on his arm. "Look, don't worry about the maid," I said. "I'll find one somehow. I'll go and see Belinda. She knows everybody. She travels to the Continent all the time. And you better go up to Fig."

He sighed and plodded up the stairs. I didn't like to go out again, in case Darcy telephoned or turned up in person only to be met by the hostility of my sister-in-law. But as I had no way of contacting him and I had learned from experience that Darcy was, to say the least, unpredictable, I decided I needed to get to work on the maid situation immediately. Perhaps Belinda had returned to London now that the fog had lifted. I decided it would probably not be wise to upset Fig even further by using her telephone so I walked through the rain to Belinda's mews cottage.

To my delight the door was opened immediately by Belinda's maid. "Oh, your ladyship," she said, "I'm awful sorry, but she's taking a rest. She's going out tonight and she said she wasn't to be disturbed."

I had trudged all this way in a bitter rain

and wasn't about to go back empty-handed.

"Oh, what a pity," I said in ringing tones, projecting as we were taught to in elocution class. "She will be sorry that she missed me, especially when I came to tell her about the royal wedding I'm to attend."

I waited and sure enough there was the sound of shuffling upstairs and a bleary-eyed Belinda appeared, satin sleep mask pushed up on her forehead and wearing a feather-trimmed robe. She made her way gingerly down the stairs toward me.

"Georgie, how lovely to see you. I didn't realize you were back in London. Don't keep Lady Georgiana standing on the doorstep, Florrie," she said. "Ask her in and make us some tea."

She staggered down the last of the stairs and embraced me. "I'm so glad you're here," I said. "I came by a couple of days ago and the place was all shut up."

"That's because Florrie couldn't get here through the fog," she said, glaring after the departing servant. "Left me in the lurch. No sense of duty, these people, and no backbone. You and I would have made it, wouldn't we? Even if we had to walk from Hackney? I tried to survive without her, but in the end I had no choice, darling, but to

74

check into the Dorchester until the fog lifted."

She led me into her delightfully warm sitting room and I peeled off outer garments. "I'm actually surprised to find you here. I should have thought Italy was so much nicer at this time of year."

A spasm of annoyance crossed her face. "Let's just say that the climate in Italy turned decidedly frosty all at once."

"Meaning what?"

"Paolo's horrid fiancée learned about me and put her foot down. She announced that she wants to get married right away. So Paolo's father told him to shape up and do his duty, or else. And since Pappa controls the purse strings it was *arrivederci* to poor little *moi*."

"You know, you're beginning to sound like my mother," I said. "I hope you're not turning into her."

"I think she's had a divine life," Belinda said, "all those playboys and racing car drivers and Texan oil millionaires."

"Yes, but in the end what does she have?"

"Some lovely jewels at the very least, and that little villa in the south of France."

"Yes, but in terms of family? Only Granddad and me and she ignores us both."

"Darling, your mother is a survivor like

me," Belinda said. "I was upset for a day or so when Paolo showed me the door, but then I decided there are plenty more fish in the sea. But enough about me, what's this I hear about a royal wedding?" She sank into the art nouveau armchair. I perched on the most uncomfortable modern sofa. "Don't tell me you've been forced to say yes to Fishface."

"Not if he was the last man on the planet," I said. "No, much more exciting than that. I've been asked to attend a royal wedding in Romania, as official representative of the family. And I'm to be in the bridal party."

"I say." Belinda looked suitably impressed. "What a coup! That's a step up in the world for you, isn't it? One day you're living on dry toast, the next you're representing our country at a royal wedding. How did this come about?"

"The bride specifically asked for me," I said. "Since we are old school friends."

"Old school friends? From Les Oiseaux?"

"It's the only school I ever went to. Until then it was all governesses."

Belinda frowned, trying to think. "An old school friend, in Romania? Who was that?"

"Princess Maria Theresa," I said.

"Maria Theresa — oh, God. Not Fatty Matty."

"I'd forgotten you used to call her that, Belinda. That wasn't very nice, was it?"

"Darling, one was only being honest. Besides, she wasn't a very nice person, was she?"

"Wasn't she? I know she was annoying, following us around and wanting to be included in everything. I used to call her Moony Matty, I remember, for the moon face and the way that she drifted around one step behind us all the time."

"And she was always pestering me to tell her about sex. Utterly clueless. Didn't even know where babies came from. But don't you remember, when we did include her, she betrayed our trust and ratted on me to Mademoiselle Amelie. Nearly got me expelled."

"She did?"

"Yes, that time I climbed out of the window to meet that ski instructor."

"That was Matty who told Mademoiselle?"

"We were never quite sure, but I always suspected. She had this smug look on her face when I was hauled into Mademoiselle's study," Belinda said.

"Well, let's hope she's improved by now. She's bringing in a couturiere from Paris to design our gowns."

"Oh, God. She'll look like a bally great meringue in a wedding dress," Belinda said. "Who is she marrying?"

"Prince Nicholas of Bulgaria, apparently."

"Poor Prince Nicholas. I'd forgotten she was a princess, but then I suppose a lot of our classmates were some kind of royalty, weren't they? I was one of the few commoners."

"You're an honorable. Hardly a commoner."

"But not in your league, darling. I say, what a scream — a bridal attendant to Fatty Matty. Let's hope the other attendants aren't her size or you'll be squished to death among them."

"Belinda, you are awful." I had to laugh. We broke off as tea was brought in. I watched Florrie serve it efficiently then depart.

"Your maid," I said, "she doesn't have a sister, does she?"

"Florrie? I've no idea, why?"

"Because I have been instructed by Her Majesty to take my maid with me to Romania. And since I don't have a maid to take with me, I'm going to have to beg, borrow or steal one from someone else, or hire one from an agency. I don't suppose you could do without Florrie for a week or so?"

78

"Absolutely not," Belinda said. "I nearly starved to death during that fog. If I hadn't been able to make a run on Harrods' food hall for pâté and fruit, it would have been the end of me. Besides, if Florrie wouldn't dare to cross London during a fog, I don't think she'd have the spunk to make it across the Channel, let alone to Romania."

"What about when you go abroad?"

"I leave her behind. I can't really afford a second ticket. There are usually enough servants to take care of me at the sort of villas I like to visit."

"Then do you have any suggestions as to where I might find a maid? Anybody you know who might be going on a cruise or to the south of France and leaving their maid behind?"

"People with money never leave their maids behind," Belinda said. "They take them along. You could probably pick up the right sort of girl in Paris, if you go a few days ahead."

"Belinda, I have no idea where one would find a maid in Paris. My mother took me there a couple of times when I was little and we went once with the school. Besides, I'd have to pay a French maid money that I don't have."

"That's true," Belinda agreed. "They are

79

frightfully expensive. But worth it. If I wasn't living this miserable existence, I'd have a French maid like a shot. My dear stepmother has one, but then Daddy gives her everything she wants." She dropped a sugar cube into her teacup. "Speaking of mothers, why don't you ask yours to cough up the money for a French maid?"

"I never know where to find my mother," I said. "Besides, I don't like asking her for things." A thought crossed my mind. "We could try asking Florrie if she knows any girls who are looking for work and want a taste of adventure."

"Anyone Florrie knows wouldn't want a taste of adventure," Belinda said. "She must be one of the most boring creatures on earth." But she rang the bell.

Florrie came rushing back into the room. "Did I forget something on the tea tray, miss?" she asked, anxiously clutching at her apron.

"No, Florrie. Lady Georgiana has a request of you. Go ahead, Georgie."

"Florrie," I said, "I am looking for a maid. You don't happen to know of any suitable girls who are out of work, do you?"

"I might, your ladyship."

"And would be up for a little adventure, traveling abroad?"

"Abroad? What, like France, you mean? They say it's terrible dangerous over there. Men pinch your bottom." Florrie's eyes opened wide.

"Farther away than France. And even more dangerous," Belinda said. "All the way across Europe on a train."

"Ooh, no, miss. I don't know no girls who'd want to do that. Sorry, your ladyship." She bobbed an awkward curtsy and fled.

"You needn't have played up the danger," I said. "We'll only be on a train and in a royal castle."

"You don't want one who's going to lose her nerve halfway across Europe and beg you in tears to be taken home," Belinda said. "Besides, what if the train is attacked by brigands — or wolves?"

"Belinda!" I laughed nervously. "Things like that don't happen anymore."

"In the Balkans they do — all the time. And what about that train buried in an avalanche? They didn't dig them out for days." She looked at me, then burst out laughing. "Why the somber face? You're going to have topping fun."

"When I'm not suffocating in an avalanche or being attacked by brigands or wolves."

"And Transylvania is part of Romania

these days, isn't it?" Belinda was warming to her subject. "You might meet a vampire."

"Oh, come on, Belinda. There are no vampires."

"Think how intriguing that would be. I understand it is utter ecstasy to be bitten on the neck. Even more of a rush than sex. Of course, I believe one then becomes one of the undead, but it would be worth it just for the experience."

"I have no wish to become undead, thank you," I said, laughing uneasily.

"Come to think of it, I'm sure Matty told us that their ancestral home was actually in the mountains of Transylvania, so there you are. Vampires everywhere. How I envy you the experience. I do wish I were coming with you." Suddenly she sat up straight, nearly knocking over the little tea table. "I have a brilliant idea. Why don't I come along as your maid?"

I stared at her and started to laugh. "Belinda. Don't be absurd," I said. "Why on earth would you want to be my maid?"

"Because you're invited to a royal wedding in Transylvania and I'm not and I'm bored and it sounds as if it could be loads of laughs and I'm dying to meet a vampire."

"Some maid you'd be." I was still grinning. "You don't even know how to make tea."

"Ah, but I know how to press things, thanks to my clothes design business. That's the important part, isn't it? I could press and dress you. And in case you have forgotten, I played the part of your maid once before and I did it jolly well," she said. "So why not? I'm itching for an adventure and you're providing one. You wouldn't even have to pay me."

I have to admit I was sorely tempted. It would be fun to be in a strange country with Belinda beside me.

"In other circumstances I'd take you up on your offer like a shot," I said, "and it would be a lot of fun, but you've overlooked one small detail — Matty would recognize you instantly."

"Nonsense," Belinda said. "Nobody looks twice at servants. I'd be in your room or in the servants' quarters. Her Highness and I would never have to meet. Come on. Do be a sport and say yes."

"I know you too well," I said. "You'd soon tire of being left out of the fun and festivities, wouldn't you? You'd only be there ten minutes and you'd find some good-looking foreign prince, reveal your true identity and leave me in the lurch."

83

"I am cut to the quick," she said. "Here am I, making you a generous and unselfish offer, and you keep finding reasons to turn me down. Wouldn't it be a lark to be there together?"

"A fabulous lark," I agreed, "and if I were going as an ordinary person, I'd take you along in an instant. But since I'm representing the royal family and my country, I have to observe protocol in every aspect. Surely you can see that?"

"You are becoming as stuffy as your brother," she said.

"Speaking of my brother, you'll never guess in a million years. Fig is in the family way again."

Belinda grinned. "I suppose in their case it's he who has to close his eyes and think of England when he does it. So you'll be bumped back to thirty-fifth in line to the throne. It doesn't look as if you'll ever make it to queen."

"You are silly." I laughed. "It will be good for Podge to have a brother or sister. I remember how lonely it was to be a child living at Castle Rannoch." I put down my teacup and got up. "Anyway, I must go on my quest for a maid. I've no idea where I'm going to find one."

"I've offered my services and been rejected," she said. "But the offer still stands if you can't come up with anyone better by the end of the week."

CHAPTER 7

A semidetached in Essex with gnomes in the garden
Still Thursday, November 10

This was turning into a tricky problem. There was nobody else in London I knew well enough to ask to borrow their personal maid. I realized when I reconsidered that it would be the most frightful cheek to turn up on somebody's doorstep and ask to borrow a maid, even if I did know them well. I wondered if I might get by with traveling alone and telling the dreaded chaperon that my maid had come down with mumps at the last moment. Surely they'd have enough servants at a royal castle to spare me an extra one. And I had become quite good at dressing myself. But probably not dressing myself in the sort of gown to be worn at weddings, with a thousand hooks or so down the back. There was nothing for it. I'd have to find an agency and hire a suitable girl, hoping that I could find some way to pay her at the end of the trip.

I was still dressed in my visiting-the-palace clothes so I set off again, scouring Mayfair for the right sort of domestic agency. I didn't dare return to the one that had supplied me with Mildred once before. The proprietress was so impossibly regal that she made the queen look positively middle class. I wandered along Piccadilly and up to Berkeley Square. Luckily the rain had slowed to a misty drizzle. I finally found what looked like a suitable agency on Bond Street. The woman behind the desk was another dragon — perhaps it was a requirement of the profession.

"Let me get this straight, my lady. You wish to employ a lady's maid to accompany you to Romania?"

"That's right."

"And when would this be?"

"Next week."

"Next week?" Her eyebrows shot upward. "I think it would be highly unlikely that I could find you the right sort of young woman to fill this position within one week. I can think of one or two who might be persuaded, but you'd have to pay her a premium."

"What sort of premium?"

Then she named an amount that I should have thought sufficient to run Castle Rannoch for a year. She must have seen me swallow hard, because she added, "We only handle the highest caliber of young women, you know."

I left in deep despondency. My brother could never find that sort of money, even if Fig would ever let him hand it over to me. It would have to be Belinda or nobody. As I walked through the growing twilight I pictured Belinda and all the sort of things that could go wrong with that arrangement. I was doomed whatever I did. Then I heard a newsboy calling out the headlines of the day in broad Cockney. That immediately made me think of the one person I had not yet turned to. My grandfather always had an answer for even the toughest problems. And even if he couldn't conjure a maid out of thin air, it was like a tonic just to see him. I almost ran to the Bond Street tube station and was soon speeding across London into darkest Essex.

I suppose I should explain that whereas my father was Queen Victoria's grandson, my mother had started life as the daughter of a Cockney policeman. She had become a famous actress and left her past behind when she married my father — only to bolt from him again when I was two.

The tube train was packed by the time it left central London and I emerged rather the worse for wear. It was raining hard again as I left the train. I was always glad to see my grandfather's little house, with its neat, pocket handkerchief–sized lawn and its cheerful garden gnomes, but never more so than that evening. A light shone out of the frosted glass panes on the front door as I trudged up the path. I knocked and waited. Eventually the door opened a crack, and a pair of bright boot-button eyes regarded me.

"Whatcher want?" a gravelly voice demanded.

"Granddad, it's me, Georgie."

The door was flung open wide and there was my grandfather's cheerful Cockney face beaming at me. "Well, I'm blowed. Talk about a sight for sore eyes. Come on in, ducks. Come in."

I stepped into his narrow front hall and he hugged me in spite of my wet overcoat.

"Blimey, you look like a drowned rat," he said, holding me at arm's length and grinning at me, his head to one side like a cheerful sparrow. "What on earth are you doing here, out on such a miserable night? 'Ere. You're not in some kind of trouble again, are you?"

"Not really in trouble," I said, "but I do need your help."

"Let me take your coat, love. Come into the kitchen and take a load off your plates of meat."

"My what?"

"Yer feet, love. Ain't I taught you no Cockney rhyming slang yet?"

He hung up my coat then ushered me down the hall to his tiny square of kitchen, which was already occupied by one person. "Look what the cat brought in, 'ettie," he said. It was his next-door neighbor, Mrs. Hettie Huggins, who had been setting her cap at him for ages and finally seemed to have succeeded.

"Pleased to see you again, yer ladyship," Mrs. Huggins said, dropping me a curtsy, although there wasn't really room for her ample hips to bend. "I've been taking care of your granddad, since he had a nasty bout of bronchitis."

"Oh, no. Are you all right now?" I turned to look at him.

"Me? Yeah. I'm right as rain, ducks. Couldn't be better, thanks to 'ettie 'ere. She fed me up like I was a prize chicken. In fact, we were just going to have some of her stew, weren't we, Hettie? Want to join us?"

"Her ladyship won't want stew, Albert. It

ain't what posh people are used to."

"I'd love some, please," I said. Then added, "Just a little," in case they didn't have much. But Mrs. Huggins ladled out a big bowl with barley and beans and lamb shank and they nodded with satisfaction as I wolfed it down.

"Anyone would think you hadn't seen a decent meal in a month of Sundays," Granddad said. "You're not still growing, are you?"

"I hope not. I'm taller than some of my dancing partners," I said. "But I do love a good stew."

They exchanged a look of satisfaction.

"So what are things like up in the Smoke?" Granddad asked.

"Smoky. We've had horrible fogs. I've hardly been out."

"Same down here. That's what done in Albert's chest," Mrs. Huggins said.

"So what can we do for you, love?" Granddad asked, looking at me fondly.

I took a deep breath. "I'm looking for a maid, in rather a hurry, I'm afraid."

Granddad burst out laughing. "I didn't mind pretending to be yer butler, love, but I ain't wearing a cap and apron and being a maid for you."

I laughed. "I wasn't expecting you to. I

was wondering if you knew anyone who had experience in service and who was out of work."

"I reckon we can come up with half a dozen girls who'd jump at the job, don't you, 'ettie?" Granddad turned to her and she nodded.

"A maid for you, yer ladyship? Your own personal maid, like?"

"Precisely."

"I shouldn't think the position would be hard to fill. You'd have girls lining up to work for a toff like you. Why don't you just put an advertisement in the newspapers?"

"There are some complications," I said, realizing as he said it that an advertisement might be a jolly good idea. Why hadn't I thought of it before? "Firstly, it's only a temporary position. I want a girl to accompany me to a royal wedding in Europe."

"In Europe?"

"Romania, to be exact."

"Blimey" was all Granddad could find to say to that.

"And I can't pay her much. I'm hoping I'll be able to pay her something when I return."

Granddad shook his head, making tut-tutting sounds. "You are in a bit of a pickle, aren't you? What about your brother and his snooty wife, can't they spare you a servant?"

"Nobody at Castle Rannoch wants to travel to London, let alone abroad. I'm looking for an adventurous girl, but I can't afford to pay her much."

"Seems to me," Granddad said slowly, "that a girl might want to take up this position so that she could use you as a reference. Former maid to royalty. That might be worth a darned sight more than money."

"You know, you're right, Granddad. You're brilliant."

He beamed.

"My niece Doreen's girl is looking for work, as it happens," Mrs. Huggins said quickly. It was clear that her brain had been ticking as he made that suggestion. "Nice quiet little thing. Not the brightest, but it might help her land a good position if she had a reference from a toff like you. Why don't I speak to her about it and send her up to you if she's willing to give it a try."

"Brilliant," I said. "I knew I was doing the right thing coming to you two. You always have an answer for me."

"So you're going to a royal wedding, are you, your ladyship?" Mrs. Huggins asked.

"Yes. I'm going to be in the bridal party, but I have to leave next week, so that doesn't give me much time to hire a maid to travel with me. This girl you mentioned — she has had some domestic service training, has she?"

"Oh, yes. She's had several jobs. Not anything like as grand as your house, of course. This will be a step up in the world for her. But like I said, she's a quiet, willing little thing. And you wouldn't have to worry about her having an eye for the boys. She don't have an ounce of what they refer to these days as sex appeal. Face like the back end of a bus, poor little thing. But you'd find her keen enough to learn."

My grandfather chuckled. "If she was in the theater, I wouldn't hire you as her manager, 'ettie."

"Well, I have to tell it straight for her ladyship, don't I?"

"I won't be judging her on her looks, and at the moment I feel it really is a case of beggars not being choosers."

"So I'll tell her she can call on you at yer house, shall I?"

"By all means. I look forward to meeting her." I finished my stew and started to stand up. "I really should be getting back to London, although I can't say I'm looking forward to it. I have my brother and sister-in-law at the house."

94

"You're welcome to the spare bedroom," Granddad said. "It's a nasty night out there."

I was tempted. The safety and security of Granddad's little house versus the doubly frigid atmosphere of Rannoch House occupied by Fig. But I had a wedding to plan for, and I didn't want Fig suspecting that I'd spent the night with Darcy.

"No, I really should get back, I'm afraid," I said. "It was so good to see you."

"We'll want to hear all about it when you come back from wherever it was," Granddad said. "You take care of yourself, traveling in foreign parts."

"I wish I were a man, then I could take you as my valet," I said wistfully, thinking how much nicer it would be traveling across a continent with him at my side.

"You wouldn't catch me going to heathen parts like that," Granddad said. "I've been to Scotland now, and that was quite foreign enough to last my lifetime, thank you kindly."

I laughed as I walked up the front path.

CHAPTER 8

I arrived home, cold and wet, to be told by an almost gloating Fig that Mr. O'Mara had called and been told that Lady Georgiana would be attending a royal wedding in Europe, at the request of Their Majesties, and should be left in peace to make her preparations. She also hinted that she'd admonished him for preying on innocent girls and suggested that he should not stand in the way of my making a suitable match.

This made me furious, of course, but it was too late. The damage had been done. All I could do was console myself with the thought that Darcy would probably have found Fig's lecture highly amusing.

The next morning they left, abandoning me for the warmth and luxury of Claridge's for their last night in London. I breathed a long sigh of relief. Now all I had to do was to pack for my trip to Europe and hope that the promised maid materialized. A telephone call from the palace informed me that my chaperon had had to put forward her traveling date, so it was hoped that I could be ready by Tuesday next. Tickets and passports would be delivered to me and, yes, tiaras would be worn. I had to telephone Binky at Claridges and I imagined Fig was gnashing her teeth at the expense of sending a servant down from Scotland with my tiara. But one couldn't exactly have put it in the post, even if we had the time. Then I realized that I would now not have time to place an advertisement in the *Morning Post* or the *Times.* It would have to be Mrs. Huggins's relative or nothing.

For a while it looked as if it was going to be nothing and I was just about to rush to Belinda and confess that I had changed my mind when there was a timid tap at my tradesman's entrance. Luckily I was in the kitchen at the time or I would never have heard it. I opened the door and standing outside in the dim and damp November twilight was an apparition that looked like a giant Beatrix Potter hedgehog, but not as adorable. It then revealed itself to be wearing an old, moth-eaten and rather spiky fur coat, topped with a bright red pudding basin hat. Underneath was a round, red face with cheeks almost matching the color of the hat. When she saw me a big smile spread ear to ear.

"Whatcher, love. I'm 'ere to see the toff what lives here about the maid's position, so 'ere I am. So nip off and tell her, all right?"

I tried not to let her know that I found this amusing. I said in my most superior voice, "I happen to be the toff that lives here. I am Lady Georgiana Rannoch."

"Blimey, strike me down with a feather," she said. "Begging your pardon, then, but you don't expect to find a lady like you opening the back door, do you?"

"No, you don't," I agreed. "You'd better come in."

"Awful sorry, miss," she said. "No hard feelings, I hope? I don't want to start off on the wrong foot. My mum's aunt 'ettie knows your granddad and she told me you was looking for a personal maid and she said why didn't I give it a try."

"I am looking for a personal maid, that's correct," I said. "Why don't you take off your coat and I'll interview you here. It's the warmest place in the house at the moment."

"Right you are, miss," she said and took off the fur coat, which was now steaming and smelling rather like wet sheep. Under-

98

neath the coat she was wearing a rather too tight mustard yellow home-knitted jumper and a purple skirt. Color coordination was not her strong point, clearly. I indicated a chair at the kitchen table and she sat. She was a large, big-boned cart horse of a girl with a perpetually surprised and vacant expression. The thought passed through my mind that she'd be expensive to feed.

"Now, I've told you my name. What is yours?"

"It's Queenie, miss," she said. "Queenie 'epplewhite."

Why did the lower classes seem to have all these surnames starting with *H* when it was a letter they simply ignored or couldn't pronounce? And as for her Christian name . . .

"Queenie?" I said cautiously. "That's your Christian name? Not a nickname?"

"No, miss. It's the only name I got."

I could see that a maid called Queenie might present problems for one about to attend a royal wedding, where there would be several real queens, but I told myself that most of them wouldn't speak English and would probably never run into my maid.

"So tell me, Queenie," I said, taking a seat opposite her, "you have been in domestic service, I understand?"

"Oh, yes, miss. I've already been employed in three households so far, but nothing like as grand as this one, of course."

"And did you serve in the capacity of a lady's maid?"

"Not exactly, miss. Sort of general dogsbody, more like it."

"So how long were you with your former employers?"

"About three weeks," she said.

"Three weeks? Which employer were you only with for three weeks?"

"All of 'em, miss," she said.

"Why such a short time, may I ask?"

"Well, the last one was her at the butcher's, and she only wanted help during her confinement, so as soon as the baby came she told me to push off."

"And the other two?"

She chewed on her lip before saying, "Well, the first one got pretty upset when I knocked over her bottle of perfume when I was dusting. It went all over the mahogany dressing table and took the surface off, but that wasn't what really upset her. It was a really expensive bottle of perfume, apparently. She'd brought it back from Paris. Oh, miss, you should have heard the words she used. You don't hear words like that from a fishmonger down the Old Kent Road."

"And the third employer?" I hardly dared to ask.

"Well, I couldn't very well stay there," she said. "Not after I set her evening dress on fire."

"How did you do that?"

"I dropped a match on the skirt by accident when I was lighting the candles," she said. "It wouldn't have been too bad, but she was wearing it at the time. She made a terrible fuss too, although she was hardly burned at all."

I swallowed hard and wondered what to say next. "Queenie, it appears that you are an absolute disaster," I said. "But it so happens that I'm desperate at the moment. I expect your aunt told you that I am due to go abroad to a very important wedding and I leave next Tuesday. It is essential that I take a maid with me to look after my clothes, help me dress and do my hair. Do you think you could do that?"

"I could give it a bloody good try, miss," she said.

"Then let us get a couple of things straight — one, there will be no swearing or any kind of bad language, and two, I am Lady Georgiana so you are expected to call me 'my lady' and not 'miss.' Do you understand?"

"Right you are, miss. I mean, my lady."

"And you do understand that this job means going abroad with me, to a foreign country?"

"Oh, yes, miss. I mean, my lady. I'm game for anything. It will be a bit of a lark, and wait till I see Nellie 'uxtable down the Three Bells, her what's always boasting that she took a day trip to Boulogne."

At least one had to admire her pluck, or maybe she was just completely clueless.

"And as to money — I do not intend to pay you any money at first. You will travel with me and receive your uniform and of course all your meals. If you prove satisfactory I will pay you what you are worth on our return and what's more I shall write you a letter of reference that will guarantee you a good job anywhere. So it's up to you, Queenie. This is your chance to make something of yourself. What do you say? Will you accept my terms?"

"Bob's yer uncle, miss," she said and thrust a big meaty hand in my direction.

I arranged for her to come to Rannoch House on Monday. She plonked the shapeless hat on her head and turned back to me at the door. "You won't regret this, miss," she said. "I'll be the best ruddy chambermaid you've ever had."

So I was due to undertake a journey fraught with avalanches, brigands and wolves with possibly the world's worst chambermaid who was likely to set fire to my dress. It would be interesting to see if I came out of it alive.

CHAPTER 9

Rannoch House
Monday, November 14
Due to leave for Continent tomorrow. Still no
maid. Still haven't heard from Darcy. Still rain-
ing.
How tiresome life can be.

By Monday morning I had still not heard
from Darcy. Now I would be going abroad
without letting him know. Really he was a
most infuriating man. I simply didn't know
what to make of him. Sometimes I thought
he was really keen on me, and then other
times he'd disappear for ages. Anyway, there
was nothing I could do about him now. If
he hadn't chosen to give me his address or
even come to see that I had survived the
visit from Binky and Fig, then too bad.

Queenie turned up a little after nine. It
took some time rummaging through the
housekeeper's closet to find a uniform that
fitted and looked suitable, because she was

a hefty girl, but eventually we poured her into a black dress, white cap and apron. She looked very pleased with herself as she stared in the mirror.

"Stone me. I look just like a real maid now, don't I, miss, I mean, me lady?"

"Let's hope you learn to act like one, Queenie," I said. "I take it you have brought your case with you with the items you'll need to travel. You can now come up to my room and pack the clothes I shall need. Bring that tissue paper with you so that they don't become creased."

We spent a rather fraught morning as I stopped her from wrapping my boots with my velvet dinner gown, but eventually all was ready. Tickets, passports and letters of introduction were delivered from the palace. My tiara arrived by courier from Castle Rannoch and Binky had generously slipped a few sovereigns into the package with a note saying *I expect you'll need some expenses for the journey. Sorry it can't be more.*

He was a sweet man, useless but sweet.

The money at least allowed us to take a taxi to Victoria Station on the morning of Tuesday, November 15. As I followed a porter to the platform where the boat train departed, I felt a sudden surge of excitement. I was really going abroad. I was going to be part of a royal wedding, even if it was Moony Matty's. My compartment was found and the porter set off for the baggage car with my trunks, leaving me with my personal luggage. I knew that in normal circumstances I would have entrusted my jewel case to my maid but I thought that Queenie might try dressing up in my tiara or let the rubies slip down the sink in the lavatory.

"You should go and find your own seat now, Queenie," I said. "Here is your ticket."

"My own seat?" A look of panic crossed her face. "You mean I'm not traveling with you?"

"This is first class. Servants always travel third class," I said. "Don't worry. I'll meet you on the platform with our luggage when we reach Dover. And I expect my chaperon's maid will be sitting with you so you'll have someone to talk to. Oh, and Queenie, please don't let the other maids know that you've only been in my employ for a day or that you set fire to your last employer's dress."

"Right you are, miss," she said, then put her hand to her mouth, giggling. "I still can't get the hang of saying 'my lady.' I always was a bit thick. My old dad says I was dropped on my head as a baby."

Oh, brilliant. Now she told me. She probably had fainting spells or fits. I was beginning to wish I'd taken up Belinda's offer after all. I had gone to see her to tell her the funny story of my new maid, but neither Belinda nor her maid was at home. It had to mean that she had probably fled somewhere warm again. I couldn't blame her.

A very nervous Queenie made her way down the platform to find the third-class carriages. As I watched her go I pondered on the irony that my maid was wearing a fur coat, whereas I only had good Scottish Harris tweed. Some girls were given a fur coat for their twenty-first birthday. I had been tempted to buy one with the check from Sir Hubert, the one of Mother's many husbands and lovers of whom I had been the most fond, but luckily I had banked it instead. It kept me in funds for over a year but had finally run out. The thought of Sir Hubert sparked an exciting memory. He was still in Switzerland, recuperating from a horrible accident (or was it attempted murder? — now we'd never know). I could visit him on the way home. I'd jot him a line as soon as I reached my destination.

As I stood there alone in the carriage I realized two things. One was that my chaperon had not appeared and the other was that I had no idea of the actual destination to which we were going. If she didn't turn up I didn't even know at which station we were to alight. Oh, dear, more things to worry about.

The hour for departure neared and I paced nervously. I was just double-checking that my jewel case was securely on the rack when the compartment door was flung open and a voice behind me said, "You, girl, what are you doing in here? Maids belong in third class. And where is your mistress?"

I turned to face a gaunt, horsey-looking woman wearing a long Persian lamb cape. Standing behind her was a most superior-looking creature in black, laden with various hatboxes and train cases. Both were staring at me as if I were something they had just discovered on the sole of their shoe.

"I think you've made a mistake. I am Lady Georgiana Rannoch, and this is my compartment," I said.

The horsey face turned decidedly paler. "Oh, most frightfully sorry. I only saw your back and you have to admit that that overcoat is not the smartest, so naturally I assumed . . ." She mustered a hearty smile and stuck out her hand. "Middlesex," she said.

"I beg your pardon?"

"That's the name. Lady Middlesex. Your

companion for the journey. Didn't Her Majesty tell you?"

"She told me there would be a chaperon. She never gave me your name."

"Didn't she? Dashed inefficient of her. Not like her. She's usually a stickler for details. She's worried about the king, of course. Not at all well."

She pumped my hand energetically all the time she was speaking. Meanwhile the creature in black had slunk past us and was busy loading cases onto the rack.

"All is done, my lady," she said with a strong French accent. "I shall retire to my own quarters."

"Splendid. Thank you, Chantal." Lady Middlesex leaned closer to me. "An absolute treasure. Couldn't travel without her. Completely devoted, of course. Worships me. Doesn't mind where we go or what hardships she has to endure. We're on our way to Baghdad now, y'know. Dashed awful place, baking in summer, freezing in winter, but m' husband has been posted there as British attaché. They always post him to a spot where they expect trouble. Damned strong man is Lord Middlesex. Doesn't allow the natives to get away with any kind of nonsense."

I wondered how Chantal and Queenie

would get along. Our door was slammed shut and a whistle sounded.

"Ah, we're off. Right on time. Jolly good show. I do like punctuality. Absolutely insist upon it at home. We dine at eight on the dot. If ever a guest dares to show up late, he finds we have started without him."

I almost reminded her that she had nearly missed the train herself, but I consoled myself that she would not be coming to the wedding with me. I'd disembark and she would travel on to Baghdad where she would boss around the natives. We started to move, first slowly past dingy gray buildings, then over the Thames and picking up speed until the backyards became a blur and merged into bigger gardens and then to real countryside. It was a splendid autumn day, the sort of day that made me think of hunting. Clouds raced across a clear blue sky. There were sheep in meadows. Lady M kept up a nonstop commentary about the places to which Lord Middlesex had brought British law and order and she herself had taught the native women proper British hygiene. "They worshipped me, of course," she said. "But I have to say that living abroad is a sacrifice I make for my husband. Haven't had a decent hunt in years. We rode with the hunt in Shanghai, but it was only over

110

the peasants' fields and that's not as jolly as good open countryside, is it? And all those silly little people shouting at us and waving their fists and scaring the horses."

It was going to be a very long journey.

At Dover we alighted from the train and found Queenie and Chantal.

"Dear God in heaven, what is that?" Lady Middlesex demanded on seeing Queenie, who was wearing the spiky fur coat and red hat again.

"My maid," I said.

"You let her look like that?"

"It's all she has."

"Then you should have outfitted her suitably. My dear girl, if you let servants go around looking like oversized flowerpots you'll be a laughingstock. I only allow Chantal to wear black. Colors are reserved for people of our class. Come along now, Chantal." She turned to the maid. "My train cases. And I want you to stay with those porters every inch of the way until the trunks are safely on board the ship, is that clear?"

"You do the same, Queenie," I said.

"I ain't never been on a ship, miss," Queenie said, already looking green, "apart from the *Saucy Sally* around the pier at Clacton. What if I get seasick?"

"Nonsense," Lady Middlesex said. "You simply tell yourself that you are not going to be ill. Your mistress will not allow it. Now off you go and no dillydallying." She turned to me. "That girl wants bringing in line rapidly."

Then she strode out ahead of me toward the gangplank. It was a pleasant crossing with just enough swell to make one realize one was on a ship. Lady Middlesex and I had lunch in the dining room (she had a hearty appetite and devoured everything within sight) and emerged in time to see the French coast ahead of us. We found Queenie, who was clinging to the railing as if it were her only hope of survival.

"It don't half go up and down, don't it, miss?" she said.

"Your mistress should be addressed as 'your ladyship,' " Lady Middlesex said in a horrified voice. "I can't think where she found such an unsuitable maid. Pull yourself together, girl, or you'll be on the next boat home."

Oh, dear. I'm sure that was exactly what Queenie wanted at this moment.

"Queenie is still learning," I said quickly. "I'm sure she'll soon be splendid."

Lady Middlesex sniffed. We sailed into Calais Harbor and then we sailed through the hassle of customs and immigration thanks to Lady M and the royal warrants, which allowed us to bypass the long lines and the customs shed. I had to admit she was marvelous — frightening, but worthy of admiration as she chivvied French dock-workers and porters until luggage was loaded and we were safely in our wagons-lits compartments of the Arlberg Orient Express.

"Run along now," Lady Middlesex said, waving Chantal away as if she were an annoying fly. "And take Lady Georgiana's maid with you."

I was relieved to find I had my own sleeping berth and didn't have to share with Lady Middlesex. I was about to come out into the corridor when I heard words I never would have expected to escape from Lady Middlesex's lips.

"Ah, there you are at last, dear heart."

I simply couldn't imagine Lady Middlesex calling anyone dear heart, and I knew her husband was already in Baghdad, so I was brimming with curiosity as I slid my door open. Coming up the corridor, clutching a bulky and battered suitcase, was a middle-aged and decidedly frumpy woman. She was wearing what was clearly a home-knitted beret and scarf over a shapeless overcoat and she looked hot and flustered.

"Oh, I've had the most awful time, Lady M. Most awful. There were two terrible men sitting across from me on the ship. I swear they were international criminals — so swarthy looking and they kept muttering to each other. Thank God it was not a night crossing or I'd have been murdered in my bunk."

"I hardly think so, dear heart," Lady Middlesex said. "You haven't anything worth stealing and they were not likely to be interested in your body."

"Oh, Lady M, really!" And the woman blushed.

"Well, you're here now and all is well," Lady Middlesex said. "Ah, Lady Georgiana, let me introduce you. This is my companion, Miss Deer-Harte."

"I am honored to meet you, Lady Georgiana." She bobbed an awkward curtsy, as she was still clutching the large suitcase. "I'm sure we'll have some jolly chats on the way across Europe. Let us just pray that there are no snowstorms this time and that none of those dreadful Balkan countries decides to make war with its neighbor."

"Always such gloom and doom, Deer-Harte," Lady Middlesex said. "Buck up. Best foot forward and all that. Your cabin is just down there. Why you had to struggle with that suitcase yourself instead of employing a porter is beyond me."

"But you know how hopeless I am with foreign money, Lady M. I'm always terrified of giving them a pound when I mean a shilling. And they always look so sinister with those black mustaches, I'm frightened they'll take off with my bags and I'll never see them again."

"I've told you before, nobody would want your bags," Lady Middlesex said. "Now, for heaven's sake go and get settled and then we'll find the dining car and see if they can produce a drinkable cup of tea."

As she finished speaking she looked down the corridor and opened her mouth in horror. "What in heaven's name?"

Queenie was rushing toward us, blindly pushing past people. She reached me and clutched at my sleeve like a drowning person. "Oh, me lady," she gasped, "can't I come in with you? I can't stay down there. It's all foreign people. Speaking foreign and acting foreign. I'm scared, me lady."

"You'll be fine, Queenie," I said. "You have Chantal, who has traveled on these trains many times and speaks the language too. Ask her if you need anything."

"What, 'er with the hatchet face?" Queenie

demanded. "She gives me a look that would curdle milk. And she speaks foreign too. I had no idea it was going to be so — well, foreign."

Lady Middlesex faced the terrified girl. "Pull yourself together, girl. You are embarrassing your mistress by making a scene. There is no question of your remaining in first class with your betters. You will be perfectly safe with Chantal. She travels with me all over the world. Now go back to your own compartment and stay there until Chantal tells you to disembark. Do I make myself perfectly clear?"

Queenie let out a whimper but she nodded and scurried back down the corridor.

"Have to be firm with these girls," Lady Middlesex said. "No backbone, that's the problem. Disgrace to the English race. Now let's go and see if any of these French people can make a decent cup of tea."

And she strode out ahead of me down the corridor.

CHAPTER 10

On a train, crossing Europe
Tuesday and Wednesday, November 15 and
16
Thank God Lady Middlesex is traveling on to
Baghdad. I don't think I could stand her
company for more than one night. Reminds
me of a brief and unhappy episode when I
tried to join the Girl Guides and failed my
tenderfoot test.

Soon we were sitting in a lounge car drinking what passed for tea — the light brown color of ditch water with a slice of lemon floating in it.

"No idea at all," Lady Middlesex said. "I don't know how the French exist without proper tea. No wonder they always look so pasty faced. I've tried showing them the correct way to make it, but they simply won't learn. Ah, well, one must suffer if one has to travel abroad. Never mind, Deer-Harte, you'll have decent tea once we reach the embassy in Baghdad."

"And what exactly is your destination, Lady Georgiana?" Miss Deer-Harte asked, taking what must have been her fifth biscuit.

"Lady Georgiana is to represent Her Majesty at a royal wedding in Romania."

"In Romania? Good heavens — such an outlandish place. So dangerous."

"Nonsense," Lady Middlesex said. "I thought I mentioned it to you in my last letter."

"You might have done, but unfortunately my mother's naughty little doggie, Towser, found the post and chewed off one corner of your letter. He's such a scamp."

"No matter. We're all here now and we are going to accompany Lady Georgiana to her destination in the mountains of Transylvania."

"I'm sure there is no need for you to interrupt your journey," I said hastily. "I trust a car will be waiting for me at the station."

"Nonsense. The queen specifically asked me to deliver you safely to the castle and I am not one to shirk my duty."

"But Lady M, a castle in the mountains of Transylvania, at this time of year too," Miss Deer-Harte said, her voice quivering. "We shall be set upon by wolves, at the very least. And what about vampires?"

"What tosh you do talk, Deer-Harte," Lady Middlesex said. "Vampires. Whatever next."

"But Transylvania is an absolute hotbed of vampires. It's common knowledge."

"Only in children's fairy stories. There is no such thing as vampires in real life, Deer-Harte, unless you mean the bats in South America. And as for wolves, I hardly think they can bite their way through a solid motorcar on a well-traveled road."

Lady Middlesex drained her teacup and I stared out of the window at the twilight wintry scene. Rows of bare-branched poplar trees between bleak fields flashed past us. The lights were already shining from farmhouses. I felt a thrill of excitement that I was abroad again.

"What are you staring at, Deer-Harte?" Lady Middlesex asked in her booming voice.

"That couple across the aisle," she said in a stage whisper. "I am sure that young woman is not his wife. Look at the brazen way he's holding her hand across the table. Such goings-on the moment one is on the Continent. And that man in the corner with a beard. He is obviously an international assassin. I do hope our cabin doors can be locked from the inside or we'll be murdered

119

in our beds."

"Do you have to see danger everywhere we go?" Lady Middlesex demanded irritably.

"There usually is danger everywhere we go."

"Fiddlesticks. Never been in real danger in my life," Lady Middlesex said.

"What about that time in East Africa?"

"Just a few Masai waving spears at us. Really, you do fuss about nothing. You're just a bundle of nerves, woman. Snap out of it."

I tried not to smile. It was such an improbable relationship — I wondered why on earth the overbearing and hearty Lady Middlesex had chosen such a simpering busybody as a companion, and why Miss Deer-Harte had accepted a position that took her from one uncomfortable place of danger to the next.

We approached Paris just as darkness fell. I peered out of the window, hoping to catch a glimpse of the Eiffel Tower or some familiar monument but all one saw through the darkness were little side streets with shutters already closed and the occasional café-tabac on a corner. If only I had money, I thought, I'd go and live in Paris for a while and pictured myself as a risqué bohemian.

The French failings at tea making were more than made up for with a superb dinner of coquilles St. Jacques and boeuf Bourguignon just after we left Paris. Lady M continued her monologue, interrupted only by Miss Deer-Harte spotting another international criminal and reiterating the fear that we should all be murdered in our beds. Toward the end of the meal, when we were savoring a spectacular bombe glacé, Miss Deer-Harte leaned toward us. "Someone is spying on us," she whispered. "I thought it earlier and now I am sure. Someone was watching us through the door to the dining car and when I tried to have a good look at him, he moved hastily away."

Lady Middlesex sighed. "For heaven's sake, Deer-Harte, don't be so silly. No doubt it was some poor fellow coming to see if anyone interesting was in the dining car, deciding he didn't want to dine with boring types like us and taking himself off to the bar for a while. Must you read drama into everything?"

"But our doors don't lock properly, Lady M. How do we prevent ourselves from being murdered in our beds? You hear what happens on these international trains, don't you? People vanishing in the night or found dead in the morning all the time. I think we should take turns in guarding Lady Georgiana. It may be an anarchist, you know."

"No anarchist would want to kill Lady Georgiana." Lady Middlesex gave a disparaging sniff. "She's not next in line to the throne, you know. I could understand your concern if it were one of the king's sons, but if someone is spying on us, he is probably a Frenchman with an eye for a pretty girl and wants a chance to meet our Lady Georgiana without two old fogies dogging her every step. I fear he will be unlucky because I have sworn to watch over her like a hawk."

I was grateful that Lady Middlesex suggested we retire to our sleeping berths early. As I came out of the bathroom at the end of the car I had the oddest sensation that I was being watched. I spun around, but the corridor was empty. It's that awful Deer-Harte woman, I thought. She is making me jumpy now. And I have to confess that I found myself wondering if there was any truth in what Lady Middlesex had said about a Frenchman wanting a chance to meet me away from the chaperons. That was an interesting thought. Belinda had always maintained that Frenchmen made the best lovers. Not that I intended to invite him in, but a harmless flirtation might be fun.

I lingered in my doorway but no Frenchman materialized, so I went to bed. Deer-Harte had been right, however. There was no way of locking the compartment. Then it occurred to me that maybe a Frenchman would be more interested in my jewel case than in me. Perhaps Queenie had confided to Chantal that I was carrying my tiara. Perhaps she had announced this loudly enough that everyone around them heard. This was a disturbing possibility. I put my jewel case at the back of my bunk, behind my head, and propped my pillow against it. Although the bed was comfortable enough, I couldn't sleep. As I lay there, being gently tossed by the rhythm of the train, I thought about Darcy and wondered where he was and why had hadn't contacted me since his encounter with Fig. Surely he wouldn't have been intimidated by her. Then I must have drifted off to sleep because I was standing in the fog with Darcy and he went to kiss me and then I found that he was biting my neck. "Didn't you know I was really a vampire?" he asked me.

I woke with a start as the train went over a set of points with great jolting and shrieking, and I lay there, thinking about vampires. Of course I didn't really believe in them, any more than I believed in the fairies and ghosts that the peasants in Scotland were convinced were real. Poor old Miss Deer-Harte was convinced they existed. Apart from reading *Dracula* long ago, which I'd found horribly creepy, I really knew very little about them. It might be rather exciting to meet one, although I wasn't sure I wanted my neck bitten and I certainly didn't want to become undead. I chuckled to myself, remembering that conversation with Belinda. Of course now I really wished that I had taken the risk and brought her along as my maid. We'd have had such a lark, and now I was stuck with a maid who was a walking disaster area and nobody to laugh with.

I was just drifting off again when I thought I heard someone at my door. We had been assured that the border agents would not disturb us during the night when we crossed from France into Switzerland and then into Austria. It could, of course, be Lady Middlesex, checking on me.

"Hello," I said. "Who's there?"

The door started to slide slowly open, and I was conscious of a tall, dark shape outside. Then I heard a stringent voice echoing down the corridor. "You there, what are you doing?"

Then a deep voice muttered, "Sorry. I

must have mistaken my compartment."

Lady Middlesex's head appeared around my half-open door. "Some blighter was trying to enter your sleeping berth. The nerve of it. I shall have a word with the conductor and tell him that he should keep better watch on who comes into this car. Maybe I should keep you company, just in case he tries it again."

"Oh, no, I'm sure I'll be all right," I said, deciding that a night with Lady Middlesex would be worse than any international jewel thief or assassin.

"I won't sleep," she said with determination. "I shall sit up all night and keep watch."

In this knowledge I finally drifted off to sleep. In spite of Miss Deer-Harte's predictions that we'd be murdered in our beds, I awoke to a perfect Christmas card scene that was familiar to me from my days at finishing school. Adorable little chalets perched on snow-covered hillsides, their roofs hidden under a thick blanket of snow. As I watched, the sun peeked between mountains, making the snow sparkle like diamonds. I opened my window and stood on my bed, breathing in crisp cold mountain air. Then the train plunged into a tunnel and I hastily shut the window again.

We breakfasted somewhere just after Innsbruck and came back to find our beds stowed and normal seats in our compartments. Luckily the scenery was so breathtaking as we climbed through spectacular mountain passes that conversation was not necessary until we moved into the flat country before Vienna. Here there were only patches of snow and the countryside was bare and gray. We had luncheon between Vienna and Budapest and when we came back to our compartments after a long and heavy meal, we found Chantal and Queenie already packing up our things, ready to disembark.

"I ain't half glad to see you, miss," Queenie said, apparently forgetting already how to address me. "I've been that scared. I didn't sleep a wink among all them foreign types, and you should see what muck they eat — sausages so full of garlic that you could smell them a mile away. There was no decent food to be had."

"Well, I expect we'll have decent food at the castle," I said, "so cheer up. The journey's almost over and you've done very well."

"I wouldn't have come if I'd known," she muttered. "Give me a nice café in Barking any day."

"All ready?" Lady Middlesex's face appeared around my door. "Apparently the train is making a special stop for us. So they don't want to wait around too long. We must be ready to disembark the moment it comes to a halt."

I looked out of the window at the gray countryside. It had become mountainous again and flakes of snow were falling. There was no sign of a city.

"Aren't we going to the capital?" I asked.

"Not at all. The princess is being married at the royal ancestral castle in the mountains. That is why it is most important that I see you safely to your destination. I gather it is quite a long drive from the station."

As she spoke, the train began to slow. We could hear the squealing of brakes and then it jerked to a halt. A door was opened for us and we were escorted down onto the platform of a small station. Peasants wrapped up against the cold stared at us with interest, while our trunks were unloaded from the baggage car. Then a whistle blew and the express disappeared into the gloom.

"Where the devil is the person they've sent to meet us?" Lady Middlesex demanded. "You stay there with the bags and I'll go and find a porter."

A local train came in, people got off and

on and the platform emptied out. Suddenly I felt the back of my neck prickle with the absolute certainty that I was being watched. I spun around to see a deserted platform with swirling snow. Of course someone is watching us, I told myself. We must be frightfully interesting to peasants who have never gone farther than the next town. But I still couldn't shake off the uneasiness.

"They can't know we're coming," Miss Deer-Harte said. "They've probably mixed up dates. We'll have to spend the night at a local inn and I can't even imagine how awful and dangerous that will be. Bedbugs and brigands, you mark my words."

At that moment Lady Middlesex reappeared with several porters. "The stupid man was waiting with his car, outside the station," she said. "I asked him how we were supposed to know he was there if he didn't present himself. Did he expect us to walk around looking for him? But he doesn't appear to speak English. You'd have thought the princess might have taken the trouble to send an English-speaking person to welcome us. A proper welcoming party would have been nice — with little peasant girls in costume and a choir maybe. That's how we would have done it in England, isn't it? Really these foreigners are hopeless." Sud-

128

denly she yelled, "Careful with that box, you idiot!" She leaped up and slapped the porter's hand. He said something in the local language to the others and they gave a sinister laugh and took off with our bags. Miss Deer-Harte's suspicions were beginning to rub off on me. I half expected the porters to have run off with our things, leaving us stranded, but we met up with them in a cobbled street outside the station.

Before us was a large square black vehicle with tinted windows. A chauffeur in black uniform stood beside it.

"My God," Miss Deer-Harte exclaimed in a horrified voice. "They've sent a hearse."

CHAPTER 11

Bran Castle
Somewhere in the hills of Romania
Wednesday, November 16
Cold, bleak, mountainous.

"Is this the only motorcar?" Lady Middlesex demanded, waving her arms in the way that English people do when speaking with foreigners who don't understand them. "Only one automobile? What about the servants? They can't ride with us. Simply not done. Is there a bus they can take? A train?"

None of her questions produced any response at all and in the end she had to concede that the maids would have to sit in the front with the chauffeur. He didn't seem to like the idea of this and yelled a lot, but it became clear that braver men than he had quailed before the force of Lady M's determination. Chantal and Queenie tried to squeeze into the other front seat, but there simply wasn't room. In spite of the spacious interior of the motorcar, there was only one seat and we three women fit rather snugly. In the end Chantal was given the front seat and poor Queenie had to sit on the floor with her back to the driver and the train cases and hatboxes piled beside her. The rest of the baggage was eventually loaded with some difficulty into the boot of the motorcar. It wouldn't close, of course, and string had to be found to tie it together. We looked anything but regal — more like a traveling circus — as we finally set off from the station.

It was now almost dark but from what I could see we were driving through a small medieval city with narrow cobbled streets, picturesque fountains and tall gabled houses. Lights shone out and the streets were almost deserted. Those few pedestrians we passed were bundled into shapeless forms against the cold. As we left the town behind, snow started to fall in earnest, blanketing the ground around us with a carpet of white. The driver mumbled something in whatever language he spoke, presumably Romanian. For a while we drove in silence. Then the road entered a dark pine forest and started to climb.

"I don't like the look of this at all," Miss

131

Deer-Harte said. "What did I tell you about brigands and wolves?"

"Wolves?" Queenie wailed. "Don't tell me we're going to be eaten by wolves!"

The driver perked up at a word he understood. He turned to us, revealing a mouth of yellow pointed teeth. "*Ja* — wolffs," he said, and gave a sinister laugh.

Up and up we drove, the road twisting back and forth around hairpin bends with glimpses of a sickening drop on one side. Snow was falling so fast now that it was hard to see what was road and what might have been a ditch beside it. The driver sat up very straight, peering ahead through the windshield into murky darkness. There was not a light to be seen, only dark forest and rocky cliffs.

"If I had any idea it was this far, I would have arranged for a night in a hotel before we began the trip." For the first time Lady Middlesex's voice sounded tense and strained. "I do hope the man knows what he's doing. The weather is really awfully bad."

I was beginning to feel queasy from being in the middle and flung from side to side around those bends. Miss Deer-Harte's bony elbow dug into my side. Queenie tried to brace herself in a corner but had a handkerchief to her mouth.

"You are to tell us if you wish to vomit," Lady Middlesex said. "I shall make him stop for you. But you are to contain yourself until you can get out of the vehicle, is that clear?"

Queenie managed a watery smile.

"I'm sure it's not far now," Lady Middlesex said cheerfully. She leaned forward. "Driver, is it far now? *Est it beaucoup loin?*" she repeated in atrocious French.

He didn't answer. At last we came to the top of the pass. A small inn was beside the road and lights shone out from it. The driver stopped and went around to open the bonnet, presumably to let the motor cool down. Then he disappeared inside the inn, leaving us in the freezing car.

"What's that?" Miss Deer-Harte whispered, pointing into the darkness on the other side of the road. "Look, among the trees. It's a wolf."

"Only a large dog, I'm sure," Lady Middlesex said.

I said nothing. It looked like a wolf to me. But at that moment the inn door opened and several figures emerged.

"Brigands," Miss Deer-Harte whispered. "We'll all have our throats slit."

"Ordinary peasants," Lady Middlesex

sniffed. "See, they even have children with them."

If they were peasants they certainly looked like a murderous bunch, the men with big black drooping mustaches, the women large and muscular. They poured out of the inn, a remarkably large number of them, peering into the motorcar with suspicious faces. One woman crossed herself and another held up crossed fingers, as if warding off evil. A third snatched a child who was venturing too close to us and held it protectively wrapped in her arms.

"What on earth is the matter with them?" Lady Middlesex demanded.

One old man dared to come closer than the rest. "Bad," he hissed, his face right at the window. "Not go. Beware." And he spat on the snow.

"Extraordinary," Lady Middlesex said.

The chauffeur returned, driving back the people, of whom there was now quite a crowd. He closed the bonnet, climbed into the driver's seat and started the engine again. Words were shouted at us and we took off to a scene of people gesticulating after us.

"What was that all about, driver?" Lady Middlesex asked, hoping that he miraculously now understood English, but the man stared straight ahead of him as the road dipped precariously downward.

I was now feeling rather uneasy about the whole thing. Had Lady Middlesex misunderstood and made us disembark from the train at the wrong station? Were we in fact in the wrong car? Surely no royal castle could be at such a godforsaken spot as this. Clearly Miss Deer-Harte was echoing my thoughts.

"Why on earth would they choose to hold a royal wedding at such an isolated place?" she said.

"Tradition, apparently." Lady Middlesex still attempted to sound confident but I could sense she was also having doubts. "The oldest daughter always has to be married at the ancestral home. It's been done for centuries. After the ceremony here the wedding party will travel to Bulgaria, where there will be a second ceremony at the cathedral and the bride will be presented to her new countrymen." She sighed. "Ah, well, if one will travel abroad, one is bound to encounter strange customs. So primitive compared with home."

We were slowing down. The driver grinned, showing his pointy teeth. "Bran," he said.

We had no idea what Bran was but we

could see that there were lights shining from a rocky outcropping towering over the road. As we peered out of the window we could make out the shape of a massive castle, so old and formidable looking that it appeared to be part of the rock itself. The motorcar stopped outside a pair of massive wooden gates. These slowly rolled mysteriously open and we glided through into a courtyard. The gates shut behind us with loud finality. The motorcar came to a halt and the driver opened the doors for us.

Miss Deer-Harte was first to step out into the snow. She stood, peering up in horror at the towering stone battlements that seemed to stretch into the sky all around us. "My God," she said. "What have you brought us to, Lady M? This is a veritable house of horrors, I can sense it. I've always been able to smell death and I smell it here." She turned to Lady Middlesex, who had just emerged on the other side of the motorcar. "Oh, please let's leave straightaway. Can't we pay this man to drive us back to the train station? I'm sure there will be an inn in the town where we can spend the night. I really don't want to stay here."

"Fiddlesticks," Lady Middlesex said. "I'm sure it will be perfectly comfortable inside and of course we must do our duty to Lady

Georgiana and present her properly to her royal hosts. We can't leave her in the lurch. It's simply not British. Now buck up, Deer-Harte. You'll feel better after a good meal."

I too was staring up at those massive walls. There seemed to be no windows below a second or third floor and the only chinks of light shone between closed shutters. I have to admit that I also swallowed hard and all the snippets of conversation came rushing back to me — Binky saying the king and queen didn't want to send their sons because it was too dangerous, and even Belinda making jokes about brigands and vampires. And why had those people at the top of the pass looked at us with fear and loathing and even crossed themselves? I echoed Lady Middlesex's words to myself. Buck up. This is the twentieth century. The place might look quaint and gothic but inside it will be normal and comfortable.

Queenie clambered out of the car and stood close to me, clutching at my sleeve. "Ain't this a god-awful-looking place, miss?" she whispered. "Gives you the willies. It makes the Tower of London look like a nice country cottage, don't it?"

I had to smile at this. "It certainly does, but you know I live in an old castle in Scotland and it's perfectly nice inside. I'm sure we'll have a grand time. Look, here comes somebody now."

A door had opened at the top of a flight of stone steps and a man in black and silver livery with a silver star-shaped decoration hanging at his neck was descending. He was silver haired and rather grand looking with high cheekbones and strange light eyes that glinted like a cat's.

"Vous êtes Lady Georgiana of Glen Garry and Rannoch?" he asked in French, which threw us all off balance. *"Bienvenue.* Welcome to Bran Castle."

I suppose I had forgotten that French tended to be the common language of the aristocracy of Europe.

"This is Lady Georgiana," Lady Middlesex said in the atrociously English-sounding French of most of my countrymen. She indicated me. "I am her traveling companion, Lady Middlesex, and this is my companion, Miss Deer-Harte."

"And for companion Miss Deer-Harte has somebody?" he inquired. "A little dog, maybe?"

I suspected he was attempting humor but Lady Middlesex said coldly, "No animal of any kind."

"Allow me to present myself," the man said. "I am Count Dragomir, steward of this castle. I welcome you on behalf of Their Royal Highnesses. I hope you will have a pleasant stay here." He clicked his heels and gave a curt little bow, reminding me of Prince Siegfried, my would-be groom, who was also related to the royal house of Romania. Oh, Lord, of course he'd be here. That aspect hadn't struck me before. The moment I had this thought, another followed. This couldn't possibly be a trap, could it? Both my family and Prince Siegfried had been annoyed when I had turned down his marriage proposal. And Siegfried was the type who likes to get his own way. Had I been specially invited to this wedding so that I'd be trapped in a spooky old castle in the middle of the mountains of Romania with a convenient priest to perform a marriage ceremony?

I looked back longingly at the motorcar as Count Dragomir indicated we should follow him up the steps.

We entered the castle into a towering hall hung with banners and weapons. Archways around the walls led into dark passageways. The floor and walls were solid stone and it was almost as cold inside as it was out.

"You will rest after exhausting journey," Dragomir said. His breath hung visibly in the cold air. "I will have servants show you to your rooms. We dine at eight. Her Highness Princess Maria Theresa looks forward to renewing acquaintanceship with her old friend Lady Georgiana of Rannoch. Please do follow now."

He clapped his hands. A bevy of footmen leaped out of the shadows, snatched up our train cases and started up another flight of steep stone steps that ascended one of the walls with no railing. My feet felt as tired as if I'd been on a long hike and I realized it was a long way down if I were to stumble. At the top we came out to a hallway colder and draftier than anything at Castle Rannoch, then up a spiral staircase, round and round until I was feeling dizzy. The staircase ended in a broad corridor with a carved wooden ceiling. Again the floor was stone, and it was lined with ancestral portraits of people who looked fierce, half mad or both. Queenie had been following hard on my heels. Suddenly she gave a scream and leaped to grab me, nearly sending us both sprawling.

"There's someone standing behind the pillar," she gasped.

I turned to look. "It's only a suit of armor," I said.

"But I could swear it moved, miss. I saw it raise its arm."

The suit was indeed standing holding a pike with one arm raised. I opened the visor. "See. There's nobody inside. Come on, or we'll lose our guide."

Queenie followed, keeping so close that she kept bumping into me every time I slowed. A door was opened, curtains were held back and I stepped into an impressively large room.

Queenie was breathing down my neck. "Ooh, heck," she said. "It looks like something out of the pictures, don't it, miss? Boris Karloff and Frankenstein."

"Come," the footman now said to Queenie. "Mistress rest now. Come."

"Go with him, Queenie," I said. "He'll take you to your room. Have a rest yourself but come back in time to dress me for dinner."

Queenie shot me a frightened glance and went after him reluctantly. The curtains fell into place and I was alone. The room smelled old and damp, in a way that was not unfamiliar to me from our castle at home. But whereas the rooms at Castle Rannoch were spartan in the extreme, this room was full of drapes, hangings and heavy furniture. In the middle was a four-poster bed hung with velvet curtains that would have been quite suitable for the Princess and the Pea. Similar heavy curtains covered one wall, with presumably a window behind them. More curtains concealed the door I had just come through. A fire was burning in an ornate marble fireplace but it hadn't succeeded in heating the room very well. There was a massive wardrobe, a dressing table, a bulky chest of drawers, a writing desk by the window and a huge painting on the wall of a pale, rather good-looking young man in a white shirt, reminding me of one of the Romantic poets — had Lord Byron visited these parts? But then Byron had been dark and this young man was blond. The lighting was extremely poor, dim and flickering, coming from a couple of sconces on the walls. I looked around, still feeling queasy from the ride and uneasy from the strange tension that had been building ever since that man had tried to enter my compartment. It wasn't the pleasantest feeling standing in a room with no obvious window or door and I decided to go and pull back the curtains on the far wall.

As I crossed the room I detected a movement and my heart lurched as I saw a white face looking at me. Then I realized it was only a pockmarked old looking glass on the wardrobe door. I pulled back the curtains enough to reveal the window, managed to open the shutters and stood looking out into the blackness of the night. Not a single light shone out from the dark forested hills. Snow was still falling softly and cold flakes landed on my cheeks. I looked down. My room must have been in the part of the castle built on the edge of the rock, because it seemed an awfully long way down into nothing. Far away I detected the sound of howling coming through the stillness. It didn't sound like any dog I had ever heard and the word "wolves" crept into my mind.

I was just about to close the window again when I stiffened, then peered intently into the darkness trying to make out what I was really seeing. Something or somebody was climbing up the castle wall.

CHAPTER 12

Bran Castle
Somewhere in the middle of Transylvania
Wednesday, November 16

I couldn't believe my eyes. All I could make out was a figure all in black with what looked like a cape blowing out behind it in the wind moving steadily up the apparently smooth stone wall of the castle. Then all at once it vanished. I stood there, staring for a while until the wind picked up, carrying with it the howling of wolves, and snow started to blow into the room. Then I closed the window again. I lay on the bed and tried to rest but I couldn't. Drat that Deer-Harte woman. If she hadn't brought up the subject of vampires, my thoughts wouldn't be running wild at this point. I lay looking around the room. The top of the wardrobe appeared to be carved with gargoyles at each corner. There were faces in the crown molding and — dear God, what was that? A piece of furniture I hadn't noticed, half hidden behind the door curtains. It looked like a large carved wood chest. A very large carved wood chest big enough to conceal a person. Or . . . it couldn't be a coffin, could it?

I got up and tiptoed across the room. I had to know what was inside that chest. The lid was infernally heavy. I was just struggling to get it open when I felt a draft behind me and a hand touched my back. I yelled and spun around. The lid crashed shut with a hollow thud and there was Queenie looking scared.

"Sorry, miss. I didn't mean to startle you. I came in real quiet-like, in case you were still sleeping."

"Sleeping? How can I sleep in a place like this?" I asked.

She looked around. "Blimey. I see what you mean. This is a spooky old place, ain't it? Gives me the willies. Reminds me of the Chamber of Horrors at Madame Tussauds. Except for the bloke on the wall. He's a bit of all right, ain't he?"

"I'm not sure I like him looking at me when I'm in bed," I said, and as I said it I realized that the portrait was directly above the chest/coffin. "What's your room like?"

"A bit like Holloway Prison, if you want my opinion. Plain and cold. And way up in

145

one of the turrets. I don't see myself getting much sleep up there. And you have to go round and round this windy staircase to reach it. I got lost several times on the way down. I'd have ended up down in the dungeons by now, if it hadn't been for one of them blokes in the smashing uniform who rescued me and brought me here. I don't know how I'm ever going to find my way back." She stared at me. "Are you all right, miss? You look awful pale."

I was about to tell her about the thing climbing up the castle wall but then I realized that I couldn't. That Rannoch sense of duty kicked in and I was sure that Robert Bruce Rannoch or Murdoch McLachan Rannoch wouldn't have been frightened by a figure climbing up a wall. I had to appear to be calm and in control.

"I'm absolutely splendid, thank you, Queenie," I said. "Now, I wonder when my baggage will arrive."

Almost on cue there was a tap on my door and the bags were brought in by more tall, dark-haired footmen, all seeming to look identical.

"You might as well put away my clothes and then help me get dressed for dinner," I said. "I wonder where you're supposed to find water for me to wash."

146

We scouted out the hall and found a bathroom not too far away — a massive cavern of a room with great stone arches rising to a vaulted ceiling. The claw-footed tub in the middle was big enough to go swimming in. A geyser contraption over it presumably supplied hot water.

"I think I'll have a bath before dinner," I said. "Why don't you start running me a bath and then see if you can locate my robe."

I undressed while Queenie unpacked and hung up my things. That's when we discovered that she hadn't packed a robe for me. "Never mind," I said. "I'll have to walk down the hall in my nightdress. There doesn't seem to be anyone else around."

I scooted rapidly back to the bathroom, feeling rather self-conscious in my nightdress, and found the whole place full of steam and the bath temperature hot enough to boil a steamed pudding. What's more the window was jammed shut and it took ages for me to run out half the bathwater and fill it with cold. After that I had a lovely long soak, got out feeling refreshed and looked around for a towel. There wasn't one. Now I was in a pickle. The nightdress that I had worn had become so sodden with steam that it was almost as wet as I was. I had no way to dry off. I'd have to make a run for it.

I pulled my nightdress over my head with great difficulty. It clung to my wet body like a second skin. I opened the bathroom door, looked up and down the hallway then sprinted for my own bedroom. That was when I realized I couldn't remember how many doors down the hallway was mine. It was two, surely. Or was it three? I was conscious of the trail of drips behind me, of the puddle forming around me, and my feet freezing on the stone floor. I stood outside the second door and tried to open it. It wouldn't open.

I tapped on it firmly. "Queenie, let me in, please."

No answer.

I rapped louder. "Queenie, for God's sake open the door."

The door was flung open suddenly and I found myself staring into the bleary-eyed face of Prince Siegfried. He had obviously just woken from sleep. He looked me up and down, his eyebrows raised in horror.

"I'm so sorry. I must have the wrong room," I mumbled.

"Lady Georgiana," he exclaimed. "*Mein Gott.* What is the meaning of this? You are not wearing clothes. Most inappropriate.

What has befallen you? You have had an accident and fallen into water?"

"I am wearing something but it's rather wet. You see, there were no towels in the bathroom and I forgot which door was mine and . . ." I was babbling on until I heard Queenie's voice hissing, "Psst. Down 'ere, miss."

"Sorry to trouble you," I said and fled.

Of course when I reached the safety of my room, I discovered that there were towels on the top shelf of the wardrobe. I dried off still feeling utterly stupid and embarrassed. Of all doors, I had to knock on Siegfried's. All in all it had been a long and trying day.

It was lucky that I had had oodles of practice in dressing myself, as Queenie was more hindrance than help. She got my dress stuck trying to put my head through one of the armholes. Then her idea of doing my hair made me look like I was housing a bird's nest. But eventually I looked presentable, wearing burgundy velvet and the family rubies, and I was ready by the time the first gong sounded.

"I'm going down to dinner now, Queenie," I said. "I'm not sure where you go for your supper, but one of the servants will show you."

Her eyes darted nervously and I felt sorry

149

for her. "I can't be late on the first evening here," I said. "Honestly you'll be all right. Just go down to the kitchen."

I left her looking as if she wanted to follow me and made my own way, with some difficulty, to the predinner gathering in the long gallery. The gallery was hung with more banners, and adorned with the heads of various animals, ranging from wild boar to bears, but it looked bright and festive with hundreds of candles sparkling on crystal chandeliers. The assembled company was dripping with braid, medals and diamonds, reminding me of one of the more extravagant Viennese operettas. I felt the wave of nervousness that always comes over me on such occasions, tinged with the worry that I'll do something clumsy like trip over the carpet, knock over a statue or spill my drink. I am inclined to be clumsy when I'm nervous. I was wondering if I could join the company without being noticed, but at that moment I was announced and heads turned to appraise me. A young man detached himself from a group and came to greet me, his hand outstretched.

"Georgiana. How good of you to come. I don't know if you remember me but we met once when we were children. I am Nicholas, the bridegroom, and I believe we are second cousins or something like that."

His English was flawless, with a typical public school accent, and he was tall and good-looking, with the dark blond hair and blue eyes of many of the Saxe-Coburg clan. I felt an instant stab of sympathy that he was being landed with Moony Matty. He was actually a prince I wouldn't mind marrying myself — if one were absolutely forced into marrying a prince.

"How do you do, Your Highness," I said, bobbing a curtsy as we shook hands. "I'm afraid I don't remember meeting you."

"At a celebration for the end of the Great War. We spent it in England, you know. You were a skinny little thing at the time and we made short work of a box of Turkish delight under a table, if I remember correctly."

I laughed. "And felt horribly sick afterward. Oh, I do remember now. You were about to go off to school. I was envious because I was stuck at home with a governess." Then I remembered something else. "You were at school with Darcy O'Mara, weren't you? He mentioned that you were a good rugby player."

"So you know Darcy, do you? Damned good fullback himself. Plenty of speed. So how do you like the castle?" He grinned impishly. "Delightfully gothic, wouldn't you

151

say? Maria insisted on having the wedding here."

"It's a family tradition, I suppose."

"Maybe for the original family — Vlad the Impaler, reputed to be Dracula, was one of them, I believe. But Maria's family hasn't been on the throne for that long. No, I think it has more to do with Maria's fond memories of summer holidays spent here as a child, and her romantic nature — wanting to be married in a fairy-tale castle." He leaned closer to me. "Frankly I would have preferred somewhere more comfortable and accessible."

"It does seem rather — gothic, as you say," I agreed.

We broke off as a large man barged up to us. "And who is this delightful creature? Introduce me please, Nicholas." He spoke with a heavy accent.

He was pale and light haired with the flat features of the Slav and his uniform was so covered in medals, sashes, orders and braid that he appeared almost a caricature of a general from Gilbert and Sullivan. And I noticed that he had called the prince Nicholas.

A slight spasm of annoyance crossed Nicholas's face. "Oh, Pirin. Of course; this is my dear relative from England. Lady

Georgiana, may I present Field Marshal Pirin, head of the Bulgarian armed forces and personal adviser to my father, the king."

"Field Marshal. I'm pleased to meet you." I inclined my head graciously as we shook hands. His hand was meaty and sweaty and it held mine a little too long.

"So from England you come, Lady Georgiana. How is the dear old King George? Splendid old chap, isn't he, but rather boring. Hardly drinks at all."

"He was well when I last saw him, thank you," I said frostily, as I didn't like this supposed familiarity with the king, "although as you have probably heard, the king's health has not been the best recently."

"Yes, I hear this. And the Prince of Wales — is he ready to step into his father's shoes, do you think? Will he do a good job when the old man kicks the bucket, as you say in England, or will he still be the playboy?"

I really didn't want to discuss my family with a complete stranger and one not even royal. "I'm sure he'll be absolutely splendid when the time comes," I said.

The field marshal put a meaty hand on my bare arm and gave it a squeeze. "I like this girl. She has fire," he said to Nicholas. "She shall sit beside me at dinner tonight and I will get to know her better." And he gave me what could only be described as a leer.

"I'm afraid that my bride has insisted that Georgiana sit close to her at dinner. They are dear friends, you know, and they will want time to chat. Have you met Maria Theresa yet, Georgiana? I know she is dying to see you again. Let us go and seek her out."

He took my arm and led me away. "Odious fellow," he whispered when we were out of earshot. "But we have to tread carefully in Bulgaria at the moment. He is from our southwestern province of Macedonia, and there is a strong separatist movement in that area, wanting to break away from us — and Yugoslavia would like to annex our part of Macedonia to its own. So you see, it's delicate. As long as Pirin holds power, he can keep them loyal. If he goes, they will try to break away. There will be civil war. Yugoslavia will undoubtedly take the side of the break-away province and before you know it another regional, if not world, war will be on our doorsteps. So we flatter and humor him. But he's a peasant. And a dangerous one."

"I see."

"That is why this alliance with Romania is so important. We need them on our side if there is any kind of Balkan conflict. But no talk of gloomy things tonight. Tonight we feast and celebrate my wedding. Ah, there is my lovely bride now. Maria, *Schatzlein,* look who I have found."

I turned to see where he was looking but there was nobody I recognized. Only a slim and elegant creature, obviously dressed from Paris, her dark hair sleekly styled and an ebony cigarette holder in one hand, was moving gracefully through the crowd. When she spotted me, her face lit up. "Georgie. You made it. How wonderful. I am so glad to see you."

And she came toward me arms open.

She was about to embrace me when she stopped and laughed. "Your face, darling. I keep forgetting that people who haven't seen me in a while don't recognize me. It's Matty, your old friend Matty."

"I can't believe it," I said. "Matty, you look stunning."

"Yes, I do, don't I?" she said with satisfaction. "All those months in the Black Forest certainly paid off, didn't they?"

"The Black Forest?"

"They sent me for a cure at a spa, darling. Three months of utter torture, drinking carrot juice, cold baths, long runs through the forest at dawn and calisthenics for hours.

But this is the result. Thirty kilos miraculously vanished. And then I was a year in Paris to pick up sophistication and voila. A new me."

I still couldn't stop staring.

"She looks utterly beautiful, doesn't she?" Nicholas said. "I can't believe my luck."

Nicholas put his arm around her and I thought I detected a brief second of hesitation before she looked up at him and gave him a smile.

"You make a very handsome couple," I said. "I congratulate you both."

"And we will have such fun trying on our dresses, won't we?" Matty went on. "I have shipped in a wonderful little woman from Paris, you know. I do love exquisite clothes. Nicky has promised we can live part of the year in Paris, which will make me very happy. But do you remember that awful uniform we had to wear in school? It will be just like old times together with my dear school friends again."

"You have more friends from Les Oiseaux attending?"

"I do. You will never guess. Our old friend Belinda Warburton-Stoke is here."

"Belinda? Here? You invited her to your wedding?"

I was really angry. She had seen me only a

156

week ago and said nothing.

"Not exactly," she said. "The most amazing thing happened. She was touring in this region and her car broke down right outside the castle. She had no idea who lived here or that I was celebrating my wedding. Wasn't it an incredible coincidence?"

"Incredible," I agreed dryly. "So you invited her to stay for the wedding?"

"My dear, I could hardly turn her away, could I? Besides, I knew you'd be thrilled to have her here with us. Belinda was always such fun, wasn't she, and most of the people here are so horribly stodgy and correct. Ah, there she is, over in that corner."

I followed Matty's gaze to the darkest corner of the room. I could make out Belinda's back in the elegant peacock blue and emerald green dress she had designed herself. She had her head on one side, listening earnestly to another handsome and blond young man. He was smiling down at her with the rapt attention on his face that most men adopted when anywhere near Belinda.

"Who is that with her?" I asked.

"That's Anton, Nicky's younger brother. I'm afraid it's no good her setting her cap at him. He will have to marry royalty and keep the family firm going, like the rest of us." And she gave a brittle laugh.

The dinner gong sounded.

"You are sitting by me tonight," Matty said. "I want to hear all about what you've been doing since I last saw you. But you need an escort in to dinner. Anton looks as if he's otherwise occupied, so it had better be my brother."

She pushed her way through the crowd, dragging me by one hand.

"Siegfried, you know Georgiana, don't you?"

I knew that Siegfried was of the royal house of Romania but I hadn't realized that he was Matty's brother. How could I have been so stupid?

Siegfried eyed me warily. "Ah, Lady Georgiana. I am relieved to see you are fully clothed again."

"What's this, Georgie?" Matty asked, grinning in a way that reminded me of times at school when she overheard something she wasn't supposed to.

"I omitted to take a towel to the bathroom and I'm afraid Prince Siegfried saw me clad in only a wet nightgown," I said.

"Lucky Siegfried. Let's hope it gave him ideas," Matty said wickedly. "We can't seem to make him show any interest in girls. Papa despairs of him."

"I have told Papa I shall do my duty and marry," Siegfried said. "In fact, I tried to make a suitable match earlier this year. Now please let us drop this subject."

"Stop being such a stuffy old bore, Siegfried, and learn to have fun. Here, take Georgie in to dinner."

She forced my arm through his just as Count Dragomir approached us.

"Dinner is served, Your Royal Highnesses," he said. "May I suggest that you take your places to process in to the banqueting hall, naturally with you at the head, Prince Nicholas, since our own monarch and your father are not present. And may I also suggest that Lady Georgiana be escorted by His Highness Prince Anton?"

"I think Prince Anton is already taken," I said.

Count Dragomir looked horrified. "But she is a commoner. That can't be allowed. Your Highnesses should intervene right now."

"Oh, don't be so stuffy, Dragomir," Matty said. "Honestly. This is an informal occasion. My parents are not present. So stop fussing."

"As you wish, Your Highness." Dragomir bowed low and departed muttering.

"Such a bore," Matty said, shaking her

159

head. As we made our way through to the banqueting hall another couple tried to cut in front of us. It was Prince Anton, with Belinda on his arm.

"Now here's a pretty problem," Anton said, grinning at Siegfried. "Who takes precedence here? Two princes, each of them only the spare, not the heir, and each with a pretty girl on his arm."

"Then I think I win this time," Siegfried said, "because my pretty girl is of royal blood and yours is decidedly not. And what's more, this is my family seat. But good manners demand that you please go ahead of me anyway."

Belinda put on an acting performance to rival my mother. "Georgie, it's you. What a lovely surprise," she cooed. "So you got here safely. I'm so glad. I had a beastly experience. Have you heard about it? If I hadn't come upon this castle, I'd have been done for."

"Poor Belinda's car broke an axle and she had to walk for miles in the snow," Anton said, gazing down at her adoringly. "Wasn't it lucky that we were in residence? Most of the year the castle is unoccupied."

"Belinda tends to be lucky," I said. I still found it hard to forgive her trickery, although I had to admire her gall.

We entered the banqueting room. It was impressively long and high ceilinged with arches along both walls and above them high leaded-pane windows. A white-clothed table extended for its entire length, big enough to accommodate a hundred diners, and footmen in black and silver livery stood at attention behind the gilt chairs. It was all very grand. Siegfried led me to the head of the table and I was seated across from Matty.

"Are your parents not here?" I asked Siegfried, realizing that we were being given places of honor and there was apparently not a king or queen in sight.

"My parents and the parents of Nicholas are supposed to arrive tomorrow," he said. "As will all the other royal guests. We are the advance party, so to speak, and thus we are rather informal." He looked across the table in distaste as Field Marshal Pirin was pushing his way into a seat close to us.

Nicholas saw that Pirin was aiming for me and forestalled him. "I suggest that my godfather sit next to you tonight, Georgiana. I am afraid his English is not brilliant but he tells me that he knows you." He turned to summon somebody. I wondered how many more surprises there would be tonight. Then I saw that the godfather in question was

161

none other than Max von Strohheim, my mother's latest conquest.

"Georgiana, you remember Herr Von Strohheim, don't you?" Nicholas said easily. "And are you acquainted with his charming companion?"

I looked across the table into my mother's startling violet eyes.

"Yes, we are acquainted," I said.

CHAPTER 13

Later that night

It was not one of my favorite dinners. Max's English was severely limited. My mother was clearly miffed that I was there, a living proof to everyone that she was over thirty.

"You might have warned me that you were coming along for this beanfeast," she hissed at me.

"I didn't know until a week ago when the queen asked me to represent the family."

Those eyes that had wowed audiences on a thousand stages opened even wider. "Why on earth did the queen send you?"

"How about 'It's lovely to see you again, my darling?' " I said.

"Well, of course it is, although you really do need a good hairdresser. I must say I was stunned to find you were here. I would have thought the Princess Royal should have been part of the wedding party, and not you."

163

"The bride particularly requested me," I said. "We were school friends."

"Ah. Well at last something useful has come out of that school." She leaned across Max and lowered her voice. "You know, this might be a good opportunity for you. Lots of eligible princes and counts."

"Too many," I said, glancing at Siegfried, who was chatting away in German to Max.

"You have to do something with your life, darling. You desperately need a good wardrobe and the only way you're going to get it is to find yourself a rich man."

"Some mothers might actually pay for their daughter's clothes," I said dryly, "but failing that, I'd like to find a job. It's just that there don't seem to be any jobs going for someone like me."

"Girls of your station are not supposed to find jobs," she said with distaste, overlooking the first part of what I had just said.

"You had a job for years until you met Daddy," I reminded her.

"Ah, but I was an actress. I had talent. I see nothing wrong with making use of talents, if you had any."

I was glad when Matty demanded my attention and regaled those around us with tales of our school days, none of which were how I remembered them and all of which

164

put Matty center stage in the escapades. But I smiled and nodded agreement, wishing that the dinner would hurry up and be over. Of course it went on for hours — course after course. The main dish was venison and I was given a leg shank, such a sweet delicate little thing that all I could think of was fawns leaping through the forest. It was cooked very rare and blood rushed onto my plate as I cut into it.

As I pushed it around my plate, pretending to eat it and wondering if I could drop it under the table, I remembered what I had pushed to the back of my mind until now — the figure who had climbed up the castle wall. I wanted to ask Matty about it, but one can hardly say at a royal banquet, "By the way, do you have creepy things that climb up your castle walls?"

Instead I said, "So I hear there are legends of vampires associated with this castle, Your Highness."

"Vampires?" And she gave a peal of laughter. "Oh, yes, absolutely true. Half our family are vampires, aren't they, Siegfried?"

Siegfried frowned. "Since our family originally comes from Germany, that would be hardly likely. However, there are many legends associated with this castle," he said in his prissy way of talking. "Of course the

165

castle was built by Vlad the Impaler, whom the peasants regarded as being in league with the devil, and it is said that the Dracula tale began here. The local peasants are very superstitious. Ask them and they will all tell you of a relative who was bitten by a vampire or met a werewolf. They won't venture out at night, you know, and if anyone dares to venture forth after dark then it's said that person has to be in league with the undead."

"Ah, so that explains the way they crossed themselves when we stopped at the inn at the top of the pass," I said.

"So primitive and illiterate," Siegfried said. "I told Maria Theresa that she should set an example of modern behavior by having her wedding in the capital, but she wouldn't hear of it. She always was a hopeless romantic."

I personally wouldn't have called the castle a romantic spot but I dared to ask, "So do any of these undead creatures climb up castle walls?"

"Castle walls?" Matty asked sharply. "I hope not. I sleep with my window open."

Siegfried laughed mirthlessly. "I believe that vampires are reputed to climb down walls, headfirst. But do not worry, you will be quite safe — as safe as you are at your own castle in Scotland, which I understand has its share of ghosts and monsters."

He turned back to Max and I looked across at my mother. She was in a sulky mood because there was nobody near her to charm. But I saw her looking down the table on several occasions and decided that she was showing interest in Anton. That might prove interesting, watching Belinda and my mother compete for his attention. Of course Mummy was hampered by having Max in tow. Not that that ever slowed down Mrs. Simpson! Amusingly Field Marshal Pirin seemed to think that Mummy was making eye contact with him and he raised his glass to her, leering over it seductively. Mummy shuddered.

"Who is that awful man? He looks like the wicked baron from a pantomime."

"He's the head of the Bulgarian army," I said.

"How terribly democratic of them, inviting soldiers to the royal palace."

"I gather he wields a lot of power and has to be humored," I said.

"I don't intend to humor him," she said. "He keeps looking at me as if he's mentally undressing me."

"Who wishes to undress you?" Max demanded, suddenly showing interest.

"Nobody darling, except you," Mummy

said quickly. She waited until Max had resumed his conversation. "His English has improved almost too well now. I liked it when he only understood what I wanted him to."

Field Marshal Pirin obviously had no sensibilities about eating venison. He too had a leg, which he now picked up in one hand while brandishing a wineglass in the other and taking alternate bites and swigs. I felt sorry for Nicholas and Anton if they were stuck with him as a frequent dinner guest at home.

Dinner finally came to an end and we ladies were led off to a salon while the men indulged in cigars and schnapps. Lady Middlesex intercepted me. She was dressed in a fearsome black gown, topped with a helmetlike affair that was no doubt intended to inspire awe among the inhabitants of the colonies. The effect was not unlike those suits of armor I had passed in the corridors.

"Ah, there you are. All settled in, then? Jolly good. Jolly good. We'll be off in the morning. The princess is kindly arranging for a car."

"Is Miss Deer-Harte not feeling well?" I asked, not seeing her among the ladies.

"She's right as rain, as far as I know, apart from being jumpy about staying in a place like this. I had a tray sent up to her room. She couldn't very well be allowed to join a glittering company like this for dinner, could she. She's only a companion."

"Here we are, then, isn't this jolly?" Matty came up to me, her arm linked with Belinda's. "I see you've made quite a conquest there, Belinda. Anton couldn't take his eyes off you all through dinner."

"Belinda's hobby is making conquests," I said. "She has left a long stream of broken hearts across Europe."

"I hope not," Matty said. "Fun is one thing, but broken hearts quite another. I hope I never have to break another heart as long as I live."

As we came into the room I saw a group of middle-aged women, dripping with jewels and furs, examining us critically — or rather it appeared as if they were examining me. They beckoned me over to them.

"You are the Lady Georgiana from England, correct?" one asked.

"Yes, I am."

"Relative of British king?"

"Yes, my father and he were cousins."

She looked at the other ladies and nodded. "Is good. English king has much power."

"So tell me. You know Prince of Wales?"

one of them asked. She was dressed in the height of fashion with a sleek cap of Marcel waves and brilliant red lips.

"Yes, I see him often."

"One hears he has a new mistress?" she asked. "An American woman? A commoner?"

"I'm afraid so." There was little point in denying it if the rumor had already reached Romania.

"What she is like, this woman?" my inquisitor persisted. "She is beautiful?"

"Actually not. Rather boyish in features and figure."

"You see." The woman turned triumphantly to her friends. "What do I tell you? Secretly he prefers boys. He will never marry and make a good king, that one."

"Oh, I'm sure he'll do his duty, at the right time," I said.

"The right time? My dear, isn't he already forty? The right time was twenty years ago. It was suggested then that I might be a suitable match for him. But alas, he showed no inclination. Fortunately I married my husband, the count, instead and he still keeps me satisfied in bed, which I'm sure poor Prince Edward could never do."

Her friends laughed.

"They say English men are cold, no?"

170

another of the women asked me. "They cannot feel passion because they are sent to the boarding school too early. You will do well to select a European husband, my dear. More fire and passion."

"Not all of them, remember, Sophia," the first woman said, giving her a warning glance that I couldn't understand. "Maybe the English lady does not want fire and passion. She may be content with good companionship."

They were laughing at a secret joke and I looked around uneasily. Suddenly I had the same feeling I had experienced on the station — someone was watching me. There were several archways along one side of the room and the passage beyond them was in darkness. I thought I could make out a dark figure standing just beyond the archway, but then it could have been the carved stone, or even a suit of armor.

At that moment the men came into the salon to join us. Nicholas came right over to Matty and me. Anton made a beeline for Belinda, and Field Marshal Pirin for my mother, which made Mummy decide that she was getting one of her headaches and excuse herself.

"Didn't you tell me there is an oubliette in this castle?" Anton said to Matty. "We should push Pirin down it. Really the fellow is too much. Did you see his behavior at dinner? Completely boorish."

"Much as I'd like to take up your suggestion, you know he has to be humored unless you want civil war or worse," Nicholas said. "And Father relies on him."

"Relies on him too much," Anton said. "He's getting too big for his boots. If you ask me the man is dangerous. He's using us for his own ends, Nicky. He sees himself as a future dictator, another Mussolini."

"You don't need to worry about it," Nicholas said. "You can go back to your delightful existence in Paris. I might have to deal with him someday when I become king."

"That's me. The useless playboy," Anton said. "All I'm good for is providing escort to beautiful women." And he took Belinda's arm.

"I didn't ask to be born first," Nicholas said. "I don't particularly want the job, any more than our cousin Edward wants the job in England, I'd imagine." He looked at me for confirmation.

"I don't think most men would want to be king," I said.

"One hopes that Father lives for years, of course," Nicholas said.

We glanced up as Pirin laughed noisily.

"That's a good one," he said, slapping his thigh. He was talking to the man who had welcomed us, Count Dragomir, who was not smiling. In fact he looked as if he were in pain.

"Well, I'm turning in," Lady Middlesex declared, appearing at my side. "We've had a long and strenuous day and tomorrow we have to face that pass again. Poor Deer-Harte is already a bundle of nerves." She looked at me critically. "And you look as if you could do with a good night's rest too. Come along." And she took hold of my arm in a firm manner.

Rather than make a fuss I bid my hostess good night and allowed myself to be led away. I entered my room, only to find someone sleeping in my bed. For an awful moment I thought I might have barged into Siegfried's room again. I tiptoed out again hastily and checked the hallway. I was sure this was my room this time. I went back in. The sleeper was none other than Queenie. I woke her up.

"Sorry, miss, I must have dozed off," she said. "It was that cold in here I got under the covers."

"Did you have your dinner?" I asked.

"I didn't like to leave the room, not quite knowing where I was going," she said.

"Oh, dear. Let's see if one of the servants can take you down to the kitchen and get you something now."

"It's all right, miss, thank you kindly," she said. "I think I'd rather just go to bed. I don't quite fancy foreign food at the moment. It's all been a bit much in one day."

I looked at her kindly, thinking how overwhelming it had been for me and then putting myself in her place, straight from a little London backstreet. "Good idea, Queenie. Just help me off with this dress first and hang it up and then you can go. You can find out in the morning where you go to bring up my tea tray."

She went and I was alone in the room. I climbed into bed and lingered for a while before I dared to turn off the bedside lamp. I had always thought of myself as the daring one in the family. I had allowed my brother and his school friends to lower me into the castle well at home. I had sat up all night on the battlements once to see if my grandfather's ghost really did play the bagpipes. But this was different. I felt a profound sense of unease. I wished I still had a nanny in the next room. Finally I curled up into a little ball and tried to go to sleep.

I was drifting off when I thought I heard the smallest of noises — a light click. My eyes shot open, instantly awake. Although the outer regions of my room were pitch-black I was somehow sure that someone was in the room with me. The curtains around the bed obscured my view. I leaned out a little, then drew my head back quickly. The fire had died down but from the glow I could make out a dark figure, moving closer and closer. At last he stood over the bed. I opened my mouth but I was too frightened to move or to scream. The glow from the fire illuminated his face. It looked just like the young man from the portrait on the wall.

He leaned closer and closer to me and he murmured something in a language I didn't understand. He was smiling, his teeth reflected in the firelight. Everything Belinda had told me about vampires biting necks and the ecstasy of being bitten rushed back to me. In the safety of London and daylight I had laughed with her. But the face above me was all too real and it seemed as if those teeth were heading straight for my neck. However terrified I was, one thing was certain. I was definitely not about to be turned into an undead.

I sat up abruptly, making him leap backward.

"What do you think you're doing?" I demanded in a way that my great-grandmother Queen Victoria would have been proud of.

The young man gave an unearthly moan of horror. Then he turned and melted back into the shadows.

CHAPTER 14

A bedroom in Bran Castle. Darkness.
Wednesday, November 16

For a while I couldn't move. I sat up, my heart beating so rapidly that I could hardly breathe. Was the creature still in the room with me? How did one ward off vampires anyway? I tried to remember from reading *Dracula*. Some sort of herb or plant? Parsley? No, that wasn't it. I thought it might be garlic. Had I eaten enough of that on the venison to breathe on him? I wasn't about to try to find my way down to the kitchen to locate some. I also thought I remembered that crosses might work, but I didn't have one of those either. Stakes through the heart? I didn't think I could pull that one off even if I had a stake at my disposal.

Then I thought of something more solid, like maybe one of the large candlesticks on the mantelpiece. Surely even a vampire could be kept at bay with a whomp over the head with that. I slipped out of bed, made my way across the room and picked up the candlestick. Then I crossed the room cautiously until I reached the light switch. I turned it on and found nobody there. Of course then I had to lift the various curtains, one by one, experiencing at least one heart-stopping moment when a blast of cold air hit me in the face and I realized that one of the windows was open.

I tried to close it but it didn't latch properly. I told myself that Siegfried's room was next door, but I pictured myself standing at his door in a nightdress again, trying to explain that a vampire had just been trying to bite my neck. Somehow I didn't think he'd believe me. Then I noticed a large tapestry bellpull beside the bed and was half tempted to yank on it and see who it brought. But since they probably spoke no English and I would have felt equally foolish explaining a vampire attack to them, I left it and got into bed, still clutching the candlestick. At least I was relieved knowing that the bellpull was there and if he came back I could summon help before he could get his teeth into me.

The moment I was in bed I realized that I remembered the chest that I hadn't managed to open before. I could never sleep not knowing what was in there. I got up and crossed the room slowly while the portrait of the young man looked down with a mocking smile. I jumped again as I caught sight of my reflection in that wardrobe mirror and it did occur to me that I had never seen the young man's reflection as he came toward the bed. Wasn't that another thing about vampires — that one couldn't see their shadow or their reflection? I shuddered. The lid was too heavy to lift. I struggled and struggled until at last I had it open. To my intense relief it only contained clothing, including a black cape. The interesting thing was that there were some half-melted snowflakes on it, which made me suspect that my vampire visitor had climbed the wall into my room.

I stayed awake for most of the night but received no more unearthly visitors. Toward dawn I drifted off to sleep, then awoke to that strange lighting that indicates the presence of snow. I opened my window and looked out. It must have snowed hard all night, as the turrets and battlements each wore an impressive white hat. The road up the pass was untrammeled whiteness. It would have been pretty in Switzerland with the hillsides dotted with meadows and chalets. Here it just made the crags and the pine forest even more gloomy. And such a feeling of remoteness. I felt as if I were trapped in another time, another world far away from everything safe.

I looked at my watch and realized it was after eight. I would have welcomed my cup of tea but there was no sign of Queenie. In the end I got tired of waiting. I had to dress myself and found my way down to breakfast. The breakfast table was deserted save for Prince Siegfried. He rose to his feet and clicked his heels as I approached.

"Lady Georgiana. I trust you slept well."

"Not exactly," I said.

"I am sorry. Please let our people know if there is anything to do to make you more comfortable."

I could hardly request a guard against vampires, could I? I was glad I hadn't given in to panic and rushed to his room. I'd have to be really desperate before I knocked on Siegfried's door again.

"Today I take the men out shooting," Siegfried said. "Maybe we find a wild boar. But later I hope we have the chance to speak together again. There are matters I wish to discuss with you. Important matters." He got to his feet, gave that jerky little bow of his and departed. Oh, golly, he wasn't going to bring up the marriage thing again, was he? How did one find a polite way to say "Not if you were the last man on earth"?

The sound of voices coming down the hallway made me look up. Lady Middlesex and Miss Deer-Harte came in, the latter waving her arms as she talked in animated fashion. Lady Middlesex cut her off when she saw me.

"Here's a how-de-doo," she said to me. "We've just heard that the wretched pass is closed. Avalanche or something. The car can't take us to the station. We have to stay here whether we like it or not."

"I really don't think I could face another night in this place," Miss Deer-Harte said. "Did you hear the wind moaning last night? At least I suppose it had to be the wind. It sounded like a soul in torment. And then someone was creeping down the hallway in the wee hours. I couldn't sleep and I was sure I heard footsteps, so I opened my door a crack and what do you think I saw? A dark figure creeping down the hall."

"It was only one of the servants, Deer-Harte. I've told you that already," Lady Middlesex said abruptly.

"Servants don't creep. This man was creeping — slinking as if he didn't want to be seen. Up to no good, I'm sure, if he wasn't a ghost or some other kind of creature."

"Really, Deer-Harte, your imagination," Lady Middlesex said. "It will get you into trouble one day."

"I know what I saw, Lady M. Of course in a castle this size I suppose all kinds of nighttime trysts and assignations occur. One hears about foreign appetites for bedroom activities."

"Don't be so disgusting, Deer-Harte. Ah, there's Her Highness now." She bobbed a curtsy as Matty came in. "So kind of you to allow us to stay on, Your Highness. Much appreciated." And she bobbed a jerky curtsy.

"We didn't have much choice as it happens," Matty said frankly. "There's nowhere else within miles. We're completely snowed in. But there's plenty of room and you are welcome to stay. I must say the snow has put a damper on the festivities. The parents and entourage were expected to arrive today, but it doesn't look as if they'll be able to get here for a while now. Not until the local people have managed to dig out the pass."

"Oh, dear. I do hope the wedding ceremonies can take place on time," Miss Deer-Harte said.

"The actual ceremony is not until next

week, so let's hope all is back to normal by then."

"Presumably you'll have various royal representatives arriving," Miss Deer-Harte said.

"This will be a relatively small occasion, mostly relatives," Matty said. "After all, we are related to most of the royal houses of Europe. Horribly inbred, I'm afraid. No wonder we're all so batty." She laughed again and I got the impression that she was playing a part, forcing herself to be gay. "The big formal celebration will take place in Bulgaria when we return from our honeymoon. That's when there will be heads of state and an official blessing in the cathedral and I'm presented to the people as their own dear princess — all that sort of boring stuff."

"I expect you'll have to get used to the boring stuff, as you call it, when you are married to the heir to the throne," Lady Middlesex said. "I find some of my official duties as a high commissioner's wife quite taxing but one knows one's duty and does what is expected of one, doesn't one?"

"I suppose one does," Matty said, giving me a grin. "We're meeting with the couturiere from Paris this morning, Georgie. I'm looking forward to it. In the small salon. It's

lined with mirrors so we can admire ourselves."

She paused and stared at the side table
that was laden with cold meats, cheeses,
fruits and breads, then she turned away.
"Alas, just a cup of coffee for me if I'm to
fit into that wedding dress."

"Fiddlesticks! One needs a good breakfast
to start the day," Lady Middlesex said. "I
don't hold with this ridiculous fad of diet-
ing. A cup of coffee, indeed. That won't
keep your strength up." As she said this she
was piling cold meats onto her plate with
abandon. "No egg and bacon, I notice," she
added with a sigh. "Not a kidney in sight.
Not even a kipper. One wonders how you
folk on the Continent survive without a
good hot breakfast."

I helped myself and sat down at the table.
Matty poured herself a cup of black coffee
then wandered off with it.

"I hear the men plan to go hunting," Lady
Middlesex said. "How they expect to tramp
through this snow, I have no idea. Insanity,
if you ask me, but at least it keeps them out
in the fresh air for the day. And hunting's a
healthy pursuit for young men. Keeps their
minds off sex. Maybe we should see if we
can borrow snowshoes and go out for a walk
ourselves, Deer-Harte."

I was glad she wasn't including me in this plan. I ate as quickly as possible, then excused myself, only to bump into Belinda in the doorway.

"Am I glad to see you," I said.

"That's quite a change from last night, I must say," she said with a frosty stare. "You looked daggers at me for some reason. I couldn't think what I might have done to upset you. It was almost as if you thought I'd spent the night with Darcy — which I haven't, by the way."

"I'm sorry," I said. "I was put out. At first I thought that you'd been invited to the wedding and hadn't told me, and then when I found out how you'd arrived here, I was annoyed by your utter subterfuge."

"Utter brilliance, darling, if you please. You do have to admit it was quite a coup. And you yourself said it would have been a lark if I could come to the wedding with you. So when you rejected my kind offer to become your maid, I decided that the wedding sounded like too much fun to be left out. So I packed my bags, caught the next train here, then I rented the oldest, most decrepit car and driver at the station, in the full knowledge that it would be likely to break down. Of course it did, at exactly the right spot, so I was able to present myself at the castle door and register surprise and delight when I found that Her Royal Highness the Princess Maria Theresa was in residence. 'But we were schoolmates,' I exclaimed and of course was received with open arms."

"You're as bad as my mother," I said.

"Not quite, but I'm working on it," Belinda said with a grin. "There was only one small glitch to my perfect scheme and that was when I didn't recognize Matty. My dear, can you believe the transformation? I suppose it is really she? Where did all those missing pounds go? And what about the moon face?"

"I know. I didn't recognize her either," I said. "She's quite lovely, isn't she? And her bridegroom isn't bad either."

"Neither is his brother." Belinda gave me her cat-with-the-cream smile. "Very satisfactory in all departments. Too bad he's a prince or I might snap him up for keeps. But he'll have to end up marrying someone like you. I know — you could marry him, I could remain his mistress in a delightful ménage à trois."

"Belinda!" I had to laugh. "I'd share a lot of things with you, but not my husband. Besides, Anton isn't the man I have in mind, although I have to admit that among available princes he's the best so far."

"Wouldn't suit you, darling. Too naughty. He told me some of his exploits last night and they made even me blush. Not an ounce of moral fiber in him. That's why we're perfect for each other."

"So I gather you didn't sleep in your own bed last night?"

"What a question to ask a lady! But darling, at beanfeasts like this who does sleep in their own bed? All you hear is curses and grunting as people bump into each other in the dark, tiptoeing between bedrooms. It's too, too funny for words. But I suppose you slept soundly and didn't hear a thing. I gather you've been given a room on the superior floor usually reserved for the family."

"Right next door to Siegfried, as it happens," I said, "but Belinda, that's what I wanted to talk to you about. Someone came into my room last night."

"Not Siegfried!" she exclaimed. "I thought his interests lay in quite another direction."

"Oh, God, no. But worse in a way. I think it was a vampire."

Belinda started laughing. "Georgie, you are too funny sometimes."

"No, seriously, Belinda. There is a spooky portrait hanging on the wall and this man

187

looked just like him. I was half asleep and I woke to see him creeping toward me and then he stood over my bed, muttered something in a language I didn't understand then bent down toward me with this sort of unearthly smile, showing all his teeth."

"Darling! What did you do?" She yanked down my collar. "Did he actually bite you? What was it like?"

"He didn't get a chance. I sat up and demanded to know what he was doing. He gave this sort of unearthly moan and vanished."

"Vanished? As in just melted away, you mean?"

"No, merged back into the darkness, I suppose, but when I finally turned on the light he was no longer in the room. And what's more there's a large chest in the room and inside it was a cape still damp with snowflakes on it. Explain that."

"My dear, how frightfully thrilling," Belinda said. "If I didn't have other diversions to occupy me, I'd volunteer to sleep in your room tonight. I have always wanted to meet a vampire."

"So you believe me?"

"I'm more inclined to believe it was some young count or other, one of Nicky's groomsmen, who made a mistake and got the wrong room when he went to visit the lady of his choosing. It's easy to do in a place like this."

"I suppose you may be right," I said. "I'm going to watch when they set out hunting to see if I recognize him. Whoever it was certainly wasn't at dinner last night. And he didn't look — you know — earthly."

Belinda put her hand on my shoulder. "Georgie, I was only joking in London about vampires, you know. You don't really believe in them, do you?"

"Belinda, you know me."

"I do and that's what worries me. Until now I'd have said you were one of the most levelheaded people on earth."

"I know and I'd agree with you. But I know what I saw and I know the absolute terror that I felt."

"A nightmare, maybe? Understandable in a place like this. Darling, isn't it all too delightfully gothic?"

"But what about the wet cape in that chest? If you want gothic, you should see the chest in my room. Come up and I'll show you."

"If you insist," she said. "Very well. Lead on, Macduff!"

CHAPTER 15

Bran Castle
Somewhere in Transylvania
Thursday, November 17

I led her up the stairs and pushed aside the curtains. Belinda looked around the room and of course her gaze first alighted on the portrait on the wall.

"I say. He's not bad, is he? And look at that sexy open shirt. I wonder how long ago he lived."

"He still lives. That's the whole point, Belinda. I swear he was my vampire last night."

A wicked smile crossed her face. "In that case I may well volunteer to change rooms with you. I wouldn't mind being bitten by someone like him."

I looked at her and realized she was still joking. "You still don't believe me, do you?"

"I think the logical explanation is that you fell asleep with that portrait staring down at you and you had a little fantasy dream about him."

"All right, I'll prove it to you. Look, here's the chest." I stomped across the room to it. "And I bet the cape is still damp. See?"

I flung it open triumphantly, then stopped. The chest was completely empty.

"An invisible cape, how unique," Belinda said.

"It was here, I swear. And when I first came up here I saw someone crawling up the wall."

"Of this room?"

"No, the outside wall of the castle. Just over there."

"But that's impossible."

"That's what I thought. But this — whatever-it-was — climbed up the wall over there and then disappeared."

Belinda put a hand on my forehead. "No, you don't have a fever," she said, "but you must be hallucinating. This isn't like you, Georgie. After all, you grew up in a gloomy place like this."

"We had a couple of ghosts, but no vampires, at Castle Rannoch," I said. "I asked Siegfried and Matty about them. Siegfried made light of it but Matty was definitely cagey. You don't think she's been bitten and become undead, do you? And that's why she looks so gorgeous? She's sold her soul or something?"

Belinda gave that delightful tinkling laugh again. "I think it was more likely to be that expensive cure at a spa, and watching her weight. She has hardly eaten a thing since I've been here."

"Well, I think of myself as a sane, rational person but I've been uneasy since I got here. Before I got here, in fact. I think someone was following me on the train. And someone's been watching me from the shadows here."

"How deliciously dramatic, darling," Belinda said. "What a change from your boring existence in London. You wanted adventure and now you've got it. Who do you think could be following you?"

I shrugged. "I have no idea. I can't think why anybody would be interested in me. Unless vampires are particularly attracted to virgins. Dracula was, wasn't he?"

Belinda laughed again. "In that case my blood will be quite safe. You know, maybe someone is actually following that horrible woman who is chaperoning you. Perhaps her husband has paid to have her bumped off en route. I know I would."

"Belinda, you are so wicked." I had to laugh too now.

Belinda slipped her arm through mine.

"Listen. It sounds as if the men are assembling for their hunt." The sound of barking dogs echoed up from down below, mingled with the shouts of men. "Let's go down and watch them and see if your handsome vampire really is still alive and among them. We'll see if you can pick him out in daylight, shall we? Of course, if he's going hunting then he's definitely not a vampire. They can't tolerate the sunlight, you know." She led me down the stairs to a gallery where we could overlook the front hall. A good-sized party of young men had assembled, the fur hats and traditional green jackets making it hard to tell the masters from their servants.

"There you are, plenty of counts and barons and whatnots, all single and all related to you, I suspect. Take your pick."

"I don't see my vampire," I said, studying the young men, some of whom were actually quite presentable as aristocrats go. "That proves it, doesn't it? He's not a normal young count staying at the castle. Now you have to believe me."

"I believe that the local red wine is stronger than you're used to and it gave you vivid dreams," Belinda said. "I say, they're not a bad-looking bunch on the whole, are they? Of course, Anton looks wonderful in his fur hat, doesn't he? So masculine and primitive. I wanted him to take me hunting with them, but I was told it was boys only. Spoilsports. I love shooting things, don't you?"

"Actually I don't. I don't mind grouse because they are so stupid, and I love hunting on horseback but I'm always relieved when the fox goes to earth."

"So what shall we do now?" Belinda looked around the deserted hallways.

"I've got to go and have a fitting for my dress," I said. "You can come and keep me company."

"I might," she said. "It's too bad I'm not still designing dresses or I could have picked up ideas."

"You're not? You've given up your dress design business?"

"Had to, darling." She frowned. "Couldn't afford to lose any more money. Nobody wanted to pay me, you see. They'd always say breezily 'Put it on my account' and when the time came to pay, they'd come up with every excuse in the book. One woman actually told me I should be grateful I was getting free advertising from her wearing my creation and I should be paying her. So I'm now unemployed like you. Maybe I'll be glad to be a maid, soon." She looked up at me with a grin. "So tell me, did you find a suitable maid and bring her with you?"

"I have a maid, but I can't say that she's suitable. Actually she's completely hopeless. She got my head stuck in the armhole of my dress last night, I found her sleeping in my bed when I came to my room and she forgot to come and wake me this morning."

"Where on earth did you find her?"

"She's a relative of my grandfather's neighbor Mrs. 'uggins."

"Well, then, serves you right," Belinda said.

"She means well," I said. "I'm actually quite fond of her in a way. She's been put in a situation quite remote from her normal life and she hasn't had a single bout of tears or panic. But I'll have to find out about that morning tea. I really do expect that much."

As we passed the stairs leading down to the kitchens we saw the young lady in question coming up, wiping the crumbs off her uniform.

"Oh, whatcher, miss," she said. "They don't half eat funny food here, don't they? Cold meat with garlic in it for breakfast. Whoever heard of such a thing? But the rolls were nice."

"Queenie, what happened to you?" I said coldly. "I was waiting for you to bring me my morning tea and to dress me."

"Oh, blimey, sorry, miss," she said. "I knew there was something I was supposed to be doing when I went down to the kitchen. But then I saw other servants having breakfast so I decided to tuck in too before it all went. I wasn't half hungry after missing me supper last night."

I felt rather guilty about this. I should really have made sure that she had had something to eat, but I remembered Lady Middlesex's admonitions about being firm with servants. "In future I expect my tea tray to be brought up to me at eight, is that clear?" I asked.

"Bob's yer uncle," Queenie said.

"And you are supposed to call me 'my lady,' remember?"

"Oh, yeah. I keep forgetting that one too, don't I? My old dad said I'd forget my head if it wasn't joined to my shoulders." She shook with laughter at that. "So what am I supposed to do now?"

"Go up to my room and see which of my clothes need pressing. I'll want to wear a different dress for the banquet tonight."

"Righty-o," she said. "Where do I find an iron?"

"Ask the other servants," I said. "I have no idea where irons are kept."

I left her trudging up the stairs and rejoined Belinda, who had been watching from the shadows.

"Darling, utterly clueless," Belinda said. "If she were a horse, one would have to have her put down."

"You are wicked," I said.

"I know. It's such fun." She blew me a kiss. "Enjoy your clothes session. If the other bridesmaids are anything like Matty used to look, you'll be the star and all the men will notice you. Toodle-pip."

She blew me a kiss.

I found the small salon where a bevy of seamstresses were working away with a clatter of sewing machines while a formidable and unmistakably French little woman in black stalked up and down, waving her arms and yelling. A cluster of young girls stood and sat near the fire, some of them in their underslips, while the little woman took measurements. The other girls seemed to know each other and nodded politely to me. Matty came over, took my hand and introduced me in German, then in English.

"My dearest friend from school" she called me, although this was a slight exaggeration. But I didn't correct her and returned the smile she gave me. Why was I suddenly so popular when she hadn't contacted me once since we left Les Oiseaux?

The dresses turned out to be quite lovely and frightfully Parisian chic — a sort of creamy white, long, simple and elegant with a smaller version of the bride's train behind them. What's more, contrary to Belinda's prediction, the other bridal attendants were attractive girls, cousins from German royal houses. One of them was a tall, slim blond girl who looked at me with interest as if she knew me and came over to me.

"You are Georgiana, *ja?* I was supposed to go to England last summer but I became sick."

"You must be Hannelore," I said, light dawning. "You were supposed to stay with me."

"*Ja.* I heard about this. It must have been shocking for you. When we are alone you must tell me all."

I was glad to find that her English in no way sounded like an American gangster movie.

Matty came over to us, wearing her bridal gown, still pinned along the sides. "How do you like the dresses?"

"Lovely," I said, "and your bridal gown is absolutely gorgeous. You'll be the prettiest bride in Europe."

"One has to have some compensations for getting married, I suppose," she said.

"Don't you want to get married?"

"If I had my way I'd like to live the bohemian life of an artist in Paris," she said. "But princesses aren't allowed any say in the matter."

"But Prince Nicholas seems really nice, and he's good-looking too."

She nodded. "Nicky is all right, as princes go. He's kind and you're right. It could certainly have been worse. Think of some of the absolutely awful princes there are." Then she chuckled. "I gather my brother asked you to marry him."

"I turned him down, I'm afraid," I said.

"At least you had the option of saying no, which is of course what I would have done in your shoes. Who would possibly want to be married to Siegfried, unless they were desperate." She laughed again, and again I felt that she was forcing herself to be lighthearted. "So how is your room?"

I couldn't very well say gloomy and vampire ridden, could I? I was formulating a polite answer when she went on, "I gather they gave you the room next to Siegfried's. Maybe they were hoping some sparks would fly!" She chuckled again. "I always used to have that room when we came to the castle

199

for the summer holidays. I love the view from that window, don't you?"

"It's rather snowy at the moment," I pointed out.

"In the summer it's lovely. Green woods and blue lakes and far away from the city and all the stuffiness of court life. I used to ride and swim with none of the rules of court life. It was blissful." And a dreamy expression came over her face.

"There's an interesting portrait on the wall of the room," I said. "A young man. Who is he?"

"One of the ancestors of the family that owned this castle, I suppose. I've never really thought about it," she said. "Castles are always full of old portraits." And she moved on to another subject.

I hadn't realized until the end of that day how much I missed the company of other young women and what fun we'd had at school. There was a lot of giggling and chatting in various languages, mostly German, of which I spoke little, but Matty was ready to translate for me. She looked the fairy-tale princess in her wedding dress with a train yards long, which we were to carry, and a veil falling around her, topped by a coronet.

By the time we had finished, the men

came back from their hunt, exhilarated because they had shot a huge wild boar with fine tusks. I was ready for a cup of tea, but instead coffee and cake were offered. I'm sorry but if you're born British there is no substitute for afternoon tea. It's in our genes. The cake was rather rich and I began to feel sick. I suppose it was tiredness as I hadn't really slept for two nights. I went up to my room, only to find no sign of Queenie. I was now becoming annoyed. It would soon be all over the castle if I had to go and look for her every time I wanted something. I was half tempted to yank on that bellpull and send whoever came to seek out my maid, but I decided that she was probably in the servants' quarters wolfing down cake and it would be quicker to find her myself. So I went down stair after winding stair and then that terrifying wall-hugging flight with no banister. I tried to remember exactly where I had bumped into Queenie this morning, ducked under an arch and started down a straight flight of well-worn steps. As I turned into a dark hallway at the bottom I could hear the clank of pots and pans and the murmur of voices. Then suddenly I started as I saw a figure crouched in a dark corner. The figure looked up at me and gasped.

"Oh, Georgie. You startled me." She put her hand up to her mouth and attempted to wipe it hastily. "Don't mention this to anyone, please. I can't help myself. I try, but it's no good." It was Matty. Her mouth was bright red and sticky and she had blood running down her chin.

CHAPTER 16

Still Bran Castle
Thursday, November 17

I couldn't think what to say. My only thought was one of flight. I turned and went back up those stairs as quickly as possible. So it was true. She was one of them. Maybe half the castle was populated with vampires and that was why there was so much tiptoeing around at night. I was actually relieved to find my room still empty. I got into bed and pulled the covers around me. I didn't want to be here. I wanted to be safe and at home and among people I could trust. I'd even have settled for close proximity to Fig, which shows you how low I was feeling.

Tiredness overcame me and I drifted into a deep slumber, only to be shaken awake by Queenie.

"Miss, it's time to get ready for dinner," she said. "I've run you a bath and put a towel in there."

This was a great improvement. My little talk this morning had obviously worked wonders. I bathed, came back to my room and let Queenie help me into my green satin dinner dress. I looked at myself in the mirror and somehow it hung wrongly. It had been a classic long evening gown before, smooth over the hips and flaring out to a gored skirt, but now it seemed to have a bump on one side, making my hip look as if it were deformed.

"Wait," I said. "There's something wrong with this skirt. It never bunched up like this before. And it seems awfully tight."

"Oh," she said. "Yes. Well . . ."

I looked up at her face. "Queenie, is there something you're not telling me?"

"I didn't think you'd notice," she said, toying with her apron. "I had to fiddle with the skirt because it got a bit scorched when I ironed it. I'm not used to ironing nice stuff like this and the iron must have been too hot." Then she demonstrated how she'd sewn the skirt together over a patch that had two big iron-shaped scorch marks on it. One scorch mark I could understand, but what had made her go back to repeat the mistake?

"Queenie, you are hopeless," I said.

"I know, miss. But I do try," she said.

"I'll have to wear the burgundy again," I said with a sigh, "unless Belinda's got something she can lend me. Run down to her room, tell her what you've done and ask her."

I waited impatiently, wondering how a dressmaker might be able to repair the damage in one of my few good dinner dresses. Almost immediately Queenie reappeared, her face scarlet.

"I knocked and went into her room, miss, and . . . and . . . she wasn't alone. A man was in bed with her, miss, and he was, and they were . . . you know."

"I can guess," I said with a sigh. "Rule number one. Always wait until someone says 'Come in' in the future."

"Yes, miss," she said.

So it was the burgundy velvet again. I did my own hair and went down to dinner. Tonight was to be a more formal occasion, as it was originally expected that various crowned heads would have arrived. Count Dragomir had had his way and insisted on the same degree of formality because there were place cards at the table and I was told I was to be escorted into the banqueting hall by Anton.

As I waited for him to join me, I was joined instead by Lady Middlesex and in her wake Miss Deer-Harte.

"Isn't this too exciting," the latter said. "So kind of Her Highness to insist that we join in the festivities. I've never been to an occasion like this. So glittering, isn't it? Like a storybook. You look very nice, my dear."

"Same dress as she wore last night, I notice," Lady Middlesex said bluntly.

"But very nice. Elegant," Miss Deer-Harte said, smiling kindly. She was wearing a simple flowery afternoon dress, quite wrong for the occasion.

"I hope I can sleep tonight," she whispered to me. "One can only go so long without sleep but the door to my room does not lock and with all that creeping around . . ."

The dinner gong sounded. Anton came to take my arm.

"What-ho, old thing," he said.

"Did you go to the same English public school as your brother?" I asked.

"Yes, only I was expelled," he said. "Or rather, politely asked to leave. Smoking in the bathrooms one time too many, I'm afraid. But I did pick up the lingo rather well." He grinned at me. "Your friend Belinda, she is a cracker, isn't she? A real live wire."

"So I've heard."

"Too bad she is not royal."

"Her father is a baronet," I said. "She is an honorable."

He sighed. "Probably not good enough, I'm afraid. Father is such a stickler for doing the right thing and family comes first and all that bosh. As if it matters who I marry. Nick will be king and produce sons and I'll never see the throne anyway."

"Would you want to?"

"I suppose I prefer my free and easy life, actually," he said. "I've been studying chemistry in Heidelberg. Good fun."

"You're lucky," I said. "I'd have loved to go to university."

"Why didn't you?"

"I'm a girl. I'm supposed to marry. Nobody was willing to pay for me."

"Too bad."

A trumpet sounded. The doors to the dining hall were opened by two of those servants in the splendid black and silver livery and we processed through. This time I was seated with Hannelore on one side of me and Anton on the other. Nicholas sat opposite with Matty on one side, and Field Marshal Pirin had again managed to position himself on the other. If anything, Pirin was wearing even more medals and orders this time. He looked first at me, then at Hannelore and his face lit up.

"This is good. Two pretty girls tonight for me to feast the eyes upon. Very nice. Feast for eyes and feast for stomach at same time." His smile was disconcerting. As my mother had said the night before, he was mentally undressing us.

"Beware that horrid man. He was pinching my bottom yesterday," Hannelore whispered to me.

"Don't worry. I've already encountered him and I'm avoiding him," I whispered back.

I noticed Anton looking around, obviously trying to locate Belinda, who was nowhere in sight, presumably sitting at a far end of the table with the lesser mortals. I couldn't help glancing at Matty and my gaze went straight to her mouth and neck. They looked perfectly normal but then she was wearing a high-necked dress. She caught my eye and then looked down uncomfortably. I found myself checking out the guests at the table to see if any of them showed obvious bite marks on their necks. One woman at the far end was wearing a lot of strands of pearls, but apart from that their necks seemed to be pristine. Maybe vampires bit each other. What did I know?

The meal began, course after course of rich food, culminating in a procession carrying a whole roast wild boar with an apple in its mouth.

"Not the one we shot today," Anton said. "Ours was much bigger."

"Who actually shot it?"

"I did" — Anton lowered his voice — "but we let Siegfried think that he did. He cares about these things, you know."

Throughout the meal Dragomir had been hovering in the background, directing servants like an orchestra conductor. As the main course came to an end he appeared at Nicholas's shoulder and banged on the table with a mallet.

"Highnesses, lords and ladies, please rise," he announced in French, then in German. "His Royal Highness Prince Nicholas wishes to drink a toast to the health of his bride and to her wonderful country."

Nicholas rose to his feet. "If the toasts are to begin, then more champagne, if you please," he said. "How can I toast my beautiful bride with anything less?"

"Forgive me. Of course. Champagne." Dragomir barked instructions and bottles were produced, opened with satisfying pops and poured. And so the toasts began. An endless stream of toasts. At home toasting at formal banquets is a stylized and decorous affair with the toastmaster drawling out, "Pray be upstanding for the loyal toast," and everyone murmuring, "The king, God bless him." Here it was what my mother would have called a beanfeast. Anybody who felt like it could leap up and toast whomever they pleased. So there was a great deal of scraping of chairs and shouted toasts up and down the table.

Dragomir, as toastmaster, tried to keep control of things, banging his mallet with a flourish before each speech. The toasts were conducted in a mixture of French, German and English as hardly any of the party spoke either Romanian or Bulgarian. If the two parties were close enough together they clashed glasses. If they were far apart they raised glasses and drank together, the rest of the diners often joining in with a swig of their own to show solidarity. One by one the men rose to make their speeches and toast their guests. Maria was the only woman who dared to rise and toasted her attendants, so I had to stand up and reach across the table to clink glasses with her. Then Nicholas rose to toast his groomsmen. "These men have watched me grow up from disreputable youth to serious manhood," Nicky said and various men at the table hooted and laughed. "And so I toast you now, you who know my darkest secrets. I drink to my dear brother, Anton, to Prince Siegfried, to Count Von Stashauer, to Baron . . ." Young men rose to their feet as he named them, twelve in all, reaching out to clink glasses with Nicholas. He was speaking in German and I couldn't take in all the names, until I was aware he had switched to English and was saying, ". . . and to my old friend who has valiantly arrived in spite of all obstacles in his path, the Honorable Darcy O'Mara from Ireland."

I looked down the table and there at the far end I saw Darcy rise to his feet and raise a glass. If my heart had beaten fast at finding what seemed to be a vampire bending over me, it was positively racing now. As Darcy took a sip from his wine, he caught my eye and raised the glass again in a toast to me. I went crimson. I wish I could get over this girlish habit of blushing. It's so obvious with my light complexion. I was actually glad for once when Field Marshal Pirin rose unsteadily to his feet.

I had noticed that he'd been drinking more than his share of red wine all evening, holding up his glass to be refilled again and again. He had had a good swig at all the toasts whether they applied to him or not. Now he grabbed his glass and launched into a speech in what had to be Bulgarian. I don't think anyone else understood, but he went on and on, his speech slurred a little, his face beetroot red, then he thumped the table and finished with what was obviously a toast to Bulgaria and Romania. He drained his glass in one large glug. Then his eyes opened wide in surprise, he made a gagging noise in his throat and he fell forward into what remained of his plate of wild boar.

The company behaved exactly as one would have expected of those who were brought up to be royal. A few eyebrows were raised and then guests went back to their meal and their conversation as if nothing had happened, while Dragomir fussed around, directing the servants to lift the unconscious man and carry him through to a couch in the anteroom. Nicholas had also risen to his feet.

"Please excuse me, I should see if there's anything I can do for him," he said quietly.

At the far end of the table Lady Middlesex had also risen. "I don't suppose there's a doctor in the house. Let me take a look at him. I was a nurse in the Great War, you know." And she strode down the room after them. I noticed that Miss Deer-Harte followed in her wake.

I could hear the murmurs of conversation.

212

"He was drinking far too much," Siegfried said. He had been sitting on the other side of Field Marshal Pirin. "Every time the servers came past he had them refill his wineglass."

"The man drinks like a fish," Anton agreed, "but I've never seen him pass out before."

"He was disgusting," Hannelore muttered to me. "The way he eats. No manners. And the wrong forks."

I noticed that Darcy had also excused himself from the table and was making his way toward the anteroom. Ice cream was served, then the cheese board was brought around and still neither Nicholas or Darcy reappeared.

When the meal was almost over, Nicholas came back to the table, leaned across and muttered something to Anton in German. I looked to Anton for a translation. He had a strange expression on his face. Before he could say anything Nicholas spoke in a loud, clear voice to the dinner guests.

"I regret to inform you that Field Marshal Pirin has been taken seriously ill," Nicholas said carefully. "May I suggest that, given the circumstances, we ask you all to leave the table and retire to the withdrawing room. I'm sure our hosts, Prince Siegfried and Princess Maria Theresa, will be good enough to arrange for coffee and drinks to be served there."

The only sound was that of the scraping of chairs as the dinner guests rose to their feet.

"Please follow me," Matty said with regal composure that I had to admire.

Anton pulled out my chair for me and I stood with the rest, feeling rather sick and shaky that the event had taken place so close to me. Anton was staring into that anteroom with a strange expression on his face — a mixture of horror and delight.

"Was it his heart, did your brother say?" I asked.

He took my arm and drew me close to him. "Don't say anything to the others, but old Pirin has kicked the bucket," Anton muttered into my ear.

"He's dead, you mean?"

He nodded but put a warning finger up to his lips. "I can't say I'm exactly sorry. Couldn't stand the bastard, but Papa is not going to be thrilled. I suppose I should go in there and support my brother, although I can't stand the sight of dead bodies in general and I'm sure that Pirin's will be more revolting than most of them."

He held out his arm to me. "I should

probably be gentlemanly and escort you to the safety of the drawing room first, in case you faint or something."

"Do I look as if I'm about to faint?" I asked.

"You look a little green," he said, "but I expect I do too. At least he had the courtesy to wait until the meal was over before he died. I'd have hated to miss that wild boar." And he gave me a grin that reminded me of a naughty schoolboy.

"I'm all right. I'll find my own way," I said. "I expect your brother would like to have you with him."

Everyone was behaving with the greatest decorum, leaving the table quietly, some of them glancing across at the archway to the anteroom where Pirin's feet could be seen sticking off the end of the couch. I heard my mother's clear voice over the discreet murmur. "The way that man wolfed down his food and drink he was a heart attack waiting to happen."

I wanted desperately to be with Darcy, but I couldn't think of a good reason to intrude, as a mere guest at the castle. But I lingered as long as I dared until most of the company had passed through the big double doors and then slowly followed Anton toward the anteroom. As I neared the entrance of the anteroom I heard Lady Middlesex's strident voice saying, "Heart attack, my foot. It is quite clear that the man was poisoned."

CHAPTER 17

Bran Castle plus dead body
Still November 17

I needed no further reason to enter that room. After all, I had experienced more of my share of murder than most young women of my station in life. I was just about to follow Anton inside when Darcy came out, almost colliding with me.

"Hello," he said. "I was just coming to find you."

"Why didn't you tell me you were coming here?" I demanded.

"At the time of our last conversation I had no idea that you were planning to attend the wedding," he said. "And your terrifying sister-in-law made it quite clear I was never to communicate with you again."

"So when did you ever do what anyone told you?" I asked.

He smiled and I felt some of the tension of the past days melting away. Now that he was here I felt that I could tackle vampires, werewolves or brigands. I was brought back to frightening reality when Darcy pushed past me and grabbed the nearest footman who was starting to clear the table.

"No," he said. "Leave it. Leave everything." The servants looked up at him, confused and suspicious. Darcy poked his head back into the anteroom and beckoned to Dragomir. "I need your help right away," he said. "I don't speak Romanian or whatever they speak in these parts. Please tell the servants not to touch anything and to leave the table exactly as it is."

Dragomir stared at him suspiciously. Darcy repeated the command in remarkably good French.

"May I ask what authority you have here? You are from the police, monsieur?" Dragomir asked.

"Let's just say I have some experience in these matters and my one wish is that we handle this in a way that does not embarrass the royal houses of Romania or Bulgaria," Darcy said. "The servants should not be told the truth at this point. This is a most delicate matter and is not to be spoken about, is that clear?"

Dragomir looked long and hard at him, then nodded and barked a command at the servants. The men hastily put down the plates they were collecting and stepped back from the table.

"Tell them that nobody else is to come into the dining room, and tell them I would like to speak to them shortly so they should not go anywhere."

That command was also repeated, although in surly and unwilling fashion, and I saw inquiring glances directed at Darcy, who didn't appear to notice.

"We should go back in there." Darcy turned to me. "Nicholas will find himself in a pretty pickle, I'm afraid, if we don't do something quickly."

"Is it true, do you think?" I whispered to Darcy. "Was Field Marshal Pirin poisoned?"

"Absolutely," Darcy said in a low voice. "All the signs point to cyanide. Flushed face, staring eyes."

"He always had a flushed face," I said.

"And the unmistakable smell of bitter almonds," Darcy finished. "That's why it's important that nothing is touched on that table."

With that he stepped back into the anteroom with me at his heels. Field Marshal Pirin's body lay on the couch exactly as Darcy had described him, his face bright red and his eyes open and bulging horribly.

He was a big man and the couch was delicate gilt and brocade so that his feet hung over the end and one arm was dangling to the floor. I shuddered and forced myself not to turn away. The other occupants of the room appeared to be frozen in a tableau around the body: Nicholas staring down at Pirin, Anton standing behind Nicholas while Lady Middlesex and Miss Deer-Harte hovered near Pirin's highly polished boots. Miss Deer-Harte looked as if she wanted to do nothing more than escape.

"You must telephone for the police at once," Lady Middlesex said. "There is a murderer in our midst."

"Impossible, madam," Dragomir said, reappearing behind us. "The telephone line has come down with all this snow. We are cut off from the outside world."

"And there is not a police station within reach to which you could send a man?"

"A man could probably go on skis over the pass," Dragomir said, "but I advise that we should not summon the police, even if we could, before Their Majesties have been told."

"But there has been a murder," Lady Middlesex said. "We need someone who can find the culprit before he gets away."

"As to that, madam," Dragomir said, "anyone who tried to leave the castle would not get far in snow like this. Besides, there is only one way out of the castle and a guard is at the gate at all times."

"Then for heaven's sake make sure the guard knows that nobody is to leave," Lady Middlesex said angrily. "Really, you foreigners. Too slipshod in everything."

"Lady Middlesex, I'm sure Prince Nicholas would appreciate it if you didn't broadcast the facts all over the castle at the moment," Darcy said. "I assure you that we will do everything in our power to get to the bottom of this as soon as possible. And nobody is going to be slipshod."

"And you are . . . ?" she asked, turning to focus on him. If she'd had a lorgnette she would have stared at him through it. One almost expected her to utter the words "a handbag?"

"He is my groomsman and good friend Darcy O'Mara, Lord Kilhenny's son," Nicholas said shortly. "A good man to have around if you're in trouble. He was at school with me — the backbone of our rugby team."

"Oh, well, in that case." Lady Middlesex was quite happy now. Anyone who was the backbone of an English public school rugby team had to be all right. "So what do you want us to do?"

"I've told the servants not to touch the table," Darcy said. "One of the first things is to have the cause of death confirmed by a competent physician. I don't suppose there is one of those within reach, is there?" He repeated the question in French.

Dragomir shook his head.

"Then we must find out how the poison was administered. I don't suppose we have any scientific testing at our disposal?"

"I believe you need iron sulfate; that turns cyanide Prussian blue," Anton said, then again he gave that boyish smirk. "So you see, big brother, I did learn a thing or two at university. I'm not sure what iron sulfate is used for — something to do with wood-working or steelworking I believe. So possibly there may be some stored in the castle outbuildings or the forge or something. We could ask Siegfried and Maria."

"No," Nicholas said shortly. "I'd much rather they didn't know yet. Not until I've thought things through."

"Too bad they no longer have a royal food taster at your disposal," Darcy said, then he saw Miss Deer-Harte's shocked face and laughed. "It was an attempt at humor," he said.

"There may be some animals on which we could test various foods," Dragomir said. "I can send a servant to see if any stable cats have had a litter of kittens recently."

"Oh, no," I interrupted hastily, "you're not going to poison kittens. That's too horrible."

"You English with your sentimental attachment to animals," Dragomir said, then he appeared to be aware of me for the first time. "Lady Georgiana. It is not seemly that you should be here. Please return to the other ladies in the drawing room."

"I asked her to be here," Darcy said. "Believe it or not she has also had some experience with this kind of thing. And she's a good head on her shoulders."

Of course I blushed stupidly as they looked at me.

"First things first," Nicholas said. "You must understand that this is a very delicate situation for us and one that could have serious ramifications if the news leaked out. Pirin was a powerful man in my country. It was only his influence at court that kept a whole province from breaking away. If word gets out that he's been murdered — why, we could have a civil war on our hands by the end of the week, or, worse still, Yugoslavia could decide this would be an opportune moment to annex our Macedonian province. So I would prefer it that the true circumstances not be made known outside of this room."

"In that case we should let it be generally thought that he died of a heart attack," Darcy said. "We can't bring him back to life but I presume it was well known that he liked his food and drink, so his death will come as no great surprise."

"That was the general consensus of opinion as we were leaving the dining room anyway," I chimed in. "If nobody else overheard Lady Middlesex then I don't think you'll have much trouble with convincing everyone that he died of a heart attack."

"That's certainly helpful," Nicholas agreed.

Anton said nothing. He was still staring at the body in fascination and revulsion. Suddenly he looked up, his clear blue eyes fastening on his brother's. "I don't think anyone should be told that he's dead before Papa finds out," Anton said. "We should keep up the pretense that he's gravely ill until our parents get here."

Nicholas frowned. "I don't know if we can do that," he said. "I'm sure some of the servants overheard this lady's outburst."

"One assumes they don't speak English," Darcy said.

"Another thing you should consider," Anton said, still looking directly at his brother, "is that Papa may well want to call off the wedding."

"Call off the wedding, why?" Nicholas asked.

"Think about it, Nick. He will want to make a grand show of mourning for Pirin — to let our Macedonian brothers know how highly he regarded him. It would be most unseemly to have any kind of festivities during such a solemn time."

"Oh, damnation, you're right," Nicholas said. "That's exactly what he'll want to do. And Romania could take it as a slight if we postpone the wedding. And think of the expense — we've already invited all the crowned heads of Europe to the ceremony back home in Sofia. And poor Maria. She's so looking forward to her big day. What a horrible mess. Trust Pirin to get himself poisoned at the most inopportune moment."

"What we have to do is keep up the pretense," Anton said, warming to his subject now and strolling past the corpse. "We'll let Papa know that Pirin is ill, but he shouldn't find out that he's dead until we've had the wedding ceremony."

Nicholas gave a nervous laugh. "And exactly how are we going to do that? He'll want to visit the sickroom, I'm sure."

"Then Pirin will be sleeping. In a kind of coma maybe."

"He looks dead, Anton, and in case you haven't noticed, he's not breathing."

"We'll have to have someone hidden behind the curtains and snoring for him," Anton said. "We can do it, Nick. We can pull it off at least until Papa realizes it's too late to call off the wedding."

"You know how thorough Papa is. He'll want to summon his own doctor."

"It will take several days to get him from Sofia."

"He'll at least want to know that a doctor has been consulted," Nicolas insisted.

"Then one of us will have to play the part. Darcy, perhaps."

"He's met me before," Darcy said. "He could have just missed the doctor who has been called out to a confinement in the mountains."

Nicholas laughed again. "You are turning this whole thing into a farce. It can't work. You know what court life is like. It will probably be all around the castle by morning that he's dead. Servants will come into his room — and who knows when Papa will get here? We can't leave a corpse lying around for days, you know. He'll begin to smell."

"How revolting," Lady Middlesex said.

Nicholas looked up at her, I think just realizing that strangers were present at what was a very private discussion. "We have no guarantee that the people in this room will not say the wrong thing."

"Unfortunately we all know the truth," Darcy said. "You can count on Georgie and me. That leaves Dragomir and the ladies. I'm sure Dragomir wants what is best for his princess and for Romania, but you may have to lock away the ladies until after the ceremony. There are plenty of dungeons here, aren't there?"

"Lock us away? Are you out of your mind, young man?" Lady Middlesex demanded, while Miss Deer-Harte whimpered the word "dungeons?"

"Then they must swear not to divulge anything they have overheard. I'm sure we can trust the word of the wife of a British high commissioner."

"You most certainly can," Lady Middlesex said.

"I must have the word of every one of you here that nothing that has been discussed in this room is ever repeated to anyone else," Nicholas said solemnly. "The future of my country is at stake. Can I trust you? Do I have your word?"

"I've already said you have mine," Darcy said. "I don't see how you're going to pull this off, but I'll do everything in my power to help you."

"Mine too," I said.

"Very well," Nicholas said. "And you, ladies?"

Lady Middlesex frowned. "I would normally not agree to go along with any kind of subterfuge or underhand behavior, but I can see the ramifications could be most difficult for your country, so yes, you have my word. Besides, Miss Deer-Harte and I shall be leaving as soon as transportation can be provided for us over the pass. I am expected by my husband in Baghdad."

"And I can be trusted to hold my tongue," Miss Deer-Harte said. "I have a long history of living in other people's houses and of hearing things not meant for my ears."

Nicholas looked at Count Dragomir. "And you, my lord steward. For the good of our two countries and the happiness of your princess?" Nicholas said to him, holding out his hand. Dragomir nodded and reached out his own hand. "I shall not let you down,

Highness. However, I should like to choose a couple of my most trusted servants to be in the know and ready to assist us, should the need arise."

"That makes sense. Choose wisely and let us get to work." Nicholas sighed. "The first thing to do is to get Pirin up to his room. That in itself will not be an easy task. He was a big man when alive. Now he'll be a dead weight."

"I will call in those two servants I suggested," Dragomir said. "Both strong men and loyal to me and the crown. I will station one of them outside his door and I shall keep the key."

"Thank you, Dragomir. Much appreciated," Nicolas said.

"I don't know what you hope to achieve with this, Your Highness," Dragomir said. "It seems like a hopeless endeavor to me."

"Not so hopeless," Anton said. "I've been studying a bit of chemistry at Heidelberg. The longer you leave it, the more chance cyanide has to dissipate from the system. A heart attack will be tragic but nobody can be blamed for it but the man himself. My father needs time to think out his strategy. We are giving him time."

I had been the silent onlooker until now but I took a deep breath. "It seems to me there is one thing you are all overlooking," I said. "And that's the murderer. Who wanted Pirin dead so strongly that he was prepared to take a risk and kill him in public?"

CHAPTER 18

Still Thursday, November 17
Still snowed in.

They all stared at me, as if I were putting a new thought into their heads.

Then Anton gave an uneasy chuckle. "As to that, the only two people who were glad to see the last of him were Nicholas and myself, and we are not stupid enough to risk our country's future by bumping him off."

"I can't think of anyone else here who actually knew the man, let alone would have had a motive to want him dead," Nicholas said.

"There are always ongoing feuds and hatreds seething in the Balkans," Darcy said. "Who is to say that one of the servants here does not come from an area where they have a longtime feud with Macedonia, or whose family has not suffered at the hands of Pirin?"

Dragomir shook his head. "That is most unlikely," he said. "These men belong to the castle, not the royal family. Local men. They live and work here year-round. Our men are Transylvanian through and through."

"Money can always buy loyalty," Darcy said. "The people of this area live a harsh life. If an instigator or anarchist were to pay them enough money, which of them might not be tempted to slip a little pill into food or drink?"

"That, of course, is the big question, isn't it?" I said. "How was the poison administered? We were all sitting together at table. We all ate the same food and drink."

The others nodded thoughtfully.

There was a sound from outside the archway and a servant appeared saying something to Count Dragomir. Dragomir looked up. "This man says that Prince Siegfried sent him to see what was happening. The prince was about to come in himself. He was annoyed at being told to stay away."

Nicholas stepped forward to block the man's view of Pirin's body. "Please tell the prince that Field Marshal Pirin is being taken to his room," he said to Dragomir in French. "He appears to have suffered a heart attack and there is regrettably nothing that anyone can do, other than wait and see if he pulls through. Sleep and perfect quiet are what he needs."

Dragomir repeated this and the man withdrew. Dragomir turned back to us. "I have asked the two men in question to present themselves. They will carry the field marshal's body to his room."

"Excellent," Nicholas said.

"But what about the tables?" Dragomir asked, looking through at them. "Our men will become suspicious if they are left untouched. They will know that something is wrong."

"That's true," Darcy said. "Then we will rescue Pirin's plate and glasses while we can, and they can take the rest. We have to assume that the poison was designed for one person and not randomly sprinkled on some part of the meal."

"The meal was at an end, anyway," Anton said. "Besides, I don't see how anyone could have poisoned the food. It was served to all of us from the same platters. The risk of setting aside one slice of poisoned meat or one poisoned potato to be put on a particular plate is too great."

"It is impossible," Dragomir said. "The platters come up from the kitchen in the dumbwaiter. They are handed to servers who whisk them to the table as rapidly as possible so that the food stays hot. There are too many links in this chain."

"I suppose it's possible that a particular server could put a cyanide capsule on one special morsel of food as he came through from the serving area," Darcy said thoughtfully, "but as you say, the risk of making a mistake is great." He broke off as two burly men appeared at the door. Dragomir intercepted them and spoke to them for a while in a low voice. They looked across at the body and nodded. Then they went over to him and lifted him between them. It was clearly heavy going.

"You and I had better help, or they'll never get him up the stairs," Nicholas said to his brother. "It may be easier if we seat him on a chair and carry him that way."

"Your Highness. That would be most unseemly," Dragomir said.

Nicholas laughed. "I'm afraid this is an occasion on which we put protocol aside, if we wish to succeed," he said. "Your job is to go ahead of us and make sure the coast is clear." He looked at the rest of us.

"And your job is to go back to the party and act normally. If asked about Pirin's health be vague. And remember the vow you made."

"But what about the investigation?" Lady Middlesex demanded. "And the plates that should be tested?"

"I'll retrieve them now and keep them safe," Darcy said. He went through to the dining room and wrapped Pirin's china and glasses inside a couple of napkins. "I moved the dishes around a bit to create some confusion," he said. "The removal of one place setting might make the servants suspicious. And if you don't mind, Count Dragomir and Prince Nicholas, I think I should have a word with the servers before they disperse and can gossip among themselves. I'll need you to translate for me, Dragomir."

"So your job is to keep the stiff upper lip, as they say in England, ladies," Nicholas said. "Go back to the party and be merry and gay."

"I think we should go straight to bed, Deer-Harte," Lady Middlesex said. "This has been most distressing for all of us. I sincerely hope that we can get away tomorrow and resume our journey back to normal life."

Miss Deer-Harte nodded. "Oh, I do hope so. I told you when we arrived that I sensed this was a place of death, didn't I? I am seldom wrong in my intuition."

And so they left. Darcy turned to me. "You should go back to the party. Above all keep talking to Maria and Siegfried so that they don't follow us. I'll come and join you when I can."

And so our group dispersed.

I tried to slip into the drawing room without being noticed but it seemed that everyone was on edge and Siegfried got to his feet as I came in.

"What news, Lady Georgiana?"

"I'm afraid I'm no medical expert," I said, "but everyone seems to think that the poor man suffered a heart attack. They have carried him to his room. There's not much more that can be done for him apart from letting him rest."

"I feel desolate that there is no doctor in our midst and no way of summoning one other than sending one of the cars back to Brasov. And given the condition of the pass, that could not be accomplished until morning."

The group was still sitting in subdued silence.

"Well, I'm not at all surprised he had a heart attack," my mother said, loudly and cheerfully. "That bloated red face is always a sign. And the way he ate and drank."

236

"He is a peasant. What can you expect," Siegfried said. "Nothing good ever comes of elevating these people to positions of power. It goes to their heads. Let those who are bred to rule do the ruling — that's how I was brought up."

"Siegfried, you are so stuffy," Matty said. Then she stood up. "I'm sorry the poor man has been taken ill, but enough gloom for one evening. It is my wedding celebration after all. Let's bring in some music and dance a little."

"Maria, do you think that's seemly?" Siegfried asked.

"Oh, come on, Siegfried, it's not as if there's been a death in the house. He may be right as rain by tomorrow and he won't be disturbed by us down here. These friends have come from all over Europe to celebrate with me and I want to dance."

She gave a command and the carpet was rolled back. A pianist and violinist appeared and soon a lively polka was played. I stood beside Siegfried as Matty dragged one of the young counts onto the dance floor. Siegfried always looked as if there were a bad smell under his nose. At this moment the expression was exaggerated. Then he turned to me and clicked his heels.

"I should see if the patient requires any-

237

thing of me," he said. "After all, I am the host in my father's absence. It is not right that I neglect Prince Nicholas in his hour of need."

"Oh, I think that Dragomir has organized everything beautifully," I said. "He's a good man. Everything runs like clockwork here."

"Yes, he is a good man," Siegfried said.

"Is the administration of this castle his only responsibility, or is he usually in Bucharest with the royal family?"

"No, his duties are confined to this place," Siegfried said. "He is not of Romanian birth, which would make him unpopular with the people."

"But you are not of Romanian birth either," I said, laughing. "None of the royal families in this region are natives of their countries."

"Ah, but we are of royal blood. That is what matters. People would rather be ruled by true royalty, wherever they come from, than by upstarts who would abuse their power."

"So where does Count Dragomir come from?"

Siegfried shrugged. "I can't quite remember. One of those border areas that has changed hands many times, I think. Just as Transylvania itself used to be part of the

Hapsburg Empire."

"Interesting," I said. "The history of this whole area is fascinating, don't you think?"

"One long disaster," Siegfried said. "One long history of being overrun by barbarians from the East. Let us hope that Western European civility will finally bring peace and prosperity to these war-torn lands." He looked around again as he spoke. "I really feel that I should at least go up to the sick man's bedroom to make sure that he has all he needs."

He was about to leave. I did the unthinkable. "Oh, no, dance with me, please." And I took his hand and led him onto the floor.

"Lady Georgiana!" His pale face was flushed, apparently affronted by my boldness. "Very well, if you insist."

"Oh, I do. I do," I said with great enthusiasm.

He placed one hand upon my waist and took the other in his. His hand felt cold and damp, rather like clutching a fish. So my decision to dub him Fishface had been quite accurate. It wasn't just his face that was fishy. I forced my mouth into a bright smile as we glided around the floor.

"So," he said, "can one assume that you have finally come to your senses? You have seen the light, *ja?* Realized the truth about the situation?"

What situation was he talking about? Did he know something about Pirin's murder? Had he arranged for it? Or was he talking about vampires, by any chance? He wanted to know whether I had discovered the horrid truth about his family. I had to tread carefully. I was, after all, a guest in a snowed-in castle, with the telephone lines down and miles from any kind of help except for Darcy and Belinda.

"What situation is this, Highness?" I asked.

"You have realized that it is important for you to follow your family's wishes and make the correct match. You understand the importance of duty."

What exactly was he talking about? Then he went on and light dawned.

"Of course I realize that ours would be a marriage of convenience, like so many royal marriages, but you would find me a considerate husband. I would allow you much freedom, and I think you would have a pleasant life as my princess."

The words "not if you were the last man on earth" were screaming through my head, but I couldn't let him stomp off to find Pirin, could I?

"Highness, I am flattered that you even

240

consider me as your bride when there are many ladies present of higher status than I. Surely Princess Hannelore would be a better match for you — a fellow German and a princess, not just a relative of the royal family."

"Ah," he said, his face clouding. "She would, of course, have been an excellent choice, but she has let it be known that she does not wish to settle down yet."

She's turned him down, I thought, trying not to smile. Good old Hannelore!

"She is very young," I said tactfully. "She may wish to experience life a little before she takes on the responsibilities of royalty."

Siegfried sniffed. "This I find ridiculous. Girls of her station marry at eighteen all the time. It is not good to let them have too much freedom and to become too worldly. Look at my sister. She was allowed to spend a year in Paris and now —" He broke off, checked himself then said, "At least she too has come to her senses. She realizes where her duty lies and has made an excellent match."

At the edge of the dance floor I saw Belinda's face light up and realized that Anton had rejoined the crowd. So had Nicholas. But there was no sign of Darcy. The music ended to polite applause. Siegfried clicked his heels to me. "I enjoyed our dance and our little talk, Lady Georgiana. Or now I shall call you simply by your first name, and you may call me Siegfried when we are in private. In public I still expect you to call me 'sir' or 'highness' of course."

"Of course, sir," I replied. "Oh, look, Prince Nicholas has returned. I wonder if he has news about the patient."

Luckily Siegfried took the hint and strode over to Prince Nicholas. I saw the latter gesturing and explaining, presumably preventing Siegfried from taking a look at the patient for himself. Belinda and Anton passed close to me.

"You and Siegfried looked awfully pally," she muttered. "If you're trying to make Darcy jealous, it's not going to work. I gather he's sitting at Pirin's bedside all night."

"That's as pally as I ever plan to get with Siegfried," I said. "Let's just say that I did it for a good cause."

I looked around the room, my head suddenly spinning with the conversation and bright lights and the whole strain of the evening. If Darcy was spending the night playing guard to Pirin, then there was no point in my staying awake. Suddenly all I wanted was to be quiet and safe and away from danger. I slipped away unnoticed and made my way up to my bedroom. There was no sign of Queenie, which didn't surprise me. She was probably snoring by now. I checked the window to make sure the shutters were fastened securely from the inside. I even opened the wardrobe and, after several deep breaths, the chest, and, satisfied that I was the only person in the room, I pushed a heavy chair against the door and undressed. But I was loath to turn the light off. Did vampires come through walls, I wondered; or through locked shutters? Anything that could crawl up that castle wall could probably do a lot of improbable things. I climbed into bed and pulled the covers up around me. The fire still glowed in the fireplace but had done little to take the chill off the room. I couldn't close my eyes. I kept checking first one corner then the next, seeing those faces glaring down from the molding and the corners of the wardrobe, and then my gaze drifting to that chest.

"You are letting your imagination run away with you," I told myself. "There is a good explanation for all of this, I'm sure. It's an ordinary room and you are quite safe and —"

I broke off and sat up suddenly. There was

now a completely different portrait hanging
on the wall.

CHAPTER 19

Night in the chamber of horrors, Bran Castle
Thursday, November 17

Instead of the attractive and rakish young man there was now a different face staring down at me. This one looked as if it came from an earlier time, with a stylized royal sneer, not unlike Siegfried's, a high collar and a velvet hat like a powder puff perched on his head. I got out of bed to examine it more closely. The paint was cracked and lined like in so many old paintings. That's when I realized something about the other picture — the paint had been daubed on, in the manner of more recent art. And there was something about the freedom of the strokes that indicated French impressionists or later. It had been a relatively new painting.

I lay in bed, trying not to look at the supercilious stare of the man in the portrait, and tried to calm my racing thoughts. Too much had happened since I set out from London. There had been the man watching me on the train, the man who had tried to come into my compartment. Then that same feeling of being watched on the station platform. Then the creature crawling up the wall, the young man from the portrait bending down over my bed, his teeth bared, Matty with blood running down her chin and now a dead field marshal. Miss Deer-Harte had called it a house of horrors and it seemed she wasn't wrong. But how did they link together? What possible reason could someone want for following me on a train? If the place was really populated with vampires, why kill someone with poison? Nothing made sense. I curled up into a little ball and wished I had never come. I also wished I knew which room was Field Marshal Pirin's because Darcy was there and all I wanted was his reassuring arms around me. It did cross my mind to wonder what he was doing here. Had Nicholas really invited him to be part of his wedding party or had he pulled off another spectacular wedding crash? After all, when I first met him he had dragged me to crash an important society wedding and he made it clear that he did this kind of thing on a regular basis. It was his way of ensuring that he had a good meal once a week, and, I suspect, he liked the thrill of it too.

At last exhaustion overcame me and I must have drifted off to sleep because I awoke to an almighty crash, and not of a wedding. I leaped out of bed so fast I almost levitated, instantly awake and regretting that I hadn't slept with the candlestick beside me this night. All I could make out from the glow of the fire was a large, bulky figure in white, standing just inside my door.

"Who's there?" I demanded, trying to sound fierce and confident and realizing that whoever it was stood between me and the light switch.

Then a voice said, "Sorry, miss."

"Queenie?" I said, anger taking over from fear. "What on earth are you doing? If you came to undress me, you're about two hours too late."

"I wouldn't have disturbed you, miss, and I didn't mean to knock anything over," she said, "but I had to come down to you. There's a man in my room."

"At any other time I would have said that was wishful thinking," I said.

"No, miss, honest truth. I woke up and he was just standing there, inside my door. I was that scared, miss, I didn't dare move."

"What did he do?" I asked, not wanting

to hear the answer.

"Nothing. Just stood there, as if he was listening. Then I must have given a little gasp, because he turned and looked at me, then he opened the door and crept out, just like that. I came straight down to you, miss. I ain't going back in there for nothing." She had come over to the bed by now and was standing beside me, a rather terrifying figure in her own right in a voluminous flannel nightgown, her hair in curling papers. "You do believe me, don't you, miss?"

"As a matter of fact I do," I said. "I also had a man in my room last night." And a man had just been killed tonight, I didn't add. Was a stranger in the castle, attempting to hide out in the servants' quarters, or was it the resident vampire, who drifted around as he pleased?

Suddenly I decided that I was angry. I was not going to be a timid little mouse any longer. My Rannoch ancestors wouldn't have run away just because of a few vampires. They would have gone to find the nearest wooden stake, or at least a clove of garlic.

"Come on, Queenie," I said. "We're going back up to your room. We're going to get to the bottom of this right now."

With that I wrapped my fur stole around

me and stepped out into the corridor.

"Lead on, Macduff," I said.

Queenie looked confused. "My name's 'eppelwhite, miss," she said.

"It's from the play we don't name," I said, quoting my mother, the actress. "Never mind. Come on. If we hurry we may catch him. Did you get a good look at him?"

"Sort of," she said. "The shutter doesn't close properly and the moon was actually shining in through my window. He was young, fair haired, thin." She paused. "That's about it, really. I couldn't see his face. But there's no point in going back up there now, is there? By the time I left my room he'd gone. And I didn't spot no one on the way down 'ere."

"We'll check it out, just in case," I said and strode down the hall so fast she had to run to keep up with me. Up a long and winding stair we went, round and round until we came out into what had to be one of the towers. Cold silvery moonlight filtered past the shutters, creating strange dark shadows. I have to confess that I was already feeling less brave than I had been in my room. When I saw the shadow of a man standing behind a pillar, my heart almost leaped into my mouth until Queenie said, "It's another of those suits of armor, miss.

It nearly scared the pants off me the first time too."

"I was just being cautious," I said and tried to walk past it nonchalantly. It wasn't easy to do, with the empty eye slits in that visor staring at me. I could have sworn those eyes followed me. We reached Queenie's room, and I flung open the door and turned the light on. It was, as she had described it, spartan in the extreme. A narrow cotlike bed, two shelves, a hook on the wall and an old-fashioned washstand. Not even a jolly picture on the wall to cheer things up.

"Well, there's certainly nowhere to hide in here," I said. "And I can't see any reason why anyone would want to come in here, either."

"Me neither, miss. Unless he was just ducking in here because he didn't want to be seen."

"Queenie, you're surprisingly bright sometimes," I said.

"Really, miss?" She sounded surprised. "My old dad says I must have been twins because one couldn't be so daft."

I went across to her window, opened the single shutter and looked out. Moonlight had turned the snow into a magical scene — deep and crisp and even sprang to mind. The only sound was the sigh of the wind around the turrets, then I thought I detected from far away a howl. It was answered by another howl, close by, this time. And I thought I saw a wolf slinking into the forest.

Of course my mind went straight to werewolves. If vampires appeared to really exist, then why not other creatures of the underworld? This was, after all, Transylvania. Was it in any way possible that the man Queenie had just encountered had now climbed down the castle wall and transformed himself into his wolf form? Or did that only happen at the full moon? The sensible part of me, that sound Scottish upbringing, was saying "rubbish" very loudly in my head, but on a night like this, in a place like this, I was prepared to believe anything.

As I leaned out farther and looked around I saw something snakelike and gleaming in the moonlight, dancing close to me with a life of its own. I leaped back until I realized that it was only a rope, hanging down the wall. If someone had climbed up here, he had been aided and abetted by a person already in the castle. And if someone had entered this way, he had gone again.

"You're right, Queenie. There is no sense in standing around getting cold," I said. "I'm sure your mystery man is long gone. I'm going back to bed."

"Can't I come with you, miss?" She grabbed at my nightie sleeve. "I can't sleep up here, all alone, after what happened. I know I wouldn't sleep a wink. Honest."

"You want to come downstairs to my room, with me?"

"Yes, please, miss. I'll just sit on the rug by the fire if you like. I don't care. I just don't fancy being alone."

I was about to say that it simply wasn't done but she looked as white as a sheet, and I wasn't feeling too steady myself.

"Oh, very well," I said, not wanting to admit that I too was grateful for the company. "I suppose I can make an exception this once. Come on, then."

We retreated back to my room, encountering nobody along the way. Once in my room I got into bed. Queenie sat dutifully on the hearth rug, hugging her knees to her chest, giving a good imitation of Cinderella. My kind heart won out over every ounce of my upbringing. "Queenie, there is actually plenty of room in this bed. Come on, you'll freeze sitting there."

Gratefully she climbed into bed beside me. I found the warmth of another body beside me comforting and fell asleep.

CHAPTER 20

Bran Castle
Friday, November 18

I was awoken by the blaring of horns. It was the sort of sound I associated with an army going into battle or alerting a castle's occupants to the enemy's advance and it caused me to leap out of bed. I didn't think that conquering armies showed up unannounced these days in central Europe, but one never knew and I didn't want to be caught in my night attire. I fumbled with the shutters, which had iced up, and flung them open just in time to see a procession of big black motorcars flying royal standards crawling up the snowy ramp to the castle. Heralds were standing on the battlements blowing on long, straight horns. The pass must have opened and the kings and queens had arrived.

I closed the shutters hastily to keep out the bitter chill and decided that morning tea would be welcome before I had to be presented to visiting royalty. It was quite light and surely tea should have arrived by now. . . . That was when I remembered Queenie. I looked back at my bed where Queenie still lay blissfully sleeping, mouth open. It was not a pretty sight.

"Queenie!" I yelled, standing over her.

She opened her eyes and gave me a vague smile. "Oh, 'ello, miss."

"The royal party has just arrived. I should be ready and dressed to be presented. Oh, and I'd like my morning tea. So up you get."

She sat up slowly, yawning her head off. "Right you are, miss," she said, not moving.

"Now, Queenie."

With that she staggered to her feet, then looked down at herself. "Lawks, miss, I can't go walking around in me nightie, can I? What would people say? I wouldn't half get an earful!"

"No, I don't suppose that would be an acceptable thing to do, but I don't have a robe I can lend you. Because you didn't pack me one." I opened my wardrobe. "Here, you'd better have my overcoat. Bring it back when you come up with my morning tea."

She paused at my doorway. "This tea bit. What am I supposed to do?"

"Go to the kitchen, tell them you've come

for Lady Georgiana's tea tray and carry it up to my room. Now, is that too hard?"

She frowned. "Okay, bob's yer uncle, miss." And with that she sauntered out. That girl will have to go, I thought. Thank heavens I hadn't taken her on for the long term.

I decided not to count on help with my morning toilet, so I was washed and dressed by the time she reappeared, red faced and panting, carrying my tea tray. "There ain't half a lot of stairs in this place, miss," she said. "Oh, and there was a bloke asking after you."

"What kind of bloke?"

"Ever so handsome, miss. Dark hair and he spoke proper English too. Not like one of them wogs."

"And what did he say?"

"He said it was about time you roused yourself and he was waiting for you in the breakfast room."

"Oh," I said, feeling my cheeks going pink. "Then I'd better get straight down there, hadn't I?"

" 'Ere, what about the tea what I just brought up for you?" Queenie demanded.

"You drink it," I said. "Oh, and my shoes need polishing."

With that I ran down the hallway. One of these days I'd better learn to be masterful with servants. Lady Middlesex was quite right. Not that I thought that Queenie would ever learn.

Darcy was alone, sitting with a cup of coffee in front of him as I came into the breakfast room. He rose to his feet as I entered.

"Well, if it isn't Sleeping Beauty," he said. "What sort of time do you call this?"

"I don't know. What time is it?"

"Almost ten."

"Oh, crikey," I exclaimed. "I had a disturbed night last night. I must have been making up for it."

"And what disturbed you?" He was looking at me in that special way, half laughing, that made my insides go weak.

"My maid woke me up to say there was a man in her room."

"Lucky maid. What did she want you to do about it? Give her your blessing or come and watch?"

"Darcy, it's not funny," I said. "She was terrified, poor thing. I went up to see, but of course he'd gone."

"Was it a hot-blooded Romanian who fancied a prim English miss?"

"I told you it wasn't funny, Darcy," I snapped. "I know exactly how she felt because the same thing happened to me the night before."

"Who was it? I'll see to him."

"Nobody I knew," I said, secretly delighted by this response. "In fact I think it might have been a vampire."

I saw the smile spread across his face.

"Don't you dare laugh," I said and hit him. He caught my hand in his and held me, looking down at me.

"Come on, Georgie. I know this is Transylvania, but you don't believe in vampires any more than I do."

"I didn't, until I came here," I said. "But there was definitely a strange young man bending over my bed, smiling at me and saying something in a strange language, and when I sat up, he just melted away into the shadows."

"Then I'd have to say that he was probably in the wrong room and got as big a shock as you did when you sat up. That sort of bed hopping goes on quite a lot in places like this, you know. Or perhaps you don't. You've led a sheltered life."

"But he looked just like the man in the portrait on my wall," I said. "Only last night the portrait had been changed, and someone was climbing up the castle wall. . . ."

"Up the wall? That's a pretty suicidal thing to do."

"Well, someone did it and there was a cloak in the chest in my room, with snowflakes still on it, and then it vanished."

"Dear me, it all sounds very dramatic," he said.

"Don't you believe me?"

"I'd suspect that the rich food has given you vivid dreams, my sweet."

"It wasn't dreams," I said. "I've felt a sense of danger since I came here. Lady Middlesex's companion said that she sensed death as we arrived. And explain to me why all these other strange things have been happening."

"What strange things?" His tone was suddenly sharp and his grip tightened on my wrist.

"Well, to begin with there was someone spying on me on the train. He tried to come into my compartment and then at the station —" I broke off because he was grinning again. "What now? Don't you believe me?"

"Oh, absolutely. I have to confess something. The person on the train was I."

"You?"

"Yes, I got wind of which train you were traveling on and I thought it would be a good idea to keep an eye on you. I hadn't counted on the old battle-ax keeping me at bay."

"But wait a minute," I said. "If you were on the same train as us, how did you get here? An avalanche blocked the pass right after we came through."

"It certainly did," he said. "By the time I'd found a car willing to drive me to the castle, the wretched road was blocked."

"So how did you manage to make it here?"

"Used my initiative, my dear. Got a lift as far as I could, then bargained for some skis and skied over the pass. I must say it was a delightful run all the way down to the castle."

"You're pulling my leg."

"Absolutely not. Would I lie to you?"

"Sometimes, I'm afraid."

He was still holding my wrist and we stood there, staring at each other. "I don't ever remember lying to you," he said. "Omitting some of the truth, maybe, on occasions when I wasn't allowed to tell you everything."

"So tell me the truth now. Are you here because Nicholas invited you to be his groomsman, or to keep an eye on me, or because you decided to crash another wedding?"

Darcy smiled. "What would you do if I

said I couldn't tell you?"

"I'd say you've probably been sent here, by somebody you can't tell me about. Undercover, for some reason."

"Something like that. Let's just say that certain people felt it would be good to have some eyes and ears on the spot, in case of trouble."

"So you were expecting trouble?"

"Come for a walk with me," he said, taking my hand.

"Where?"

"In the castle grounds."

"There is deep snow, in case you've forgotten."

"Then go and put on your boots and coat. I'll meet you down here in five minutes."

"But I haven't had breakfast," I said, looking longingly at the spread on the sideboard.

"Breakfast can wait. We may not have another chance to be alone together. At this minute Their Royal Highnesses are greeting their respective parents and relatives, so we can slip away undetected."

"All right," I said. "Just let me pour myself a cup of coffee."

I gulped it down, then hurried up to my room, where, of course, I discovered that Queenie had forgotten to return my overcoat and thus had to wait while she went to her room to find it. Darcy was waiting impatiently at the foot of the stairs. The guards at the door saluted us as they opened it. Snow had been cleared from the court-yard, where the various motorcars now stood. We crossed it to the big outer gates. The gatekeeper looked at us with surprise when we indicated we wanted to go out. Much snow, he said in German. And no-body was to leave.

"We just go for a small walk. English people need fresh air," Darcy replied. So having decided we were mad English people, he opened a small door beside the big gates and we stepped through into the outside world. Pristine snow stretched before us. The boughs of the fir trees were bent heavy with snow and every now and then there was a soft whoosh and thud as snow slid off to the ground below. It was so bright that it was dazzling. Darcy took my hand and we crunched across the snow, keeping to the tracks the motorcars had made until we were among the trees at the base of the great crag on which the castle stood. An icy blast whistled down from the pass, freezing my nose and ears. The silence was absolute, except for the rattle of a dead branch in the wind.

"This is nice," I said, my breathing hanging like smoke in the chill air. "Nice but cold."

"I wanted to talk to you away from prying eyes and ears," Darcy said. "I wanted to sound you out on Pirin's death. Nicholas's parents arrived this morning. His father will want to know the truth sometime. Nicholas can't keep on pretending forever, and I'd like to have found out who might have killed Pirin before then, so that hopefully an international incident can be averted."

I nodded.

"You must have some ideas on the subject," he said.

"Actually I don't," I said. "I was sitting opposite him at dinner. And I don't see how he could have been poisoned. The only people who came anywhere near him were servers and Dragomir. The servers put food from the same platter on everyone's plate, and as for wine, well, the rate he was drinking it, his glass was being constantly refilled."

"You saw it being refilled, did you?"

"Yes, I did. From the same carafe as everyone else."

Darcy frowned. "Cyanide takes effect almost instantly," he said, "so it's unlikely to have been in the food because he'd cleaned his plate pretty well. Unfortunately he knocked over and spilled the remnants of his wine when he collapsed, but there doesn't seem to be any residue in his glass."

"Is it possible to put cyanide into some kind of capsule, so that it wouldn't work on the system until it was digested?"

Darcy nodded. "Possible, I suppose, but at the rate he was chomping and drinking, it seems likely he would have bitten through a capsule much earlier."

I nodded. "I suppose he would."

"Baffling," Darcy said. "Well, now that the pass is open I can send out the utensils to the nearest laboratory for testing and perhaps we'll know where the cyanide was hidden. But that still brings us to motive."

"Oh, I can think of a lot of people who'd want Pirin dead," I said.

"Can you?" He looked at me sharply.

"Well, he was an odious man, wasn't he?" I laughed uneasily. "He ogled women, he insulted men. He called Nicholas by his first name, you know. In public. Imagine an English general calling the Prince of Wales David. Only Mrs. Simpson dares to do that."

"I'm well aware that Nicholas and Anton disliked him," Darcy said, "but they are both intelligent young men. They realized his importance to the stability of the region.

And if one of them wanted to kill him, there would have been better opportunities. They were out hunting, I gather. Why not mistake him for a wild boar? For that matter why not push him out of the train on the way here?"

"You're a bloodthirsty person at heart, aren't you?" I asked.

He grinned. "Oh, no, my dear, I'm a romantic. But I've seen plenty of hard reality in my life. So who else would have wanted him dead?"

"What about the servers?" I asked. "Did you have a chance to talk to them?"

"Only very briefly, but I have their names, and again, I can have someone look into their backgrounds further when we are back in communication with the outside world. But as far as I could gather they all seemed to be as that Dragomir chap described them: local men, long in the employ of this castle and thus with no reason to be concerned with what happened in Bulgaria."

"Which leaves Dragomir himself," I said. "He was standing behind the table. I wouldn't have noticed if he'd moved forward and dropped something onto Pirin's plate or into his glass. What do you know about him?"

"Dragomir? Very little."

"Do you know, for example, that he is not from Romania?"

"He's not?"

"Siegfried told me. He said that was why he hadn't risen higher in Romanian government. He comes from a border area that has changed hands several times. He could be in the pay of another government."

Darcy's eyes lit up. "He certainly could be. Good thinking, old bean."

I had to laugh.

"What?"

"I didn't know you thought of me as 'old bean.' I'd hoped for something a little more romantic."

He moved closer to me and slipped his arms around my waist. "I'll reserve those words for the bedroom at some more opportune moment," he said and then he kissed me. "Mmm, what deliciously cold lips. They need warming up." The second kiss was not so gentle and left us both breathing hard. "I suppose I should be getting back to help Nick and Anton," Darcy said, releasing me with reluctance from the embrace. "Any minute now their father is going to want to visit the field marshal's bedside. I've no idea how we're going to pull this off, and I just wish that I had something concrete to tell them about Pirin's death. I can ask Siegfried about Dragomir, but again I can't find out much more about him until the telephone service is restored."

"And Siegfried will want to know why you are interested in Dragomir's past," I said. "He may be obnoxious but he's not stupid. He wanted to go up to the field marshal's room to check on him last night, and I had to dissuade him with my feminine wiles."

Darcy burst out laughing. "I don't think that feminine wiles work particularly well on Siegfried," he said.

We started to walk back up the slope to the castle.

"Siegfried talked about marriage again last night," I said.

I'd expected him to find this amusing. Instead he said, "Perhaps you should accept. You might not get a better offer. Princess Georgie, maybe Queen Georgie one day."

"Don't say that, even in jest," I said. "You wouldn't wish me married to Siegfried, would you?"

"I'm sure he'd let you keep a lover, since his own interests lie elsewhere."

"He actually said that. I suppose it's the way it's done in royal circles, but it's not for me."

I felt Darcy's grip tighten on my hand. "Georgie, you know I'm a rotten catch," he said. "I have nothing to offer a woman. I don't even have a nice little castle in Ireland any longer. I live by my wits and I can't see how I'm ever going to support a wife. So maybe you should think more sensibly and forget about me."

"I don't want to forget about you," I said shakily. "I don't need a castle."

"I can't see you being happy in a little flat in Putney," Darcy said. "And I don't think your family would be too happy either. But anyway, I'm not ready to think of settling down yet. I have to make my mark in the world first, and you have to experience more of life."

We walked the rest of the way in silence. Would I be happy in a little flat? I was thinking. Would I be able to fit into a world I didn't know, living a life only just getting by, with no luxuries, and with a husband who couldn't tell me about his career but who disappeared for long periods? I decided to put the future on hold for now.

Chapter 21

As we approached those formidable gates I looked up at the castle and a thought struck me. "Darcy, that man I saw climbing up the wall — the one who came into my bedroom. You don't think he had anything to do with Pirin's death, do you? You don't think he was sent here with that mission?"

Darcy frowned. "I don't see how any outsider could have administered the poison. As I said, death is usually almost instantaneous. And I discount your theory of vampires." He glanced at me and saw my mouth open, about to speak. "That man bending over you . . . who knows, maybe one of Nicholas's groomsmen took a fancy to you. Or more likely someone got the wrong room. It's easy to do in a place like this."

"I know," I said, remembering with embarrassment. "I went to Siegfried's door by mistake. His room is next to mine."

Darcy laughed. "Well, that explains everything, doesn't it? I'll wager the young man was paying a nightly visit to Siegfried. No wonder he was shocked to see you instead."

I considered this as we went back up the steps. It did seem a likely explanation and one that I liked better than anything supernatural. It didn't get us any closer to solving who killed Field Marshal Pirin, but at least it made sense.

The door guards stepped forward smartly to open the castle doors for us. They saluted although their expressions betrayed that we were mad for trying to venture forth on a morning like this. In the entry hall we encountered Lady Middlesex and Miss Deer-Harte, dressed in their overcoats.

"Oh, there you are. We've been looking all over for you. Where have you two been?" Lady Middlesex demanded.

"Just for a quick hike over the pass," Darcy said.

"Rubbish," Lady Middlesex said. "Nobody could go far in this sort of snow."

"We went for a little walk," I corrected.

"Oh, so a walk is possible after all. These stupid people are telling us that the snow is too deep to go anywhere and they didn't seem to understand when we asked them for snowshoes," Lady Middlesex said.

"Really these foreigners have no stamina at all."

"It is deep, actually," I agreed. "We only walked in the tracks the tires made."

"Dashed annoying," she muttered. "It seems that none of the drivers are prepared to drive us back over the pass yet. They say that it was bad on the way here and they're not going to risk it again yet, with the promise of more snow. So it looks as if we're still stuck. But at least we can be useful in your investigation into that man's death. When do we have our first council of war?"

"I'm going to find Prince Nicholas this very minute," Darcy said. "I'll let you know later." We left them and walked up the stairs to the main floor. "Those women are going to be trouble," Darcy muttered to me. "Poking their noses in and saying the wrong thing at the wrong minute. Can't you do something to distract them? Or better yet find a suitable dungeon and lock them in it?"

"Darcy." I laughed.

"I'm sure a castle like this must have an oubliette," he went on, chuckling now.

"You are terrible. And I don't see what I can do to distract them. I don't even know my own way around."

"They're going to ruin everything if they

270

are left loose," Darcy said. "For God's sake try to keep an eye on them."

"I will," I said.

"Oh, and Georgie," he said, reaching out his hand to me as I turned away. "Take care of yourself. Someone in this castle has already been killed."

I considered that statement as I went slowly down the hall to my room. Someone in this castle was a ruthless killer. Not that the killing affected me in any way. It had to be of a political nature, carried out by someone who either wished to cause trouble between Balkan states or was a communist or anarchist. Maybe our own government suspected that trouble was likely and that was why they had sent Darcy — one never knew with him. But such a killer wouldn't pose any threat to someone like me, who was only thirty-fourth in line to a distant throne. But I had been threatened in a different way, hadn't I? The vampire bending over my bed. The strange man in Queenie's room. I didn't see how the two could be related. If vampires had wanted to kill Field Marshal Pirin, I imagined they would have done a far more impressive job of it — hurled him from the battlements or sent a great statue crashing onto his head, or even bitten his neck and turned him into one of them. Poisoning with cyanide was all too human a crime. . . .

I was startled from my thoughts by the figure with the raised arm until I realized it was just the suit of armor that had frightened Queenie. Really it was almost as if someone had arranged this castle to provide the maximum amount of shocks to visitors!

In my room I found Queenie, sitting on my bed with a cup of tea in one hand and a biscuit in the other. She didn't even have the grace to jump up when I came in.

"Whatcher, miss," she said, attempting feebly to brush the crumbs from the front of her uniform.

"Queenie, you really will have to learn how to address your mistress properly," I said. "The correct thing to say is, 'Hello, my lady' or 'Welcome back, my lady.' Is that really too hard to learn?"

"I do try," she said, making me wonder whether she was a secret bolshie and doing this deliberately to let me know that she was my equal. This then started a whole train of thought in my mind. How much did one really know about servants? She had just shown up on my doorstep and I had no way of knowing who she really was. While I didn't think that anyone could pretend to be as stupid as she was, maybe the same circumstances were true for other servants in the castle. Maybe one of them had come here with the express purpose of killing Pirin.

"You can help me off with my coat and boots, Queenie," I said.

"Bob's yer — yes, me lady," she said. Maybe there was hope after all.

"Oh, by the way," she added as she took my coat, "there was a message came for you from the princess. She hoped you were feeling all right because she hadn't seen you this morning and to remind you that you were supposed to be meeting the other bridal attendants for a dress fitting at ten thirty."

I glanced at my watch. Ten forty-five. "Oh, golly," I said. "I'd better get going then. Oh, and give me that dress you scorched. Maybe one of the dressmakers can fix it for me if she has a moment."

I went back down the various staircases as fast as I dared because the steps were worn and smooth and the going was treacherous. In the great hallway at the bottom I encountered Lady Middlesex and Miss Deer-Harte, still wandering around in their coats.

"We thought we might follow your example and go for a little stroll," Lady

Middlesex said. "Since the snow was apparently not too deep for you."

"It was lovely out there," I said, trying to convey enthusiasm. "A walk is a good idea. Good fresh mountain air." I didn't add the word "freezing" to that sentence. At least I'd done what Darcy had asked and sent them out of the way for a while. I didn't think even someone as hearty as Lady Middlesex could take that kind of cold for long, however.

At the doorway to the salon I heard the sound of girlish laughter and I paused, my mind racing back to that disconcerting moment when I had stumbled upon Matty the evening before. I had seen her with blood running down her chin and she had begged me not to tell anybody. She couldn't help it, she had confessed. Was it too improbable to believe that she had been bitten by a vampire and had become one of them? Darcy had been so amused by my stories of vampires that I hadn't even mentioned Matty to him. I suppose it did sound ridiculous to anyone who hadn't experienced it personally. I would have thought it ridiculous myself if it hadn't happened to me. My nightly visitation could be explained by a case of mixed-up rooms, but then a normal room-hopper would not need to climb up walls — let's face it, would not be able to climb up walls. And where could an outsider have come from with the pass closed and no habitation nearer than that inn, and snow too deep to walk through? I am normally a sensible person, I told myself, but the things I had witnessed defied rational explanation.

I took a deep breath, opened the door and went in. Matty rose from the sofa near the fire and came to meet me. "My dear Georgie," she said. "Are you well? I was worried when nobody had seen you this morning."

She looked and sounded completely normal, but she was wearing a scarf around her neck that would hide any bite marks.

"I'm quite well, thank you," I said. "Darcy O'Mara and I went for a little walk."

"Nicky's groomsman? Ah, so that's where your interests lie. Poor Siegfried, he'll be devastated."

That's when I remembered that I had actually not discouraged Siegfried the night before. Oh, no, Siegfried didn't really think I had changed my mind, did he?

"Of course, you're lucky," she said. "Nobody would mind whom you married. It wouldn't make any difference to world peace."

"My sister-in-law is keen for me to make

the right match, and I think the queen expects me to cement ties with the right family," I said.

"It's such a bore being royal, isn't it?" She slipped her arm through mine and led me over to the other young women at the fire. "I'm really becoming convinced that communism is a good idea. Or maybe America has it right — choose a new leader every four years, from among the people."

"America maybe," I said, "but look at the mess in Russia. Communism doesn't seem to have made life for the ordinary people better there."

"Who cares, really." Matty gave one of her slightly fake laughs. "So no more talk of politics or any other boring subject. We are all going to be happy and enjoy my wedding. I could have killed that awful man for spoiling the evening last night."

"I don't think he intended to have a heart attack," I said cautiously.

"Maybe not, but I'm still angry with Nicky for inviting him. This morning Siegfried was muttering about trying to send one of the cars to Bucharest for the royal physician and Mama and Papa were distressed to hear that one of our guests had become sick."

"I don't think it was Prince Nicholas's

choice to bring Pirin along with him," I said. "He's a powerful man in that country. I rather suspect he does what he wants."

"Well, I certainly didn't invite him to my wedding," she said. "He invited himself. I rather wish he'd hurry up and die and then we could all stop worrying about him. It's like a cloud of gloom hanging over us, knowing he's lying up there."

I didn't like to say that her wish had been granted. She turned to the other girls and obviously repeated what she had said in German, as it produced a titter of nervous laughter. I observed her critically. She was so different from the needy, unconfident girl I had known at school. I was almost prepared to believe she wasn't the same person. I'd already been fooled by one imposter this year, so surely two was a little much. And her parents obviously recognized her as their daughter, so she had to be Matty, but she had certainly grown up in a hurry. The couturiere approached, clapping her hands as if she were directing a flock of chickens.

"Highnesses, we have no time to waste. So much work to be done. Now, who is ready to volunteer to be first today?"

I was anxious to get out of there and find out what was happening with Nicholas and Darcy. I was also uneasy in Matty's presence. "I will, if you like," I said.

The dress was fitted with nods of satisfaction. "This young lady has no curves, like a boy," our couturiere said to her assistant in French. "On her the dress will look right." I wasn't so sure that having no curves and looking like a boy was a compliment but I took it for one, especially as she had very little to do in the way of pinning and altering. When I glanced at myself in those walls of mirrors a tall, elegant creation stared back at me. I noticed that the room was suddenly quiet and saw that the other girls had stopped talking and were now watching me.

"Georgie, I did not think that you would grow up to be so chic," Matty said. She came to stand beside me and put her arm around my waist as we stared at ourselves in the mirrors. "Wouldn't Mademoiselle Amelie and the other teachers be surprised if they saw us now. What a shame we are wasted in a remote castle in Romania. We should be on the French Riviera, or in Hollywood, flirting with all the men-about-town, don't you think?"

I laughed with her but my cheeks were very pink. It was the first time anyone had ever suggested that I might be elegant one day. Maybe there was some of my mother's blood in me after all.

I had just been unpinned from my dress and was retrieving my more practical jumper and skirt when there was a tap at the door. One of the seamstresses was directed to go and returned with a letter. Matty looked at it, then handed it to me. "From one of your admirers." She gave me a knowing look.

I glanced up at the door as I recognized Darcy's firm black scrawl. *I need to speak to you immediately,* it said.

"I'll be back," I said.

"A midmorning tryst. How romantic. Siegfried will be jealous." Matty wagged a finger and the other girls giggled as I went to the door. I hoped she was just joking. For a second I felt a stab of a different kind of fear — had I been brought here to be bride of this particular Frankenstein after all? Frankly if it was a choice between life with Siegfried and a bite from a vampire, I think I'd prefer to be undead. But I didn't have long to consider this as Darcy was waiting outside the door for me.

"Ah, there you are," he said, drawing me to one side. "Look, something has come up and I have to go."

"Go? Go where?"

"We've run into a complication," he whispered. "Nicholas's father demanded to

279

be taken straight to see Pirin."

"Oh, Lord, so I suppose the game's up."

"Not yet. We kept the curtains drawn so that it was pretty dark. The firelight actually made his skin look reddish. I slipped into the room and hid under the bed, then I snored loudly to make it sound as if he was still breathing."

I started to laugh, it was so absurd.

Darcy smiled too. "It worked once, but the king is very concerned. He wanted to send one of the cars to bring his personal physician from Bulgaria immediately."

"How did you stop him from doing that?"

"Nick persuaded him that there was a good hospital with modern equipment in the nearest city and it would be better if Pirin were transported there immediately."

"Oh, no, what are you going to do?"

"I've volunteered to go to the hospital with him, since Nicholas can't leave his bride."

"But what good will that do? They'll pronounce him dead as soon as he arrives."

"If he arrives," Darcy said. "I'm also going to be driving and unfortunately the car is going to go off the road into a snowdrift somewhere up on the pass. By the time I've gone for help poor Field Marshal Pirin will have died, so there will be no point in summoning the personal physician. And the news of the tragic death won't reach the castle until after the wedding."

"So you're not going to be here for the wedding either?" The disappointment in my face must have shown.

"I have to do this, my love," he said. He raised his hand to my cheek. "I'm the only one who can do it, but I want you to help Nick and Anton in any way you can."

"Of course," I said. "Take care of yourself."

"You too." He leaned forward and kissed my forehead, then he went down the stairs without looking back.

CHAPTER 22

Still in Bran Castle

I returned to the salon.

"That was quick for a tryst," Matty said.

"He just had a message to give me," I said. "Your future father-in-law wants the field marshal to be taken to a hospital immediately and Darcy has volunteered to accompany him."

"Thank God he's going," Matty said. "Now we can return to enjoying ourselves."

I excused myself soon after, having decided not to ask one of the seamstresses to save my scorched dress. The way those sewing machines were clattering away indicated that they were busy enough already. Maybe when all the dresses were finished, I'd try again. I came into the hallway in time to run into Lady Middlesex and Miss Deer-Harte. "I don't know how you two managed to go for a walk in that snow," Lady Middlesex said accusingly. "We only ventured a few yards before Deer-Harte sank up to her middle. Had a dashed difficult time getting her out."

"I'm sorry," I said. "We walked in the tracks the cars had made."

"Better get you up to your room, Deer-Harte, before you catch your death of cold," Lady Middlesex said. "Saw them loading the field marshal's body into one of the hearses, by the way. And Mr. O'Mara went off with him. I hope they're taking him to a place where a proper autopsy can be performed."

I put my finger up to my lips. "Remember we're not supposed to be talking about this," I said. "Field Marshal Pirin has gone to hospital."

"Oh, yes. Right. Of course." She grinned like a naughty child. "Not that it matters. I'm sure none of the servants understand a word of what we're saying."

"I'm sure it's very easy to listen in on conversations in a castle like this," I said. "We have a laird's lug at Castle Rannoch — you know, a secret room where you can listen to conversations in the great hall. And sound carries through all the pipes in the bathrooms, so I'm sure it must be the same here."

"Well, I believe in calling a spade a spade,"

Lady Middlesex said, annoyed now that I'd caught her out. "I don't hold with trickery and deceit. Not the British way, you know. And if there is a murderer loose in this castle, then it's high time he was found."

I looked around to see who might be listening to this outburst. Luckily the hall appeared to be deserted, but at that moment I heard footsteps coming up the stairs. Prince Nicholas came toward us, taking the steps two at a time.

"Well, that's been accomplished, thank God," he said. "My father saw him off."

"How did you manage that?"

Nicholas grinned. "We carried him down to the car, wrapped head to toe in blankets against the cold. Father never had a chance to see any more of his face than a mustache peeping out. Good old Darcy. Splendid chap. Now we can hope that it takes a long time to mend the telephone wires."

"So when do we hold the council of war?" Lady Middlesex demanded.

Prince Nicholas looked wary. "War?"

"I mean when do we meet to plan strategy and work out how we are going to solve this?"

"Oh, right." Nicholas looked as if meeting with Lady Middlesex was not what he had in mind.

"We should pool our brains on this one, and our observations," she said. "Deer-Harte thought she noticed one of the servants acting shiftily."

"Very well. No time like the present, I suppose," Nicholas said. "Maria is still with her ladies and the dressmakers, I presume?" I nodded. "So I'll find Dragomir and my brother and we'll meet in the library in fifteen minutes. Agreed?"

"Just gives you time to get out of those freezing wet clothes, Deer-Harte," Lady Middlesex said.

I was making my way up to the floor that contained the library when I remembered that I hadn't had any breakfast and took a detour to the breakfast room in the hope that there was still a roll I could grab. The room was empty but for Belinda, sitting alone at the table with a coffee cup in front of her.

"Where have you been?" she asked. "I've been looking everywhere for you."

"I got up late and then went for a walk with Darcy," I said.

"How romantic. But where is everyone else? The place is like a morgue."

"Matty is having a dress fitting with her attendants and you know that the royal party arrived, don't you?"

Belinda frowned. "Oh, yes. Anton deserted me to rush to the side of his papa. And they all seemed to be heading for the sickroom of that awful man Pirin."

"Pirin's now on his way to hospital, thank goodness," I said, feeling strange about lying to my best friend.

"So why aren't you at the dress fitting?"

"I went first. And I have such a perfect lack of figure that not much alteration was involved."

"Good, then you and I can do something fun together. What shall it be?" She got up and slipped her arm through mine. "Not that this is the sort of place that I consider to be fun. No casino, no shops. Thank God for sex, or I'd be bored to tears."

"Belinda! You really shouldn't say things like that where they can be overheard."

She laughed. "There's nobody in the room but the two of us. Besides, it's the truth."

"You were the one who wanted to come here," I reminded her.

"Well, it did seem like a good lark at the time," she said. "And I have to admit that Anton is rather scrumptious. But now his parents are here, I'm afraid he'll have to behave like a good little boy. So what shall it be? Do you want to go and look for your vampires? We could find where their coffins are stored."

"Stop teasing. I know what I saw, why won't anyone else believe me?"

"But darling, of course I believe you, and I'm dying to meet a vampire." She attempted to drag me from the room.

"I'm sorry, but I can't come anywhere with you at the moment," I said. "I have to meet —" I stopped hastily. Of course I couldn't tell her that I had to meet the princes or she'd want to come along. "Lady Middlesex," I finished. "I have to meet Lady Middlesex and Miss Deer-Harte." I tried desperately to think of a reason for this meeting that would sound unappealing to Belinda. "She's writing a history of San-dringham House and she wants my insights."

Belinda wrinkled her nose. "I think I'll go and take a long bath so I can try out my new Parisian bath beads. The bathrooms seem to be unoccupied at this time of day. Toodle-pip."

I breathed a sigh of relief, put a slice of cheese onto a roll and fled. I arrived at the library to find that the others were already assembled, sitting around a big oval ma-hogany table in the center of an impressive if gloomy library. Shelves of leather-bound volumes rose into darkness, and a gallery circled the library at about twelve feet above our heads. High, narrow windows threw shafts of sunlight onto the floor, illuminating the dust motes. There was a pervading smell of must, dust and old books. I took the empty chair next to Lady Middlesex and opposite Nicholas and Dragomir.

"Sorry I'm late," I said. "I got held up by —" I broke off as I noticed that there was one person at the table I hadn't expected. Prince Siegfried was sitting beside Dragomir.

"Lady Georgiana." He nodded his head.

I looked at Nicholas. He raised his eyebrows. "Siegfried sensed that something was wrong and insisted on seeing Field Marshal Pirin, so naturally I had to tell him the truth and apologize for our secrecy in keeping this matter hushed up."

Siegfried pursed those cod lips. "This most serious matter was brought to my attention, and I now have to decide whether it should be brought out into the open, or kept from my parents."

I glanced at Dragomir. Had he been the one who had spilled the beans to Siegfried? And if he was the murderer, would that have been a wise thing to do?

"I have explained to His Highness the delicacy of the situation regarding the stability of my nation and the Balkans as a whole," Nicholas said in a clipped voice. It was clear there had been an argument about this already.

"And I have explained to His Highness that this is my country and I have to make sure that we behave as we would expect any citizen to behave — and that includes reporting a murder to the proper authorities."

"Obviously we may have to do that eventually," Anton said in a soothing manner, "but if we can solve it among ourselves here, then nobody else needs to know and the wedding can take place as planned. Surely that is what you wish, Siegfried?"

"Of course."

Dragomir cleared his throat. "But surely the simplest thing to do would be to claim that a communist or anarchist managed to climb into the castle, administer the poison and then make his getaway undetected."

"The simplest thing," Nicholas said, "would be to treat the death as a heart attack, which is what everyone else believes anyway. If they decide on an autopsy, it will be hard to trace the cyanide after that amount of time."

"If we are to believe your diagnosis that cyanide was administered," Siegfried said carefully, "then we must do our duty and find the person who committed this shocking act. Just because the occupants of this castle are royal does not put us above the justice system of our country."

"Well spoken, Your Highness," said a deep voice in guttural French, and a figure stepped from the darkness at the far end of the library. If I had been asked to describe Dracula, this man would have fit the bill perfectly. Tall, thin, hollow cheeked, hollow eyed and very pale, he was dressed head to toe in black, which accentuated the whiteness of his skin. For one ridiculous moment it crossed my mind to wonder whether Vlad the Impaler was still alive and still ruled this castle and the people in it. The man moved toward us with smooth, menacing steps. Then he looked around at us and smiled. "If the personages at this table were not of such exalted rank, I should think that I was witnessing a conspiracy and have you all arrested on the spot," he said. "However, as His Highness Prince Siegfried has just so wisely said, even royal personages are not above the law. If I understood correctly, and I admit that my English is not as fluent as it should be, you were planning to cover up a murder so that there would be no unpleasantness and the wedding could take place as planned. Am I right?"

"Who the devil are you?" Nicholas asked coldly.

"Allow me to introduce myself. I am Patrascue, head of the Romanian secret police." He pulled up a chair and squeezed himself in between Nicholas and Dragomir. "Given the importance of the occasion and the presence of foreign royalty, I elected to travel with Their Majesties to this royal wedding. How fortunate that I did, wasn't it? I had only just arrived when one of my men reported to me that he had overheard a conversation about a murder and a body being whisked away."

I looked across at Lady Middlesex, who had gone a little pink.

"So perhaps one of you would be good enough to tell me who died."

"Field Marshal Pirin," Siegfried said. "Head of the Bulgarian armed forces."

"Also senior adviser to my father and a powerful force in the politics of the region."

"Ah, so we are looking at a political murder, are we?" Patrascue licked his lips. "Very well. Understand this. I will be conducting the investigation and you will be answering my questions — royal or not. Do not think that your exalted rank puts you above the law in Romania. Dear me, no. Our country is a constitutional monarchy and you really have very little power."

"You have to understand," Anton said, "that we were not attempting to cover up a murder just so that a wedding can take place. This man's death could have significance for the future of my country and this entire region."

"And you are . . . ?" Patrascue asked insolently.

"I happen to be Prince Anton of Bulgaria," Anton said coldly. "In case you don't know, you are sitting next to Prince Nicholas, my older brother, heir to the throne and bridegroom."

"My felicitations." Patrascue nodded to Nicholas. "And these other people — your fellow conspirators. Why are they here?"

"I am Lady Georgiana, cousin to King George of England," I said, reverting to my imitation of my great-grandmother, as I always do when I feel threatened. "I am here representing Their Majesties at this wedding. These two ladies are my companions, sent to accompany me by Queen Mary."

"And the reason you sit here now? I did not think the power of the British Empire extended to central Europe." Patrascue eyed me insolently.

"Actually I'm here as a relative," I said.

"As a descendant of Queen Victoria I am related to the Bulgarian royal family and more remotely to the Romanian one. Also I was sitting opposite Field Marshal Pirin at the fateful dinner, and thus witnessed everything. My companion Lady Middlesex was the first to suspect that his death was not a heart attack."

"You say you witnessed everything," Patrascue went on. "What exactly did you see, *ma chérie?*"

I bristled at the words "my dear." I had come to believe that there is at least one obnoxious policeman in every country and he was facing me. "I saw Field Marshal Pirin give a long, rambling toast, take a swig of his wine and then seem to be choking and pitch face forward across the table."

"He seemed to be choking, you say. Was it possible that he was indeed choking and a simple slap on the back could have revived him?"

"He had finished eating at the time," I said. "There had been speeches and toasts for some minutes. Besides, he was dead almost immediately. Initially it was suspected that he had had a heart attack."

"But someone thought it might be murder?"

"I did," Lady Middlesex said. "I'm Lady

293

Middlesex, the wife of the British high commissioner in Mesopotamia. My husband has represented the British Crown all over the world. I know poison when I see it."

"And what poison would that be?"

"Why, cyanide, of course. Red face, staring eyes and the odor of bitter almonds. A classic case. I saw it once before in the Argentine."

Patrascue turned back to me. "Did you see somebody administer this poison?"

"No. I saw nobody come near the table except the servers and Count Dragomir."

Dragomir made a coughing noise in his throat and said, "I resent the implication that I was somehow involved in this farce. Why would I want to kill a man I had never met before? It is my duty to make sure all servers perform flawlessly. Naturally I was standing behind the table, in a position where I could watch them all."

"And yet you saw nothing amiss?" Patrascue asked.

"The men performed flawlessly as always."

"We have no idea how the poison was administered," Nicholas said. "I sat beside him. All food and drink was served from the same platters and carafes and with great speed. It would have been impossible to select a poisoned morsel for a particular person."

"Then I would suggest that it was placed in his glass before the meal," Patrascue said smugly.

"But we were told cyanide acted almost immediately," I said. "The field marshal had cleared his plate, had second helpings and had his wineglass filled countless times from the same carafe as everybody else."

"If the poison was indeed cyanide," Patrascue said. "I take it no doctor was present to make an accurate diagnosis. Amateurs are frequently wrong in my experience."

"There is no physician in the castle, unfortunately," Anton said. "But I have studied a bit of medicine at the University of Heidelberg and I can tell you that the telltale odor of bitter almonds was present and the face was flushed."

"Ah, a so-called expert," Patrascue said. "It is unfortunate that the body has already been transported away from the castle, or I myself could have determined what poison had been administered. I hope that somebody had the sense to put aside the utensils this person used at the dinner table. I shall send them off for testing and then we shall know."

"They did and they have been taken with the body to be examined by a competent laboratory," Nicholas said. I thought I detected a note of glee in his voice. "Naturally we didn't expect a trained policeman like yourself to arrive so soon, given the condition of the pass."

"Ah." Patrascue tried to come up with a response to something that might have been a compliment. "Then the next step is to interview those who served the meal. Count Dragomir, you are in charge of the running of this place, are you not?"

"You know very well that I am," Dragomir replied curtly. No love lost between those two, I thought.

"Then please be good enough to have those men who served at dinner brought to the library instantly for questioning."

"If we do that, then word will spread around the castle rather rapidly that the field marshal is dead, and probably murdered. That is the last thing we want at this moment," Nicholas said. "The men were questioned discreetly last night."

"And it is as I told Their Highnesses," Dragomir said. "These are all local men, simple men who have been in the service of this castle for most of their lives. Why would any of them want to poison a foreign field marshal, even if they had the means to do so?"

"Money," Patrascue said. "Enough money can persuade a man to go against his conscience and to perform in a most ruthless manner. How many footmen were there serving at dinner last night?"

"There were twelve," Dragomir said. "But we would only be concerned with those who served the field marshal. Those who waited on the other side of the table would never have come near him."

"Ah, I see." Patrascue nodded jerkily. "And it would be impossible to lean across this table?"

"Any servant who leaned across a table would be instantly dismissed," Dragomir said. "Our standards of etiquette are of the very highest."

"I will speak with these men, one at a time," Patrascue said. "I will swear them to secrecy. They know enough of my reputation to realize what would happen to them if they were rash enough to lie to me or to break their vow. And if one of them has accepted money to commit this heinous act, then I shall make him confess, I promise you." He smiled unpleasantly. I noticed his teeth were unnaturally pointed.

"Of course we could have made a mistake all along," Anton said in a different, breezy voice. "As you say, we are only amateurs.

Perhaps we were misinterpreting what was only a simple heart attack after all. It was this lady who suggested that she smelled the odor of bitter almonds, and we know that ladies are inclined to be hysterical in the presence of a body."

"I absolutely resent —" Lady Middlesex began. I kicked her hard, under the table. She looked at me in astonishment and shut up.

"As soon as the car bearing Field Marshal Pirin's body reaches civilization we shall know the truth," Anton went on smoothly. "Why don't we wait until a competent physician has given his assessment of the situation? It would be a tragedy if false rumors leaked out to my country and a regional war began for nothing. It wouldn't make you look good either, if you started a witch hunt for something that turned out to be a simple heart attack."

Patrascue stared at him, trying to assess the implications of what he was saying. There was a pitcher of water on the table. He reached forward, poured himself a glass and drank from it.

"There is something in what you are saying," he said. "I have no wish to destabilize this region or cause any unpleasantness with our neighbors at this moment of joy and celebration. We will await the doctor's opinion. But in the meantime I will keep my eyes and ears open. Nobody will be above my scrutiny. Nobody!"

He put down his empty glass firmly on the table. The participants rose to their feet. Except for me. I was staring hard as if I were seeing a vision. I had just realized something that threw a whole new light onto this situation.

CHAPTER 23

I stood staring at the table until the others had left. In my mind's eye I could visualize Field Marshal Pirin giving his drunken, rambling toast. He had reached for a glass, and he was holding it in his left hand. Hannelore had mentioned that his table manners were abysmal and he never used the correct fork. Apparently he didn't use the correct glass either. It was not his glass at all he had grabbed for, but Prince Nicholas's.

It took me a moment to grasp the implication of this. The intended murder victim was not Pirin at all, but Nicholas. And the reason Nicholas hadn't drunk his own wine and died was that he had switched to champagne when the toasts started and had not touched his red wine after that. This would indicate that the glass had originally been free of cyanide during the main course when Nicky was drinking red wine with the wild boar. Somehow, someone had introduced the cyanide after that, unfortunately not realizing that Nicholas was going to call for champagne for his toasts. And if someone had introduced the cyanide, it had to be one of the servers or Dragomir.

Wait a minute, I thought. I was discounting the other diners at the table. Pirin obviously wouldn't have put cyanide into a glass he was going to drink himself. On Nicholas's other side was his bride and she was hardly likely to want to kill off her bridegroom. Opposite him was his brother, Anton, and as Dragomir had said, it was frightfully bad form to reach across the table. It would have been noticed instantly. And besides, the brothers seemed to be on good terms. Anton wouldn't have wanted his brother dead. I paused, considering this. Anton had made jokes about not being the heir and having no purpose in life. Did he secretly wish that he'd be king someday and not his brother? And of all the people around, he would have had a knowledge of poisons. After all, he had told me that he was studying chemistry in Heidelberg. And he was the one who had persuaded Patrascue to do nothing for now. Which would give him ample time to dispose of any traces of cyanide if he needed to.

"Lady Georgiana!" Lady Middlesex's strident voice cut through my thoughts. "Aren't you coming?"

"What? Oh — yes," I stammered. Now there was the question of whom to tell. I wished that Darcy hadn't gone away.

Lady Middlesex grabbed my arm with her bony fingers. "We must go somewhere to plan strategy."

"Strategy?"

She looked around. "Obviously we must make sure that everything is kept from that odious little policeman. We must work fast before he makes a complete mess of everything. Typical bungling foreigner. No clue how to run things properly. It is up to us now to unmask the murderer."

"I don't see how we're ever going to do that," I said. "I was there, facing Field Marshal Pirin all the time. If it was Dragomir or one of the footmen who slipped the cyanide into the glass, he was very slick and I don't see how we'd ever find out who did it."

"That's if it was Dragomir or one of the servants," Lady Middlesex said knowingly. She drew me closer. "Deer-Harte thinks she saw something. Of course, she is prone to flights of fancy, as we know."

"I am an excellent observer, Lady M,"

Miss Deer-Harte said, "and I know what I saw."

"What did you see, Miss Deer-Harte?" I asked.

Her face went pink. "As you recall on the first night here I was not invited to join the company for dinner. Lady M thought it wouldn't be right for a mere companion. I was told my supper would be sent up to my room. But after a while I thought that it wasn't fair to one of the servants to have to walk up all these stairs with my tray, so I decided to come down and fetch it myself. Well" — she paused and looked around again — "as I passed the banqueting hall I heard the sound of merry voices, so naturally I lingered and took a little peek inside."

"This was the first night," I interrupted. "The night before Pirin was murdered."

"It was, but what I saw could be significant. There was somebody watching from the shadows on the far side of the hall. He was dressed in black and he was standing half hidden behind one of the arches. He just stood there, not moving and watching. I thought it was odd at the time. I remember thinking, 'That young man is up to no good.' "

"You always think things like that, Deer-Harte," Lady Middlesex said. "You think that everyone is up to no good."

"But in this case I was proven right, wasn't I? And I'd like to wager that he was the same young man I saw creeping along the corridor in the middle of the night. I couldn't see his face clearly on either occasion, but the build and demeanor were the same. And the way he was slinking along, he was clearly up to no good."

"I am inclined to think she's been letting her imagination run away with her again," Lady Middlesex said, "but at the moment we are grasping at straws, aren't we?"

"I don't believe it was simply imagination," I said. "What color hair did he have?"

She frowned, thinking. "It looked light to me. Yes, definitely light. Why do you ask?"

"Because a strange man came into my room on the first night, and then my maid came to me in great distress the next night to report that a man was in her room."

"A young man with light hair?"

"Exactly. A good-looking young man with a Teutonic face."

"I didn't see his face, but I definitely saw the hair," Miss Deer-Harte said.

"He came into your room?" Lady Middlesex demanded. "With what intention? Burglary or designs on your person?"

"I didn't take the time to ask him. I rather

fear the latter," I said. "He was bending over me with a smile on his face. But when I sat up he disappeared hastily."

"And your maid? Did he have designs on her person too? Clearly a man of great depravity."

The thought struck me that a man would indeed have to be desperate to have designs on Queenie's person. I knew it was deadly serious but I had to stop myself from giggling. I suppose it was the tension. "He didn't touch her. He stood inside her door and when she gasped, he slipped out."

"And did you report these effronteries to anyone?"

"No, I didn't." I paused.

"I would have. If any man had dared to come into my room, I should have reported him immediately."

I hardly liked to say that nobody was likely to pay a nightly visit to Lady Middlesex. Nor did I want to bring up the possibility of vampires. Miss Deer-Harte, the one who had worried about vampires on the train, did not seem to connect her lurking young man with anything supernatural. And if the same man was our poisoner, then it was unlikely that he was anything more than a normal human. Vampires don't need to poison people. In fact they wouldn't want to taint their blood supply.

"One can only conclude," Lady Middlesex went on, "that he was casing the joint, as criminals would say. It is most probable that he is a trained assassin and has been hiding out, waiting for the right moment to kill."

I considered this too. It made sense that he was a trained assassin and that he was hiding out in the castle. But as Prince Nicholas had pointed out, there were surely easier ways to kill someone in a rambling old building like this than risk being detected at a very public banquet.

"And did you happen to see him at the banquet last night?" I asked Miss Deer-Harte.

"No, but then I was included in the party last night, not standing outside as an observer. One looks down to eat, so that one doesn't risk spilling food, doesn't one? One looks at the person to whom one is speaking. And I was naturally at the far end of the table, among the least important of the diners. But the interesting thing was I checked this morning that the spot where he had been standing was exactly behind Field Marshal Pirin's seat. If you want my opinion, he was planning a dummy run, plotting when he could dart out and put the poison in the glass."

"But I would have noticed any intruder, I'm sure," I said. "So would Prince Anton and Princess Hannelore, who were sitting on either side of me."

"Are you so sure?" Miss Deer-Harte said. "Supposing, for example, that you were in the middle of being served. Your server offers you the platter and says, 'Some cauliflower, my lady?' And you nod and say, 'Thank you,' and watch while it is put on your plate. For those moments you are not watching what is happening across the table, are you?"

"No, I suppose not," I said.

"And if someone were dressed in black, not unlike the footmen's uniform, or he had actually managed to procure himself a footman's jacket, then nobody would look twice if he passed the table with a carafe in his hands. Servants are always too busy making sure they do their job to perfection to notice other servants. And it has been my observation that people simply pay no attention to servants."

"Dragomir would have noticed," I said. "He was hovering behind Prince Nicholas, directing the proceedings. As he said, he would have noticed anything slightly wrong."

"Then let us consider that this Dragomir chappy is somehow involved," Lady Middlesex said.

I couldn't see why Dragomir would want to kill Prince Nicholas any more than he would want to kill Pirin. But if he were, in fact, from the Macedonian province that was now part of Yugoslavia it was just possible that he might want to cause civil war in Bulgaria as a way to reclaim its Macedonian lands. And what better way to do that than to assassinate its crown prince? Binky had said that they were always assassinating each other in this part of the world, hadn't he? I decided that I'd risk a little chat with Dragomir myself.

"We obviously can't snoop through every room in the castle," Lady Middlesex said, "particularly now that the royal party has arrived, but it seems to me that the first task is to find out how he came by the poison and where he's hiding the vial it came in."

"I presume that any assassin could have the poison in his pocket when he came into the castle and would leave again with the empty vial," I said.

"I don't know if you've noticed," Lady Middlesex said brusquely, "but there are no footprints leading from the castle, apart from yours and Mr. O'Mara's this morning.

I checked particularly when we went on our little walk. He is still here, you mark my words." She looked down at Miss Deer-Harte and nodded.

"I shall be extra vigilant, Lady M," Miss Deer-Harte said. "If he is hiding somewhere he will have to come out eventually. He will need a bathroom and food and drink. I shall be watching for him."

"Well said, Deer-Harte. Splendid stuff. We'll show them how quickly and efficiently things are done when the flower of British womanhood takes over." She slapped Miss Deer-Harte on the back, almost knocking her over. "Onward and upward then."

And she marched down the hall like a general leading troops into battle.

CHAPTER 24

I was left alone in the cold, drafty hallway. I hadn't had time to consider what I should do about my big discovery. Whom should I tell that Prince Nicholas was the intended victim? Obviously not the two English ladies. They had caused enough trouble already. In fact, if Lady Middlesex hadn't spoken up, Pirin's death might well have been considered a heart attack and we wouldn't be in this uncomfortable situation with that horrid man Patrascue snooping on us. I couldn't tell Prince Anton because it was just possible that he was the murderer — although I found that hard to believe. But he did have knowledge of chemistry, he was agile and, as Belinda had said, he was reckless and loved danger. That left Siegfried or Matty and I rather suspected that Siegfried would report anything straight to Patrascue. Matty would probably think it was all a huge joke and not want to take it

310

seriously. So the only person I could talk to was Nicholas himself. He had a right to know and he might have his own suspicions.

I was on my way to seek him out when a clear, melodious voice echoed down the hallway. "Yoohoo, darling!" and there was my mother, hurrying toward me, her long mink coat flying out around her. "There you are, my sweet," she said. "We've been in the same building for several days and hardly had a chance to say a word to each other."

She caught up with me and we kissed, several inches from each cheek, the way we always did. In spite of the way she showed copious affection to everything in trousers, my mother was not much of a hugger when it came to other women.

"That's because you don't like being seen with me," I said. "It reminds people you are old enough to have a daughter my age."

"What a wicked thing to say. I adore spending time with you, my sweet, or I would if you led a less boring life. We must do something to liven you up. That dress at dinner last night. So absolutely last year and it hides all the best bits of you. I know you don't have much bosom, but you should make the most of what you have. You really must let the men see the goods you are offering."

"Mummy!"

She laughed, that tinkling laugh that had captivated audiences everywhere, and slipped her arm through mine. "You really are so delightfully prudish, my sweet. I put it down to Scottish upbringing. So repressed. Let's go and have a girl talk somewhere, shall we?" She started to lead me down the hallway. "If I'd known I was going to be cooped up in this dreary place for days on end, I'd never have come. Of course Max had to be here, as Nicholas's godfather, but I could have popped to Paris on my own. I do adore it just before Christmas, don't you? So sparkly."

I didn't have a chance to protest. I was borne down the hallway and into a small sitting room where a fire was blazing in a hearth. It was actually quite warm and cozy compared to the rest of the building. Trust my mother to find the one comfortable spot. She draped herself into an armchair and patted the bearskin rug at her feet. "Come and talk to me. Tell me all."

"There's not much to tell," I said. "I've been at Rannoch House, but I'm hoping to go somewhere else for the winter because Binky and Fig are going to be in residence. Fig's expecting again."

"Good God. And they already have the

312

heir. Binky really must be a saint, or blind or desperate. You don't suppose she could actually be good at it, do you? Secretly passionate when roused?"

I looked up at her. "Fig? Passionate?" I burst out laughing. Mummy laughed too.

"You must come and stay with us in Germany, darling," my mother said. "Max can introduce you to a nice German count. Come to think of it, why don't we set you up with one of Nicky's groomsmen? Young Heinrich of Schleswig-Holstein has oodles of money."

"I don't think I'd like to live in Germany, thank you," I said. "I'm amazed how you can do it and not think of the Great War."

"Darling, the people we mix with had nothing to do with it. It was those nasty militaristic Prussians. Your father's wretched cousin Kaiser Willie. No, you'd live well in Germany. Good food, if a little stodgy, and great wine, and Berlin is such a lively city. Or we could find you an Austrian and live in Vienna. Now there's a delightful city for you. And the Austrians — all so fun loving and absolutely no interest in war or conquest."

"Isn't this new chap Hitler an Austrian?"

"Darling, we met him recently. Such a funny little man. I'm sure nobody will take

313

him seriously. And there's also Nicky's brother, Anton. Now he would be quite a catch. I rather fancy him myself, but with Max as his brother's godfather — well, one has to draw the line somewhere."

"I'm surprised you're still with Max," I said. "He doesn't seem your type at all. He doesn't seem very lively. You're much more at home with people like Noel Coward — theater people."

"Of course I am, but so many of them are like dear sweet Noel — pansies, darling. And let me warn you that a certain prince in this house is one of them too. Because I have heard rumors that you're being considered for the post of princess."

"Siegfried, you mean?" I laughed. "Yes, he's already proposed and let me know that I could take lovers after I produced the heir."

"Aren't men funny?" Mother laughed again. "But I rather think your interests lie in another direction. A certain Mr. O'Mara?" She laughed at my red face. "Darling, you have bitten off more than you can chew there. He does have a reputation, you know. Wild Irish boy. I can't see him settling down and changing nappies, can you? And of course he has no money and money is rather important to happiness."

"Are you happy with Max?"

Those large china doll eyes opened wide. "What an interesting question. I get bored and think I'll leave and then the poor dear adores me so much that I simply can't do it. He wants to marry me, you know."

"Are you thinking of marrying him?"

"It has crossed my mind, but I don't think I'd like to be a Frau. I know he's nobility and a von and all that, but I'd still be Frau Von Strohheim and it simply isn't *moi*. Besides, I believe I'm still officially married to that frightfully boring Texan chappy, Homer Clegg. He doesn't believe in divorce. If I really felt strongly I could go to Reno or wherever it is that people go and pay for a quickie divorce there, but I simply can't be bothered. No, my advice to you, my darling, is that you marry well and keep someone like Mr. O'Mara on the side. Choose someone with dark hair and then the baby will match whoever the father is."

"Mummy, you say the most outlandish things. I can't believe how I came to be your daughter."

She stroked my cheek. "I abandoned you too young, I realize now. But I couldn't take another minute of that dreary castle. I never realized your father would want to spend half the year there and go tramping about

315

the heather in a kilt. Simply not me, my sweet, although I have to confess that I enjoyed being a duchess. One got such good service at Harrods."

As she twittered on I sat there uneasily, aware of all the things I should be doing. My gaze drifted from the cracking fire to the portrait above the mantelpiece. Then I blinked and gave it another look. The man in the picture looked like Count Dragomir.

I got up and stood in front of the fire, staring up at it. The man in the portrait was younger than Dragomir but he had the same haughty face, the same high cheekbones and strangely cat-like eyes. But one hardly puts a portrait of a castle servant on the wall. Then I looked at the writing at the bottom. The painter had signed his picture and it looked as if the date was 1789.

"What are you looking at, darling?" my mother asked.

"This portrait on the wall. Doesn't it remind you of Count Dragomir?"

"They all look similar in this part of the world, don't they?" Mummy said in a bored voice. "It was those Huns. They were so good at raping and pillaging that everyone now looks like them."

I was still staring at the portrait. It reminded me of someone else I knew, but I couldn't quite put a finger on it. Something about the eyes . . .

"Darling, as I told you at dinner the other night, your hair is a disaster," Mummy said. "Who is your hairdresser in London these days? You should get a Marcel wave. Come up to my room and I'll have Adele do it for you. She is a whiz with problem hair."

"Later, Mummy," I said. "I really have things I should be doing now."

"More important things than keeping your poor lonely mother company?"

"Mummy, there are plenty of other women who would love to sit and gossip with you, I'm sure."

"They love to gossip in German and I never could get the hang of that language. And I'm not too hot at French either and I do so love to be the center of things, not a hanger-on."

"You could always find Belinda. She likes all the things you do."

"Your friend Belinda?" A frown crossed that flawless face. "Darling, one hears she is nothing more than a little tramp. Did you see how she was virtually throwing herself at Anton the other night? And I gather her bed wasn't slept in after that." She gave me a knowing wink.

I was amused at the pot calling the kettle

black. Little tramp, indeed. So I suspected it was sour grapes, since Mummy had confessed to being attracted to Anton. "Well, you'll have to find someone else to amuse you, because I'm supposed to be at the fitting for my bridal attendant's dress," I said. "You heard that I was one of Matty's attendants, didn't you?" I knew that a dress fitting would count as a good reason for my mother.

"Oh, well, then you should hurry off, darling," Mummy said. "I hear that the princess has brought in Madame Yvonne, of all people. She's a trifle passé, but she still makes some divine gowns. What's yours like?"

"Divine," I said. "You'll be pleased with me. I actually look elegant."

"Then we have hope of snaring a prince or a count for you yet," Mummy said. "Toddle along then. Don't keep Madame Yvonne waiting."

I took the opportunity and fled, leaving her sitting with her legs stretched out in front of the fire. When I came out to the vast entrance hall I paused. What should I be doing? Seeking out Nicholas; speaking with Count Dragomir? It all seemed so pointless. Would Nicholas want to know that someone had tried to kill him? And what about Dragomir? Obviously my mother was right and the resemblance to that portrait was purely a coincidence. He hadn't been alive since 1789 — not unless he was one of the undead. That ridiculous thought flashed through my mind and I tried to stifle it. He had all the qualities one would expect of a vampire count — that pale, skin, elegant demeanor, strangely staring light eyes, hollow cheeks. Rubbish, I said out loud, having picked up the word from Lady Middlesex. And as I had decided earlier, no undead person would need to administer poison. Poison at a dinner table bore the mark of a desperate, daring human being.

I wandered along hallways until I heard voices and came upon a group assembled in the anteroom next to the banqueting hall. I spotted Prince Nicholas among them and was making my way through the crowd toward him when a voice said, in French, "Now, who is this charming young person?" and of course I realized that I was among the royals who had arrived earlier. Then, of course, I felt highly embarrassed, because I was dressed for warmth rather than elegance. The embarrassment was doubled when Siegfried stepped forward, took me by the elbow and said, also in French, "Mama, may I present Georgiana, the cousin of King George."

The elegant, perfectly coiffed, exquisitely dressed woman beamed at me and extended an elegant hand. "So you are the one," she said. "How delightful. You don't know how we have longed to meet you."

I curtsied warily. "Your Majesty," I murmured.

"And you speak such fluent French too."

I hardly thought the word "majesty" comprised good French and was seriously worried at the effuse greeting. I had just been introduced to Siegfried's father, the king, when the gong sounded and I was swept into luncheon without having an opportunity to speak to Prince Nicholas. I was seated between a countess and an elderly baron, both of whom spoke to me in stilted French, and then, when they realized I knew nobody that they did, they spoke across me: "So do tell me, what is Jean-Claude doing this winter? Monte Carlo again? Too overrun with riffraff these days for me. And what about Josephine? How are her rheumatics? I heard she was in Budapest for the baths. I find them so unhygienic, don't you?"

I managed to eat and answer when spoken to, while at the same time watching what happened behind the table. Servants came and went with such rapidity that I could see there was a chance that an opportune assassin could have darted out from an archway, administered a dose of poison and vanished again without being noticed. Especially if someone were speaking at the time. I looked down the room. If someone at the far end of the table had been making a toast, all eyes would have been on him. The whole thing seemed impossible. I would have been happy to call it a heart attack and leave well enough alone, but for the fact that someone had tried to kill Prince Nicholas and that person was still among us.

I managed to eat my way through a rich and creamy soup, a sauerbraten with red cabbage and some delicious dumplings stuffed with prunes and dusted in sugar. Then, the moment luncheon was over, I tried to intercept Prince Nicholas as he left the room.

"Can we go somewhere to talk?" I said in a low voice. "There's something I need to tell you privately, about Field Marshal Pirin."

"Oh, right." He looked startled, then glanced around. "I'll get Anton."

"No!" The word came out louder than I meant it to, and several people around us looked up. "No," I repeated. "This is only for your ears. It's up to you whom you decide to share it with when I've told you."

"All right." He looked amused if anything. "Where shall we go for this secret meeting?"

"Anywhere that obnoxious man Patrascue isn't likely to overhear."

"Who knows where his men are lurking?" Nicholas said. "It's so easy to spy on people in a place like this. Oh, damn, speak of the devil —" Patrascue had come into the room and appeared to be making a beeline for us.

"You, lady from England," he said. "You will come with me, please. I have something that I want you to explain to me immediately."

"Do you want me along too?" Nicholas asked.

"Just the young lady," Patrascue said.

I had no choice but to go with Patrascue, especially as he appeared to have two of his men in tow and I didn't want to cause a fuss.

"I'll see you later then," I called after Nicholas, then I turned to Patrascue, who was standing close beside me. "What's this about?" I asked.

"You will soon see," Patrascue said. He marched ahead of me with great purpose, up the stairs until we came out onto my hallway. Then he flung open my bedroom door. A frightened-looking Queenie was standing by the bed.

"You will please explain this," Patrascue said. He opened the chest and pointed at a small glass bottle lying there.

"I have no idea what it is or how it got there," I said.

"I, on the other hand, have a very good idea," he said. "I would like to deduce it was the receptacle that contained the poison." He stepped closer until he was leering down at me. "I have had my suspicions about you from the beginning," he said. "You were sitting opposite this field marshal. And why should the English king send you to the wedding? Why not send his own daughter, a princess, as would be more fitting?"

"Because Princess Maria Theresa personally asked for me to be part of her bridal procession, since we were old school friends. So the queen thought that it would kill two birds with one stone, so to speak."

"Do not worry, as soon as the telephone lines are restored I shall be calling the garden of Scotland to verify this."

The garden of Scotland? I grinned. He meant Scotland Yard.

"Please do. Are you suggesting that I came all the way from England to kill a field marshal I had never even heard of until this week?" I tried to give a carefree laugh that didn't quite come off. One heard rumors of the way justice was conducted in foreign countries, and I would certainly be an easy scapegoat for him. "What possible motive could I have? It is my first time in this part of the world. I never met any of these people before."

"As for motive, I could think of several. The young Bulgarian princes, they did not like this fellow, I have heard. You are their cousin, are you not? Perhaps you are in a conspiracy together to kill him for them."

"In that case," I said, "we could easily have labeled his death a heart attack and nobody would have challenged it. But why should I wish to get involved in Bulgarian politics, even if these are my cousins?"

"Money," he said with a horrible grin. "As I told you earlier, money can make anyone do evil acts. And you have none, so your mother's companion confided to me."

"I may not have been brought up with money, but certainly with plenty of integrity," I said haughtily. "If I were so desperate for money, I could have made a good marriage by now. Your heir to the throne here has already asked me."

"I know this," he said, waving a hand airily. "I make it my business to know everything."

"So if I married him, I'd hardly want to start off my marriage with a war between Balkan countries, would I?"

"But I heard you rejected him," Patrascue said. He turned to one of his men and said something under his breath in another language. The man took out a handkerchief, then leaned forward and removed the little bottle. He handed it, still in the handkerchief, to Patrascue.

"I assure you, you won't find my fingerprints on it," I said. "And you'll probably discover that it is an ordinary medicine bottle containing someone's headache mixture."

Using the handkerchief, Patrascue removed the stopper, sniffed, then backed away hastily. "This did not contain a headache mixture," he said. "And I do not expect to find fingerprints on it. A clever killer will have wiped them away."

"Even a stupid killer would have hurled the bottle out of the window, where it would have sunk into snow that's not going to melt for ages," I said. "By which time the killer would be back in his or her own country."

Patrascue stared at the window, digesting this, the wheels in his brain working slowly.

"Isn't it obvious, even to you, that some-one is trying to frame me?" I said. Actually I said "attach the blame to me" because the only French word I knew for "frame" was the one that held pictures on walls and I didn't think that would be right. "Why would the real killer not have disposed of the evidence? How easy that would be in a castle of this size, with so many nooks and crannies and gratings in walls and floors. Or why not keep it on his person?"

Patrascue said nothing for a while. "Be-cause only a clever criminal would absolve herself from blame by making me think that she had been framed," he said at last. "I will tell you what I think, English lady. I think that this is a clever plot between you and your fellow Englishman, who conveniently drove away with the body before I could examine it or question him."

I grinned. "He's not English, actually. He's Irish."

He waved a hand in a bored manner. "English, Irish, what is the difference. I have heard of this Mr. O'Mara before. He was involved in a scandal at a casino, I believe. And he is interested in making money. But don't worry, I will send my men after him and he will be brought back here, and the truth will come out."

"Don't be so ridiculous," I said. "The queen of England would be horrified if she heard I had been treated this way when I have been sent to represent my country. Princess Maria Theresa, my dear school friend, will also be horrified, if I tell her."

He put his fingers under my chin and drew me closer to him. "I do not think you realize the spot you are in, young lady. I have the power to arrest you and lock you up, and I can assure you that our jails are not pleasant places — rats, disease, hardened criminals . . . and sometimes it takes months or years before a case comes to trial. But given that you are here for such a festive occasion, I will be gracious. I will merely inform you that you may not leave this castle without my permission."

His fingernails were digging into my chin, but I wasn't going to show him that I was scared. "Since I'm here for a wedding next week, I'm hardly likely to do that," I said. "Besides, I understand it may snow again, in which case nobody will be leaving for a while."

He leaned his face closer to mine. His breath was rank with garlic and worse. "Since you so emphatically insist on your innocence," he said, "you must have some thoughts on who committed this terrible crime. Who do you think it was? Dragomir, for example? You say you saw everything — did you perhaps observe Dragomir slipping something into a glass? Think hard, young lady, if you wish to go home after the wedding."

I saw then that he wasn't as stupid as I had thought. His plan had been to make me so fearful for my own safety that I would be willing to point the finger at Dragomir. He was about to discover that British girls are made of sterner stuff. They do not collapse in sobs when a fierce policeman threatens them with prison. Even though I did have my suspicions about Dragomir, I certainly wasn't going to share them with this man.

"If you want my opinion," I said, "I think you should consider the possibility of vampires."

CHAPTER 25

"Ooh miss, I wasn't half scared," Queenie said as soon as the men had left. "Those horrid brutes, they barged in here and started going through your things. I didn't half give 'em an earful. 'Whatcher think you're doing?' I said. 'Them things belongs to a royal person and she won't want you mucking about with them and getting your dirty hands on them.' But it wasn't much good because they didn't speak English. What was that man saying to you?"

"He thought I'd poisoned the man who was taken ill at dinner last night," I said. "They found what looked like a vial of poison in that chest."

"I bet they planted it there themselves," Queenie said. "You can't trust them foreigners, can you? That's what my old dad says and he should know because he was in the trenches in the Great War."

"Your old dad may be right on this occasion," I said. Planting the evidence there themselves was definitely a possibility — but why choose me? Was it because I came from a faraway place and therefore would cause a local political problem if I was arrested? Or did he think that I looked vulnerable and would easily break down and confess or be willing to pin the blame on Dragomir? It was all too much like a gothic drama. I just hoped that his men didn't catch up with Darcy. I didn't think that was likely. The sky outside my window looked heavy with the promise of more snow. I glanced longingly at my bed. A quick nap sounded like a good idea, but I really couldn't put off having my chat with Nicholas. He may still have been in grave danger. Why, oh, why did Darcy have to choose this moment to leave? He could have kept an eye on Nicholas and prevented another murder.

I made my way downstairs again. The hallways seemed colder than ever, with banners actually wafting in the wind. As I looked around me I realized that servants were everywhere. Usually one does not even notice the presence of servants, but at this moment I was particularly aware of them. Which made me think — if an intruder was in the castle, someone else must know about him. It wouldn't be possible to sneak around without encountering a servant or two, so someone had to be feeding the intruder and keeping him safely hidden. That indicated that the assassin had to be from here, and not one of the guests from Bulgaria.

Of course then my thoughts turned again to Count Dragomir. I found that I was passing the door to the sitting room where I had spotted the portrait. I opened the door cautiously and found the room empty. I tiptoed over to the fireplace and stared up at the portrait. In the flickering light of the fire it looked almost alive.

"All alone, my lady?" said a deep voice behind me.

I gasped and spun around. Count Dragomir was standing there, in the flesh. "Is there something I can get you?" he asked. "Some tea, maybe? You English like your tea at this hour, I believe."

"Er — no, thank you," I stammered.

"Then perhaps you came in here to be alone or to take an afternoon snooze," he said. "I leave you to sweet dreams."

He bowed and was about to retreat when I plucked up courage.

"Count Dragomir," I said, "I couldn't help noticing that there is a bad feeling between you and the policeman Patrascue."

"I'm sure the feeling is mutual," Dragomir said. "We were at the university together
as young men. We took an instant disliking
to each other. He was a sneaky, underhand
sort of fellow even then." I felt that there
was more but he was not going to tell me.

I took a deep breath and risked the second
question. "That portrait on the wall. Have
you noticed — the resemblance to you is
striking. But I'm sure you weren't born in
seventeen hundred and something." I gave
a gay little laugh.

"You're right. The family resemblance is
strong," he said, examining it. "One of my
ancestors. We used to own this castle, you
know. In fact, we used to be rulers of Transylvania when it was an autonomous state
and not part of Romania."

"But I was told you came from Yugoslavia."

"One of my ancestors decided to risk
battle against the occupying Turks," he said.
"He was foolhardy and the Turks were all-
powerful in those days. My ancestor counted
on the help of his neighbors in what should
have been a regionwide uprising, but I'm
afraid my family had earned a reputation
for brutality and ruthlessness. No help
came. The castle was taken and my family
had to flee into exile. So it is true I was

raised in what is now part of Yugoslavia. I went to study in Vienna, where I met the present king of Romania, who was a fellow student. We struck up a friendship and later I was offered a government post when he came to the throne in his country. Times have been hard since the Great War and jobs not easy to come by, so I was glad to accept. Ironically I was put in charge of this castle, so I am now the glorified butler where my family once ruled. But that is life, is it not? Nothing is certain."

I nodded. "My family has also lost all its money. My brother is just scraping by at the family seat. Times are hard."

"I believe I would have risen higher in government circles had it not been for our friend Patrascue." He came closer to me. "Tell me — Patrascue has enlisted you to trap me, has he not? That is the way he works — he decides whom he would like to be guilty, arrests them and then invents the evidence to prove it."

"He did suggest to me that I might have seen you put the poison in a glass. I told him I saw no such thing."

"The English, they can always be counted upon to behave like gentlemen and like ladies." He smiled. "But do not underestimate this Patrascue. He wields consider-able power in my country. There is a rumor that he is a puppet of Russia. They would like to extend their arm into this region, you know. I can understand why Prince Nicholas wanted to keep the death a natural one. The least little thing can spark off an international incident in these parts." He straightened a bowl of flowers on a small table, then looked up suddenly. "So I would stay out of any unauthorized investigation or amateur sleuthing, if I were you. You are playing with fire, my lady. Enjoy your role as bride's attendant and have a good time here. This is what young ladies should do, no?"

He nodded graciously and left. His tone had been pleasant enough but the threat had been real. Was he concerned for my safety or his own? So the castle was his ancestral home. And given his family history, he could well have an ax to grind with any of his Balkan neighbors. And a desire for revenge, going back generations. Maybe a little war between countries was just what he wanted.

I followed him out of the sitting room. If Dragomir were really the one who had administered the poison, why had he seemed so helpful when we met afterward? He had helped collect the utensils, handle the servants, get the body up to a bedroom and generally behaved the way a perfect butler would. Why? Was it that he wanted to appear above suspicion, or did he know that he had carried out a clever murder and would never be caught? Or was it that he felt guilty that the wrong man had died?

With these thoughts buzzing through my head I found myself in the long gallery, where afternoon coffee was being served. My mother had found the group of older countesses and was sitting eating torte with them. She waved as I approached.

"We're about to play bridge, darling. Care to join us?"

"No, thank you, I'm useless at bridge. Is the princess still in the fitting room?"

"Oh, no, darling. She appeared about half an hour ago, poured herself a black coffee and looked with longing at the cakes. That child is starving herself, if you ask me. Now she's definitely too thin. European men do like a woman to have a little meat on her bones."

"And Prince Nicholas, have you seen him recently?"

"I haven't seen him since lunch. I gather he and Anton went out to shoot, and I expect Max went with them. They're only happy when they're shooting something —

apart from sex, of course."

"Mother!" I gave her a warning frown.

My mother glanced around at the other women, who were tucking into their torte with abandon. "They won't understand. Their English is hopeless, darling. Besides, it is about time you were acquainted with the facts of life. I've hopelessly neglected my duty in that area. Men only have two thoughts in their heads and those are killing or copulating."

"I'm sure there are plenty of men with finer feelings, who are interested in art and culture."

"Yes, darling, of course there are. They are called fairies. And they are quite adorable — so witty and fun to be with. But in my long and varied life I've found that the ones who are witty to be with are no use in bed, and vice versa."

She took a final bite of her cake, licked her fork — curling her tongue in what would have been a seductive gesture had any men been present — and went to join the other ladies, who were setting up a bridge table. I helped myself to coffee and cake and sat alone on a sofa, feeling uneasy. So Nicholas had gone out hunting again, had he? I had seen from experience how easy it was to shoot at the wrong target, and hadn't Darcy suggested exactly the same way to kill someone conveniently? But I could hardly go after Nicholas at this stage. I'd just have to wait until he returned. Dragomir had warned me against amateur sleuthing, but I was apparently the only one in the castle, apart from the killer, who knew the truth. I had to warn Nicholas as soon as he came back.

The cake looked absolutely delicious — layers of chocolate and cream and nuts. I took a slice but I found it hard to swallow. If I couldn't come up with a good answer for the first question — who wanted to kill Prince Nicholas? — then perhaps I should examine the next logical one: why? I understood that murder is committed for several reasons: fear, gain, revenge, with fear being the most compelling motive of the three. Who in this castle had something to fear from the prince, something so terrible that he had to be silenced forever? I couldn't answer that one. I knew so little about everyone here. So who had something to gain from his death? The obvious answer to that was Anton. He'd be next in line to the throne if his brother died. And he had the means — a knowledge of chemistry — and he had stood to clink glasses with his brother. No — that theory didn't work since the poison was put into the red wine when Nicholas had already switched to champagne and Anton would have observed that.

Of the other people within reach at the table, Matty wouldn't want to finish off her bridegroom right before the wedding. I was sitting opposite, so was Siegfried, and neither of us did it. So we were back to Dragomir or an unnamed server, bribed by a large sum of money to do the unthinkable. And if not these, a political assassination. That, I supposed, made the most sense, because an anarchist or communist wouldn't care about the murder taking place in such a public place — would actually prefer it to be visible and spectacular, like the assassination of the archduke in Sarajevo that had started the Great War.

This was out of my league. I had tangled once before with a team of highly trained communist infiltrators and had no wish to do so again. In fact I wanted to do as Dragomir suggested — have a good time with the other young women and enjoy the wedding celebrations. I just wished that Darcy wasn't counting on me.

CHAPTER 26

The long gallery, Bran Castle
Still November 18

I was still toying with my cake when Matty came wandering in, looking distracted. "Isn't Nicholas back yet?" she asked. I noted that she pronounced his name in the French way, "Nicolah," and didn't call him Nicky or Nick as his brother did.

"I haven't seen him," I replied.

"Really, what a ridiculous thing to do, to go out shooting in weather like this. Aren't men silly — at least some men."

She perched on the sofa beside me, her eyes on my cake.

"My mother says that men are only interested in two things, killing things and sex," I said, trying to brighten her mood.

"Not all men," she said, looking away again. "In Paris I met artists, writers, men who had a romantic side and could express themselves."

339

"My mother claims they are all fairies."

"Not all," she said. She got up and went over to a tall, arched window. Daylight was fading fast. "It's starting to snow again, you know. I hope they don't get lost. I suppose I'd better tell Dragomir and send servants out to find them."

And she left me. She had only been gone a few minutes when I heard raised voices and the clatter of boots on stairs, and Nicholas and Anton came into the room, snowflakes still dusting their hair and eyelashes. Their faces were alight and they were laughing.

"Your bride was worried about you," I said as Nicholas passed me.

"It was rather an absurd thing to do, I suppose," Nicholas said. "We got lost. Max fell into a snowdrift and had to be dug out."

"And after all that, we come home empty-handed," Anton added. "But it was great fun. And one hates being cooped up inside all day."

They made a beeline for the coffeepots and cakes, then came to sit beside me.

"What was it you wanted to tell me earlier," Nicholas asked, "when that brute Patrascue dragged you off? He wasn't arresting you for the murder or anything, was he?"

"Actually he was," I said. "He found a small glass bottle, containing what he believed was the poison, in a chest in my room."

"Good God," Nicholas said. "But surely even someone as thick as Patrascue didn't think that you'd hidden it there, did he?"

"I did point out that I could easily have thrown it out of the window into the snowy wilderness where it wouldn't have been found for months," I said.

"So the question is who planted it on you?" Anton asked.

"The assassin, I presume, as he had to make a quick getaway," Nicholas suggested.

"Or Patrascue himself, which I consider more likely," I said. "He wanted to scare me into implicating Dragomir."

"Oh, so he thinks Dragomir did it, does he? Interesting. I had the same suspicions myself," Nicholas said.

"In his case I don't think he cares whether Dragomir was guilty or not. He has a long-standing feud with the man — I couldn't exactly get to the bottom of it, but he'd love to frame Dragomir. I didn't play along and refused to be intimidated."

"Quite right," Anton said. "I love British girls, don't you, Nick? Such pillars of strength. Think of Boudicca." He reached

341

across and gave my knee a squeeze.

"Behave yourself, Toni. You can't have more than one at a time, you know," Nick said, laughing.

"I don't see why not. The more the merrier, that's my motto. In fact I'm rather miffed that I wasn't born a Turk. I'd have enjoyed a harem. It would have been a challenge to see how many I could get through in one night."

"You are offending this young lady's sensibilities," Nicholas said.

"No, really," I said, laughing, but Anton stood up. "I shall go and find Belinda," he said. "She loves to hear of my exploits and she is quite willing to add to them."

"That young man will have to learn to take life seriously one day," Nicholas said as soon as Anton was out of hearing. "Father rather despairs of him. Too bad he was born a prince. He'd have done well as a film star in Hollywood, I feel — or better yet a stunt-man."

I looked around. The ladies had begun their bridge game. An old man was holding forth to several of the young counts. I moved closer to Nicholas. "About what I wanted to tell you," I said.

"Oh, yes. You've discovered something important?"

342

"Very important, especially to you," I said and related exactly how I remembered the incident. "So it was your glass that he took," I concluded.

For a while Nicholas said nothing. Then he sighed. "It's rather sobering, isn't it? One lives with the threat of assassination, I suppose, but it's still a shock when it comes close to home. Then it's obviously some infernal anarchist. Probably did as Patrascue suggested and paid one of the servants to do his dirty work."

"You can't think of anyone else who might want you dead?" I asked. "Nobody here who bears you animosity?"

Nicholas gave a wry smile. "I've always thought of myself as a likeable sort of chap," he said. "Not the kind that makes enemies."

"But if it was a political assassination, why not aim for your father rather than you?"

"I can think of a couple of answers to that one: My father wasn't there on the night in question. His entourage had been held up by the avalanche on the pass, remember. If the whole thing had been planned for that night, maybe they decided I was the next best thing and went for it. And the second answer is that maybe it didn't matter which of us they got. Remember the archduke in Sarajevo? He was a minor player in the

343

Hapsburg dynasty and yet the incident still started a world war."

I shuddered. "It's horrible. How can you live when you never feel safe?"

"I suppose one has no choice," he said. "One likes to think that we bring stability and culture to a region, but it's always been a hotbed of intrigue and violence. They've been killing each other around here since day one. And none more violent than the family that used to own this place. Vlad the Impaler and his descendants. I'm sure you've heard of him. What a bunch they were. Talk about cruel and ruthless. I've read some of the books in this library. Some of their vile deeds would turn your stomach. And of course the books and the local inhabitants claim that Vlad became Dracula and still lives on."

And he laughed.

"There you are at last, you wicked one." Matty came into the room and bent to kiss his forehead. "I was worried about you. And you still have snow on your head."

I decided to be tactful and leave them alone. I went back up to my room and looked out of the window. Snow was now falling fast — great fat flakes whirling and swirling around the turrets. And my thoughts went instantly to Darcy, somewhere up on that pass. I hoped he'd be sensible enough to take refuge at the inn up there. In fact I just wished this whole thing were over.

It did cross my mind to wonder where Queenie was. I presumed she was still in the kitchen, stuffing her face on cake. If she came back to London with me, she'd desert me as soon as she found out that I lived on baked beans and toast. I wondered whether to go and seek her out, but I couldn't get the disturbing image out of my mind of Matty with blood running down her chin. I didn't want to believe in vampires, but I know what I saw quite clearly. If she really was a vampire, then I had no intention of being next on her menu.

I paced the room. Soon I'd need to start dressing for dinner and it was almost impossible to get into an evening dress alone. I thought of going down to Mummy and seeing if her maid could do my hair for me, as promised. It would be interesting to see what I looked like, properly coiffured. Still no Queenie. I opened my wardrobe, cautiously, as I wasn't sure what might be lurking inside something of that girth, and took out my one presentable dinner dress. I couldn't wear it for a third night in a row, yet neither could I wear the one with the scorch marks. Too bad that my mother was such a tiny little person, I thought. I know she'd travel with oodles of delicious clothes. Suddenly I had a brain wave. Knowing Belinda, she would have come with a trunkful of fashionable dresses. Maybe she'd let me wear one of her dresses tonight.

I hurried down the first flight of stairs and along the hallway to where I thought Belinda's room was. As I passed a door I heard voices — a man's voice, low and calm, and a woman's voice raised in anger and shrill. "What were you thinking?" she demanded in French. "How could you? It will be the end of everything."

I didn't hear the man's reply. Interesting, I thought, and continued down the hall. At what I hoped was Belinda's door I knocked, never knowing what might be going on in Belinda's room. I waited, and I was about to go away when the door was opened by a bleary-eyed Belinda.

"Oh," she said, eyeing me with disappointment. "I thought you might be Anton. Sorry. I was taking a much-needed nap before dinner. Is it time to dress?"

"Almost," I said.

"Come on in, then," she said and led me into a small square room. She flung herself back on the bed and closed her eyes again.

I looked around. It was plain and simple by castle standards. No terrifying wardrobe or chest for her.

"So who dresses you?" I asked. "I take it you didn't bring a spare maid along in your trunk, did you?"

"No, I left the faithful Florrie at home. She goes to pieces if I take her abroad. Luckily Matty is being sweet and sending her maid to take care of me when she's finished dressing her mistress. Her room is right next door. As you can see, I'm in what was probably a dressing room originally. Dashed inconvenient actually, as I suspect that the walls aren't exactly soundproof, and one does have the occasional nocturnal visitor."

I perched on her bed. "Belinda, the way you carry on, don't you ever worry about, you know, getting in the family way?"

Belinda chuckled. "You are so delightfully old-fashioned in your wording, my sweet. There are useful things called French letters and Dutch caps, you know. And if I were to get preggers, there is a wonderful little clinic on the coast near Bournemouth, and I'm sure the man in question would cough up the necessary funds to do the trick." The smile faded. "Don't look so horrified, darling. It's done all the time. Of

347

course it's easier for married women — no need for clinics as long as the baby looks something like the official father. Accept the fact, Georgie — bed hopping is a major sport for our class. It whiles away the long hours between hunting, shooting and fishing." And she laughed again.

"Do you ever think you'll get married?" I asked.

"If I find someone rich and boring enough, and preferably old, and short-sighted." She reached up and put her hands on my cheeks. "I enjoy it, darling. I love the thrill of the chase. I can't picture myself ever tied down to one man."

"You and my mother must come from another planet," I said. "Settling down with one man sounds awfully nice to me."

"The problem is with whom, darling," Belinda said, dropping back to her pillows with a sigh. "Your beloved Darcy doesn't have the means nor the temperament for domestic bliss. In fact I see him turning into one of these enigmatic men who flit around the globe, living by their wits into old age."

I sighed. "You may be right. I wish I hadn't fallen for him, but I have. Everyone is pushing me to marry sensibly — I could probably even have someone like Anton if I wanted. But I don't want. And I certainly don't want to live in a part of the world where I could be assassinated any day."

"Don't be silly, darling. I'm sure Anton and his family are quite safe. Who'd want to kill them?"

I realized then that she didn't know anything. I got to my feet, before I spilled any beans. "Belinda, what I actually came for was to beg a favor. My maid Queenie has managed to put a huge scorch mark in my good evening dress. I can't keep wearing the same thing at dinner every night so I wondered if I could possibly wear one of yours."

"That maid of yours is a total disaster," Belinda said. "What will she do next? Give you third-degree burns when she spills your morning tea all over you? It's too bad we're snowed in or you could send her home on the next train."

"She'd never make it across Europe alone," I said, laughing in spite of everything. "She'd wind up in Constantinople and find herself in a harem. I gather big, chubby women are the thing over there."

Belinda got up and went across to a gilt-trimmed white wardrobe. "I suppose I can spare you a dress," she said and opened it. There must have been at least ten dresses hanging there.

349

"Belinda — how long did you expect to be here?" I asked in amazement.

"One never knows how long one will be abroad," she said. "One meets somebody and suddenly there's an invitation to the south of France or a château on the Loire, so it's always best to be prepared."

I examined the dresses one by one and chose what I thought was the least flamboyant — pale turquoise, straight and simple.

"Good choice," she said, smiling at me. "Not really my style at all, but I keep it in case I need to look virginal for somebody's parents."

"You must be a better actress than my mother," I quipped back.

"It's about time you tried it yourself and then you'd know what you were missing," she called after me as I carried the dress from her room. "And don't let your maid anywhere near it with an iron."

As I came out into the hallway there was no sound coming from behind the next door. I realized with a shock that this must be Matty's room. So who was in there with her? A man with whom she spoke French? And yet I knew she spoke German when she was with Nicholas. Her father maybe? Her mother was French, after all, so perhaps that was the language used at home, and yet Siegfried also preferred to speak German. I was tempted to go and peek through the keyhole. I crept toward the door, bent down and put my eye to it. But I could see nothing. Obviously the key was still in it.

Suddenly I heard the tap of brisk footsteps behind me. Two of the older countess chaperons were coming toward me. They looked at me with interest, on my knees in a strange hallway.

"I — uh — dropped my ring," I said. "It falls off sometimes when my hands get too cold."

"Then let us help you look for it," one of them said.

"Oh, no, thank you. I have already found it again," I said, scrambling hastily to my feet. "Most kind."

I heard a muttered exchange in German as I hurried on my way, my cheeks flaming.

I made it safely back to my room and shut the door with a sigh of relief. Still no sign of Queenie. Really this was now too much. Not that she was any use in dressing me, but one expected a maid to appear occasionally. I left the dress on my bed and made my way resolutely toward the kitchen. On my way down I passed one of the servants coming up. She curtsied.

"Is my maid down there?" I asked. Then I

repeated in French, "I am looking for my maid."

"No, Highness," she answered in French. "Nobody is there."

Which probably meant that she was taking a long nap in her room. That girl could sleep more than anybody I had ever met. I chose what I hoped was the right tower and made my way up the spiral stair until I emerged to her cold and drafty corridor. If she'd snuggled under her blankets to keep warm, I couldn't blame her. As I stood there, trying to remember which door was hers, a door opened and a young woman, dressed elegantly in black, came out.

"What do you require, Your Highness?" she asked in French.

I told her I was looking for Queenie.

"She has the room next to mine. This one" — she pointed at a door — "but I do not think she is there. Excuse me. I must go to dress the princess for dinner."

I opened Queenie's door and fumbled for a light switch but couldn't find one. In the dim light from the hallway I could see that the room was unoccupied. The bed was made. Queenie was definitely not there.

CHAPTER 27

Still November 18
Have lost Queenie.

I retreated, puzzled and a little worried now. Where could she have gone? A secret tryst with a male servant? But I had little time to think about it. I'd have to hurry if I was to dress myself for dinner. I struggled into Belinda's dress, which fortunately had a zipper at the side and not hooks up the back, then I brushed my hair, powdered my nose and finished my toilette. Still Queenie didn't show up. I was alarmed and annoyed now. Where could she be?

I arrived in the gallery outside the banqueting hall to find it brimming with people and even more decorations and jewels than the night before. And tiaras. Oh, Lord, I should have worn my tiara. I was wondering whether I'd have time to sprint back upstairs to fetch it when I was grabbed by Prince Siegfried.

"You are looking enchanting, Lady Georgiana," he said. "A most suitable gown, if you permit me to say so."

"I didn't realize that tiaras were going to be worn," I said. "I left mine in my room."

"It does not matter. You look delightfully refreshing, the way you are."

Why was he being so charming? Did he think that I knew something about him that he would not wish to be repeated?

"Tonight you will allow me to escort you to dinner again?" he said and offered me his arm. I could hardly refuse and allowed myself to be led into the middle of the crowd. I was just wondering where his parents were when trumpets sounded. Dragomir, looking even more awe inspiring than ever, stepped forward. "The parents of the bride, Their Royal Majesties the king and queen of Romania, and the parents of the bridegroom, Their Royal Majesties the king and queen of Bulgaria," he announced. The crowd parted and the royal couples, the queens dripping jewels and suitably crowned, processed down the middle, while those they passed curtsied and bowed. As they passed me I curtsied. The king of Romania held out his hand to me and gave me a warm smile. "So charming," he said.

The rest of us lined up to follow the

monarchs into dinner. I was seated opposite Siegfried, not far from his parents. The seat beside me was empty and I looked around, realizing I hadn't seen Matty. She came rushing in at the last minute, looking flustered.

"Sorry, Mama, sorry, Papa. I overslept and that stupid maid didn't wake me in time," she said.

Interesting, I thought. The maid had gone down in plenty of time. And the man I had heard her arguing with had not been her father. The meal started with a rich hunter's soup. Matty took a sip or two then toyed with it. I was now intrigued. Who had been in her bedroom before dinner? I looked up and down the table at the various young counts and barons, trying to put a name to each face. Nicholas had introduced them one by one as he toasted them last night, but it seemed to me that most of them spoke German, not French. The only other option was that Matty had been speaking to someone like Dragomir; but would protocol permit that she allow a retainer into her bedroom, especially as I now knew that her maid hadn't been present at that moment? Maybe Belinda had heard more and would be able to enlighten me, but my friend was now at the far end of the table, looking bored between two elderly gentlemen who were clearly both fascinated to be sitting next to her. Interestingly enough, my mother wore a similar expression at the other end of the table. Those two were so alike. It would have been much easier if Belinda had been her daughter instead of me.

Matty's unfinished soup was whisked away and a portion of trout was placed before us. The one good thing about this whole experience so far was that I had been eating good food again, but at this moment I was having as much trouble as Matty in eating anything much. Siegfried was saying something to me. I nodded and smiled, that knot of worry still in my stomach. Where the devil was Queenie? She couldn't have left the castle, which meant she was somewhere and presumably safe. Knowing her, maybe she'd found a warm corner to curl up in and would have awoken feeling guilty by now.

I glanced across at Matty, who was now trying to hide the trout under a lettuce leaf.

"Is something wrong?" I whispered to her.

"No, nothing at all. Why should anything be wrong?" she said. "But I just heard that the old man was poisoned. My maid told me."

"Your maid told you?" I asked with concern. "How did your maid find out?"

"She overheard Patrascue talking."

"I see." I wondered how many other people in the castle had overheard something and whether everyone now knew about the murder. So much for keeping it from Nicholas's father if even servants knew about it.

I observed her face. Just how much had her maid overheard? Did Matty really know that the poison was intended for Nicholas? She didn't seem to and she went on, "It's very upsetting. My whole wedding is turning into a nightmare. I don't know why I thought it was such a good idea to come to the castle in the first place. Stupid of me. Stupid, stupid, stupid. We could have been at the palace in Bucharest, going to theaters and enjoying ourselves."

She broke off as her father, the king, rose to his feet. Dragomir rapped on the table with his gavel. "Pray silence for His Majesty King Michael."

The king proceeded to welcome all his guests, especially the bridegroom and his parents, and raised his glass in a toast to friendship between the two nations forever. We drank — those of us who were in the know a little tentatively, our eyes watching everyone else. Nobody keeled over, however, and the king went on.

"As we share in the joy of our daughter's nuptials, I am delighted to announce that there will soon be a second celebration to follow this one. My son has informed me that he too will take a bride." Murmurs of approval from around the table. "And we shall be most delighted to welcome another descendant of our esteemed Queen Victoria into the family. Her father was my good friend, and I look forward to having her as my daughter."

I had been looking up and down the table to see who he was talking about.

He picked up his glass. "So I ask us all to be upstanding and raise our glasses in a toast to my son, Siegfried, and his bride-to-be, Lady Georgiana."

Everyone was on their feet. I felt as if I were falling down a deep well shaft. I wanted to scream "No-o-o-o!" but everyone was smiling and raising their glasses to me.

"You sly one. You didn't tell me." Matty embraced me and kissed me on both cheeks. "I can't say I'd want Siegfried, but I'm so glad you're going to be my sister."

What could I do? I had been brought up with etiquette rammed down my throat. A lady would never make a fuss at a banquet. A lady would never contradict a king. But this lady would never marry Prince Siegfried in a million years. Siegfried was raising his glass to me, pursing his cod lips in a kiss. Oh, God — please don't say I've got to kiss him. The company sat down again. I hastened to sit before any kiss might be required. I hadn't realized that the steward had pulled my chair out for me. One second I was standing, glass in hand; the next I was sitting on nothing and had disappeared under the table with a startled cry. Of course then all heads turned back to me again. I was hastily rescued from my undignified position, my face burning with embarrassment, and placed in my chair. Everyone around made a fuss of me, hoping that I wasn't injured and pressing glasses of champagne at me. I heard murmurs of "Too much champagne going to her head" and "Attack of nerves, poor little thing."

Believe me, if I could have crawled under the table and escaped at that moment, I would have done so. But there were too many legs around. I was profoundly grateful when the next course was brought in — a Hungarian delicacy of flaming meats on a sword. It was applauded with oohs and aahs. I watched it as if I were looking at a film of someone else's life. This couldn't really be happening to me. When had I ever given Siegfried any indication that I might marry him? I felt a cold sweat creeping over me. I had actually come close to flirting with him last night. I had begged him to dance with me to keep him from paying a visit to Field Marshal Pirin's room. And he'd taken that as a sign that I'd changed my mind. And this evening he had asked me something that I hadn't quite heard and I'd nodded and smiled. Oh, golly — had he asked me if I'd changed my mind then? I thought he was only talking about the food or the weather. Doomed, that's what I was. The words "producing an heir" echoed around my head. Followed by Belinda's laughing suggestion that I lie back, close my eyes and think of England.

That was never going to happen, if I had to throw myself off one of the turrets first. Well, maybe not quite as dramatic as that. Run away to Argentina, disguised as a peasant, perhaps, or even go and live with Granddad in Essex. I wasn't going to marry Siegfried, but I'd have to find a way out without anyone losing face. Maybe I could just happen to discover that he was more attracted to men than women and let his parents know that I could never condone such behavior. That ought to do it. Only not tonight. Not now. At this moment I had to be Siegfried's intended.

The meal finished with no more deaths, accidents or surprises and we ladies were escorted through to the withdrawing room for coffee and liquors. I was looking around to see if I could slip away unnoticed when the queen of Romania stood before me with open arms.

"My dear child," she said. "I can't tell you how happy this has made me. It was our dearest wish and that of your royal cousins too." And she embraced me.

Suddenly I saw clearly: this whole excursion had been a plot to get me to marry Siegfried. I was never Matty's dear friend at school. The queen could more properly have sent her own daughter to the wedding and not me. I was, as they say in American gangster films, set up. Framed. Duped. Ladies swarmed around me, patting me and offering congratulations. Even my mother came to peck me on the cheek. "Very sensible," she whispered in my ear. "You'll have a lovely dress allowance and he won't bother you. A little difficult about future babies that Darcy has dark hair, but so does Siegfried's mother, so that's all right."

I looked up to see Belinda looking at me with wonder and amusement on her face. As soon as she could she dragged me aside.

"Have you lost your mind?" she demanded. "You can't be that desperate."

"I'm not and I haven't," I hissed back. "It's all a horrible misunderstanding. I never said that I would marry him, but I had to humor him last night and he took it the wrong way. What on earth am I going to do, Belinda?"

"Can I be a bridesmaid?" she asked, mirth bubbling up again.

"That is not funny," I snapped. "You've got to help me."

"You could let him know you're not a virgin," she said. "I gather that rather matters to people like Siegfried."

"But you know I am."

"Then remedy it rapidly."

"Thanks!" I laughed nervously. "And how am I supposed to do that? Darcy has gone away again, and I'm not desperate enough to want to remedy it with anybody else."

"I could lend you Anton, I suppose," she said as if we were talking about gloves.

"Belinda, you're not taking this seriously."

"You have to admit it is too, too delicious for words, darling. You becoming Mrs. Fish-face. At least you'll be a princess and Fig will have to curtsy to you."

"I hardly think that makes up for being married to Fishface," I said. "This is turning into the worst day of my life. Speaking of which, you haven't seen my maid, have you?"

"Probably sneaking off again to get at the cakes," Belinda said.

"No, I asked and she wasn't below stairs. And she wasn't in her room, either. I'm worried about her, given everything that's happened."

"What do you mean?" she asked and I remembered that she wasn't in on Pirin's murder.

"The vampires and everything," I said, making her laugh again.

"Sweetie pie, you don't really still believe there are vampires in the castle, do you?"

"In a castle like this it's easy to believe in anything," I said.

"My lady, I believe congratulations are in order," said a deep voice right behind me. I spun around to see Count Dragomir standing there. He bowed low. "I look forward to serving you as my princess."

As he went to withdraw I remembered my worry. "Count Dragomir, if you have a moment."

"Of course, Your Highness." He put his hand to his breast and bowed. So I'd now been elevated to Highness in anticipation, had I?

I beckoned him to one side. "Count Dragomir, I am concerned because my maid seems to have disappeared. She didn't come to dress me for dinner and she is not in her room. I wondered if you could ask the other servants if they had seen her and perhaps even send out a search party to look for her for me. She may have taken a wrong turn and fallen down some dark staircase."

"You are right," he said, "there are plenty of dangerous spots in a castle like this for those who wander where they shouldn't. But do not concern yourself, my lady. I will set servants to the task immediately. We will find her for you." He was about to move off again when I spotted Lady Middlesex and Miss Deer-Harte, who had come into the room together. I decided to ask one more question.

"Count Dragomir. The English lady over there — she tells me that she observed a young man creeping about the hallways at night, and then the same young man hiding in one of the archways, watching the banquet on the first evening. I just wondered if you had any idea who that might be, or if it was possible that a stranger is hiding out in the castle."

"How can a stranger have come into the castle, my lady?" Dragomir asked. "You have seen for yourself — there is only one gate and it is guarded at all times. The only other way in would be to fly."

"Or climb up the wall?" I suggested.

He laughed. "You have been listening to the rumors of vampires, have you not? No man in his right mind would attempt to climb the castle wall."

"So none of the servants has reported seeing a strange young man — pale, with fair hair?"

"No, my lady. None of the servants has seen any kind of stranger in the castle. They would have reported to me instantly if they had. I'm afraid your English lady friend is letting her imagination run away with her. Remember how upset she was when she first arrived here. Of course His Highness, your betrothed, has light hair. Perhaps she saw him."

I wrestled with taking this one stage further and telling him that I had seen the young man myself and his portrait had hung in my room until it was mysteriously changed for another one. But Dragomir decided this for me by saying, "Pardon me, Highness, but I am wanted elsewhere." And he backed away from me.

I was just considering how strange it would be if I really were a princess and people had to back away from my presence, when Lady Middlesex came over to me, with Miss Deer-Harte in tow.

"Well, there's a turnup for the books," she said. "I see you've made a good match for yourself. The queen will be pleased. My congratulations."

I managed a weak smile and nod. "I asked Dragomir if any of the servants had reported seeing Miss Deer-Harte's young man, but he dismissed the idea that there could be a stranger in the castle."

"I know what I saw," Miss Deer-Harte said emphatically. "And I'm going to prove to you all that I was right. He can't escape in this weather so I'll spot him eventually and I'm wearing my whistle. As soon as I see him I'll blow it to attract attention."

"Watch what you're saying, Deer-Harte — here comes that awful man." Lady Middlesex glanced over her shoulder. And sure enough, Patrascue, with a couple of his men in tow, had entered the drawing room. Although everyone else was dressed for the evening, he was still in a black street coat with the collar turned up. He stood in the doorway, looking around. It was as if an icy blast had entered the room. The women froze in midconversation. Patrascue waved his hand lazily. "Do not let me disturb you,

Majesties. Pray continue."

He spotted me and women stepped aside for him as he made a beeline for me. "I hear that congratulations are in order. So you changed your mind and accepted his offer, did you, English Lady Georgiana? Soon you will be one of my people. I look forward to that day."

Again I felt the threat: soon I will have control over you. But I managed a gracious nod and words of thanks.

"The men have not yet left the dinner table, Mr. Patrascue," the queen said in her clear French voice. "I suggest you leave us ladies to finish our coffee and brandy in peace."

"Majesty." Patrascue managed a semipolite nod and retreated again. I heaved a sigh of relief.

"Don't let that man upset you, my dear," the queen said, extending her hand to me. "I can't think why he is so interested in you, but ignore him. We all do. Come and have a glass of cognac. You look quite pale." And she led me back into the fold.

Soon after, the men joined us. Siegfried and Nicholas came over to us. Siegfried took my hand and pressed his cold fish-lips against it. Uck. If it was that bad against my hand, I dared not think what it would feel like actually kissing him.

"You are a very wise girl," he said. "May I congratulate you on your good taste. You will lead a happy life."

I couldn't think of a thing to say back. I merely tried to force a smile and wished that the floor would open up and swallow me. Fortunately Matty didn't suggest dancing again so I wasn't forced to dance with Siegfried. Instead a roulette wheel was brought out and what seemed to me like large sums of money were soon being wagered.

"How old are you now, Georgiana?" Siegfried asked me.

I told him I was twenty-two. He placed a stack of chips on twenty-two. "In your honor," he said. "I feel sure you will bring me luck." And sure enough, the wretched wheel landed on the number the very next spin. Siegfried smiled and pushed a mound of chips over to me. I put random chips on the board, without the slightest idea what I was doing, and it seemed that I couldn't lose. I noticed that both Patrascue and Dragomir had entered the room and were standing watching in the shadows.

"I think I had better give you back your chips before my luck turns," I said when I could stand the tension no longer.

"Your luck will not turn while you are with me," he said, "and of course the winnings are yours to keep. You will need to start preparing your trousseau."

When I went to cash them in I was amazed and delighted to find that I had apparently won several hundred pounds. On any other occasion this unexpected windfall would have brought relief and jubilation. Tonight it was like a condemned man hearing that his horse came up on the Derby.

As soon as I was able I slipped away, up to my room. Still no sign of Queenie. I felt a growing knot of fear in my stomach. People didn't just disappear without reason. One person had been murdered already. Had Queenie stumbled upon the killer and been in the wrong place at the wrong time? If it was our light-haired young man, then she had seen him in her room and could identify him. Of course then so could I, which might mean I was also in danger. I went across and peered out into the night. It was snowing gently now and outside was the silence that only comes with snow.

"I wish you were here, Darcy," I said into the night. "I hope you're all right."

I latched my shutters, pulled the heavy drapes back into place and stood staring at the dying fire. My nerves were wound as taut as watch springs. In one day the head of a secret police had threatened me with jail, I had found that I was engaged to the repulsive Siegfried and my maid had vanished. Not to mention that there had been a murder in the castle. I certainly couldn't go to bed not knowing what had happened to Queenie. I lit a candle and made my way up to her room again. But it was untouched. The hallways and stairs were deserted. I really didn't know what else I could do. I stood peering down one dark passageway after another. Dragomir had promised to send servants to look for her and I didn't know my way around half of the castle. I had no choice but to go back to my room and get ready for bed.

I lay there for a long time, unable to sleep. I was just drifting off when I heard a scraping noise outside my window, then the rattle of my shutters. I sat up, awake and alert. I had latched the shutters from inside, hadn't I? I stared into the darkness, wishing the heavy drapes weren't covering the windows, every fiber of my being poised for flight. Nothing moved. There was no more sound. I relaxed. It must have been a sudden gust of wind that had rattled the shutters, nothing more, I told myself. But just to be on the safe side, I went to the mantelpiece and retrieved that candlestick again.

I lay there, gripping the candlestick, and began to feel rather silly. I was worrying too much, I told myself. Queenie had slipped and fallen down some disused stair. She'd probably twisted an ankle and would soon be found. And there was no such thing as vampires. Even as I had this thought I felt a waft of icy air strike my face and the curtains moved. Then, as I stared in horror, a white hand appeared between the curtains and a figure slipped noiselessly into my room.

CHAPTER 28

My bedroom in the middle of the night
Friday to Saturday, November 18 to 19

I sat up, gripping the candlestick. The dark figure came closer to my bed, moving with catlike grace. As he pulled aside the bed curtain and bent toward me I raised the candlestick to strike. Then I saw his silhouette against the fire. His head and neck were covered in fur. I must have gasped as I raised the candlestick because a hand grabbed my wrist as another hand came over my mouth.

"Don't make a sound," said a voice in my ear.

I stared up at him, trying to make out his features in the firelight glow. But I recognized the voice all right.

"Darcy? What on earth are you doing here?" I demanded, relief flooding over me. "You nearly scared the daylights out of me."

"I can see that." He took the candlestick

from me. "Quite the little tiger, aren't we? If you hadn't taken a breath I'd have been lying here with my head bashed in. Rule one of the secrecy game — never breathe." And he smiled as he took off his coat and hat and perched on the bed beside me.

"I gasped because I caught sight of your head and I saw it was shaggy fur. I thought you were a werewolf."

"First vampires and now werewolves. What next — witches, fairies? Come to think of it there are some fairies in the castle already." He grinned. "For your information, it's only the sort of hat the local chaps wear to go hunting." He undid the strap under his chin. "See — it has earflaps. Wonderful for keeping out the cold."

"But what are you doing here?" I asked. "I thought you'd gone off with Pirin's body."

"I did," he said. "But I decided I didn't quite like what was going on at the castle so I thought I'd double back and keep an eye on things. Field Marshal Pirin won't mind. I left the car in a suitable snowdrift and skied back down again."

"Did you really just climb up the wall?"

"Not as impossible as it sounds," he said. "Someone had conveniently left a rope hanging down."

"What if it wasn't properly tied? You'd

373

have fallen and been killed," I said.

"A fellow has to take the occasional risk in life, you know."

"Not this fellow," I said. "I don't want to find your broken body lying on rocks, is that clear?"

He looked at me tenderly and brushed back a strand of hair from my face. "Don't worry about me. I lead a charmed life. Luck of the Irish."

"Oh, Darcy, you are so infuriating I could kill you," I said and flung myself into his arms. My cheek nestled into the wet wool of his coat as he held me tightly. "You smell like wet sheep," I said, laughing.

"Stop your complaining, woman," he said. "I've plowed through a snowstorm and climbed a castle wall to see you. You should be grateful."

"I am. Very grateful. You don't know how happy I am to see you."

"So has anything significant happened since I went away?"

"Not much, apart from discovering for whom the poison was really intended, having evidence planted on me by the secret police, oh, and finding out that I'm engaged to Prince Siegfried."

"What?" He started to laugh. "You are joking, aren't you?"

"Deadly serious about all three things."

"You didn't really agree to marry Sieg-fried. Promise me you didn't."

"No, I didn't actually, but he thinks I did. His father announced the engagement at dinner tonight, so I could hardly leap to my feet and make a scene in front of all those people, could I?"

Darcy was scowling now. "What on earth gave Siegfried the idea that you were going to marry him?"

"I suppose I gave him too much encour-agement last night."

"You encouraged him?"

"I had to find a way to keep him from go-ing up to visit Marshal Pirin," I said. "So I begged him to dance with me. Then he said something to me this evening, but Matty was talking at the same time and I didn't quite hear what he said so I smiled and nod-ded." I looked up at him hopelessly. "What am I going to do, Darcy? I have to get out of it without causing an international inci-dent."

"For now you'd better go along with it, I suppose," Darcy said. "Don't worry. We'll sort it all out somehow. At least you don't have to worry about Siegfried trying to slink into your bedroom at night. So what about the other matters? You say you've found out that the poison wasn't intended for Pirin?"

I nodded and told him about the glass. His face was grave. "So it was intended for Nicholas. Have you mentioned this to anyone else?"

"To Nicholas himself. I thought he had a right to know and to be extra vigilant. I don't know if he's told anyone else. He might have told Matty for all I know."

"That would have been a mistake. It may be all around the castle by now."

"At least the poisoner is warned that we know the truth. He'll hardly dare try it twice."

"But he may try something else instead. It's all too easy to dispose of a person in a place like this."

"I know," I said. "My maid has disappeared too. I'm so worried about her. I can't think where she's gone."

"And you said the secret police attempted to plant evidence on you?"

"What appeared to be the vial of cyanide showed up in my trunk."

"That idiot Patrascue, I suppose." Darcy scowled again.

"You know about him?"

"Oh, yes. We've met before."

"He was so angry that you'd managed to escape with the body. He was rather horrible, Darcy. He threatened me with prison."

"What on earth would have made him suspect you? I know he's not very bright, but —"

"I think he was just trying to frighten me into implicating Dragomir," I said.

"That makes sense. It sounds like his modus operandi."

"But I didn't allow him to intimidate me. I think he was rather miffed."

Darcy was staring into the firelight. "I wonder if he has anything to do with the disappearance of your maid, then. He's taken her as a bargaining chip, maybe?"

"How horrible. I shall be furious if he's done that. She's a simple girl, Darcy. She'll be scared out of her wits."

Darcy's arm tightened around my waist. "Don't worry, I'm back now. We'll sort everything out tomorrow."

I nestled my head back against his chest and closed my eyes. "I hope so," I said. "I just wish someone would find the murderer and make everything right again."

"So you're no nearer to finding out the truth?" Darcy asked.

"If the poison was intended for Nicholas, then I suppose it's possible that we're dealing with a trained assassin, or even an anarchist who climbed in, using that rope you found, planted the poison and climbed down again. The only thing against that theory is that there don't appear to be any tracks leading away from the castle."

"You're overlooking something else," Darcy said. "Someone in the castle must have let down the rope for him. That means that he had inside help. More than one person is involved."

"We know that only Dragomir and the servants were anywhere near the table," I said, "but there is a mysterious Mr. X we have to factor in. Remember I told you a strange man came into my room and bent over my bed, and I thought he was a vampire?"

Darcy nodded. "And I told you it was a case of the wrong room."

"Well, I've looked all over the castle and I haven't seen him anywhere again. Except that his portrait, or the portrait of someone very like him, was hanging on the wall when I first arrived and then someone changed it for the one you see now. Why would anyone do that?"

Darcy shook his head. "It doesn't make sense to me."

"If he wasn't a vampire, if he was a real person, then it is someone who knows the castle well. Perhaps the portrait was of one of his ancestors and he realized that it resembled him closely so he sneaked in and removed it." I sat up, suddenly realizing something. "Dragomir," I said. "He told me his family used to own this castle, and there is a portrait downstairs that looks just like him. What if this is another family member? Apparently they were driven from their castle by the Turks after a failed uprising. They expected their neighbors to help them, but nobody did. So what if this is a revenge killing?"

"Hardly," Darcy said. "That family was driven from the castle more than two hundred years ago. I know that vengeance is a strong force in this part of the world, but the current royal families of both Romania and Bulgaria only came to their thrones in the eighteen hundreds. They really have no ties to the Balkans. They were set in place by the European powers, and, as you know, Nicholas is from the Saxe-Coburg-Gotha line, like yourself. A Transylvanian dynasty could have no feud with them."

"Count Dragomir is bitter that he is now a glorified servant in a castle his ancestors used to own," I said.

"Then he'd want to strike at the Romanian royals, not a Bulgarian prince, wouldn't he?"

"Which brings us back to my mysterious Mr. X," I said. "Lady Middlesex's companion, Miss Deer-Harte —" I stopped as Darcy started laughing. "She can't help her name," I said. "Just stop it and listen. Miss Deer-Harte is a professional snooper. She claims she saw the same man creeping along one of the corridors at night and then she saw him lurking in an archway at dinner the first night. She says it was the archway immediately behind where Nicholas was sitting and she thinks he was casing the joint, as Lady Middlesex put it."

Darcy got up and walked over to the fire, taking off his wet coat and throwing it onto a chair. "Have you told anybody about this except me?" he asked.

"I didn't know who to tell," I said. "We've managed to keep it from the royals so far. Count Dragomir is the only one who could institute a thorough search of the place and he might well be involved."

"Don't tell anyone," Darcy said. He perched on the low chair by the fireplace and started to unlace his boots. "I may do some snooping of my own, but in the meantime don't let anyone know that I'm back. If you've no maid at the moment, all the better because I can hide out in here."

"You're not going to start snooping now,

are you?" I asked.

"I have just made my way through a snowstorm and climbed a long way up a rope and I'm whacked out," he said. "Move over. I'm coming to bed."

He snuggled in beside me, wrapping me into his arms. "Now that you're betrothed to the heir to a throne I could probably face the guillotine for this," he whispered and kissed me. I tried to respond to his kiss, but the tension of everything that had happened kept intruding.

"I'm sorry. It's no use," I said. "I'm so upset by everything that I can't stop thinking and worrying."

"Don't worry about this leading to anything, because it's not going to," he said. "I'm so tired that I could fall asleep on the spot. In fact . . ."

And I saw his eyelids flutter shut. He looked adorable with his eyes closed, almost like a child asleep, his eyelashes unfairly long for a man's. I leaned over and kissed his cheek.

"Damn Siegfried," I muttered, even though a lady never swears.

My own eyes were drifting shut, lulled by Darcy's rhythmic breathing, when a terrible clattering sound, accompanied by an unearthly scream, jerked me awake. It sounded as if somebody had thrown every pot and pan in the castle down a flight of stairs. I leaped out of bed.

"What was that?" I asked.

Darcy opened his eyes lazily.

"Probably a servant dropped a tray of dishes. Go back to sleep."

"No, it was worse than that," I said. I grabbed the nearest cardigan, reached for my slippers and went out into the dark hallway. It seemed that the sound was loud enough to have woken other people. Siegfried was standing there, looking like a ghost in his long nightshirt. Oh, God, imagine facing that specter every night.

"Georgiana, *mein Schatz,* did you hear that noise?"

"I did."

"Do not worry. I shall protect you," he said, moving forward cautiously.

From below came shouts. Siegfried and I made our way to the nearest staircase.

A group had already gathered at the bottom of the spiral stair. They were bending over what looked like a suit of armor.

"Who can have knocked one of our suits of armor down the stairs?" Siegfried demanded. "What is happening here?"

The servants stood reverently at the sound of their master's voice.

"Highness, I heard the noise and came running," one of them said. "It appears that —"

He never finished the sentence, as a loud moan came from within the armor. Someone wrenched the visor open and a very human pair of eyes looked up at us. And the occupant groaned again.

"What is the meaning of this?" Siegfried demanded. "What foolery were you playing?"

"I was ordered to keep watch," the man said, his face twisted in pain. "Chief Patrascue set me on guard duty. He told me to disguise myself in this way."

"Ridiculous man," Siegfried snapped. "He had no right. These suits of armor are precious state heirlooms, not to be worn like carnival costumes."

"My leg," the man groaned. "Get me out of this contraption."

Just as they were extracting him with care a figure in black came flying toward us.

"What has just transpired?" the newcomer asked. He peered down at the suit of armor. "Cilic, is that you?"

"Yes, my chief, it is I," the man said.

"What are you doing down there?" Patrascue asked. I told you he wasn't very bright.

"I missed my footing and I fell," the man

said, then groaned loudly again for maximum effect. "It is hard to see, wearing one of these visors."

"You had no right to instruct your man to wear our armor," Siegfried said. "What on earth were you thinking? Rather farcical, wouldn't you say?"

"I had my reasons," Patrascue said. "I placed my men invisibly on duty around the castle to protect your royal personages, but I didn't think this man would be foolish enough to attempt to move from his spot."

"I needed to find a bathroom," the man said, followed by an exceptionally loud groan as the armor was removed from his leg. "I didn't notice the top of the stairs."

"Get him to bed, and stop this nonsensical behavior at once," Siegfried said. "This is royal property and you have no authority here, Patrascue. Now go away and leave us in peace. You have upset my betrothed. Come, *mein Schatz.*" And he extended his arm to me.

He escorted me to my door. "I am so sorry your sleep was disturbed by this idiot," he said. "Is there anything I can have brought to your room to help you sleep better? Some hot milk, maybe? Some more coal for the fire?"

"Oh, no, thank you, Your Highness," I

stammered, conscious of Darcy presumably still lying in my bed. "I have everything I need."

"You need no longer address me as 'your highness,' *mein Schatz,*" Siegfried said. "Now it is to be Siegfried and Georgiana."

"Thank you, Siegfried," I muttered.

He clicked his heels, something that had little effect in bare feet. "That is good then. Let us hope there are no more disturbances tonight." And he took my hand and put his fish lips on it again.

CHAPTER 29

My bedroom and not alone
Still the middle of the night

I let myself into my room with a sigh of relief. Even in the darkness I could see the bed turned back and no sign of Darcy.

"Darcy?" I whispered. He must have heard Siegfried's voice outside the door and decided to hide, just in case. I tiptoed around, lifting up drapes, peeping under the bed. "It's all right, you can come out now," I said. Still he didn't appear. I glanced over at that chest. I certainly wasn't about to open that. But I did open the wardrobe and peer inside. It was big enough to hide several men.

"Are you in there?" I asked.

"Who are you talking to?" A voice right behind me made me spin around, heart thumping.

Darcy was standing there.

"I was looking for you," I said. "Don't do

that again. You're going to give me a heart attack."

"I heard the commotion and decided I better take a look for myself," he said. "As usual that fool Patrascue was making a balls-up of things. Go back to bed, you're freezing."

I got into bed and he followed. I put my head on his shoulder. It felt wonderfully comforting and safe. This is what I want and need, I remember thinking. If only . . . I suppose I must have fallen asleep because the sound of screams at first seemed to be part of my dream. Only gradually I came to the surface and realized that they were part of the real world. Darcy was already standing up.

"What now?" he demanded. "Can't a fellow get a decent night's sleep in this place?"

"I'll go," I said. "It's probably another of Patrascue's men frightening the maids by walking around in a suit of armor."

Darcy laughed. "Quite possibly. I'll stay put for now. I really don't want anyone to know I'm here."

Siegfried was standing at his door again. "I must apologize, *mein Schatz*. Two ridiculous disturbances in one night is unforgivable. I will demand that this man Patrascue take his underlings and leave our castle immediately." He strode down the hallway with me in tow. This time we went down the first flight of stairs and met nobody. Other guests in night attire were standing at their doors along the second hallway as the screaming continued, coming up from down below.

"Some hysterical maid," my mother said as I passed her. "Probably had to fight off the footman. Happens all the time."

We came under a low archway and found ourselves at the top of that final flight of steps above the entrance hall — those alarming steps that hugged the wall with no kind of banister. A group was already assembled at the bottom. One of them was indeed a maid, now sobbing instead of screaming while other servants attempted to comfort her. Beside her was a spilled scuttle of coal. The rest of the group was standing around something on the floor.

"What is it?" Siegfried called, his voice echoing through the high-ceilinged hall. "Why are we being subjected to this noise?"

The group broke apart. A couple of maids curtsied. Dragomir stepped forward. "Highness, there has been a tragedy," he said. "The English lady. She must have fallen from a great height. There is nothing to be done."

And there at the bottom of the steps lay the body of Miss Deer-Harte, her head at an unnatural angle. I had seen death before but the heightened tension of the past few days brought bile up into my throat. My head started to sing and for a second I thought I was going to faint. I leaned against the cold stone of the wall and inched my way down the stairs before I could pass out and join Miss Deer-Harte on the flagstones below.

"Someone should let Lady Middlesex know," I said, trying to master myself. "This lady was her companion."

"Poor woman," Siegfried said, eyeing the body with distaste. "I wonder what she was doing wandering around down here in the middle of the night?"

"Maybe the commotion from Patrascue's men upset her and she was coming down for a hot drink or a cognac," Dragomir said. "Or maybe she was sleepwalking. Who knows. It is unfortunate that such a thing should happen."

There was a certain smoothness to his voice that made me look at him sharply. I knew very well why Miss Deer-Harte had been wandering around. Had she actually spotted the man she was seeking this time, and been foolish enough to follow him? And was it possible that Dragomir was somehow involved? I wanted to get back to my room to tell Darcy what had happened, but perhaps my first duty should be to break the news to Lady Middlesex.

We heard her long before we saw her. "What is this nonsense now? Why am I being dragged out of bed at this godforsaken hour?" Her voice echoed down the hallway. She came out to the top of the steps. "What do I care if some other stupid foreigner has fallen and —" She broke off, her face rigid with horror.

"Deer-Harte?" she gasped. "No. No, it can't be." And she pushed her way down to the bottom of the stairs until she was standing over the body. "Oh." She put her hand up to her mouth and a great gulping sob came out. I went over to her and put a tentative hand on her shoulder. She wasn't the sort of person one would think of embracing. She continued to stare down at her friend, her body heaving with convulsive sobs. I was as shocked as everyone else. It wasn't the reaction I had expected of her over someone I thought she considered a rather annoying companion.

"I'm really sorry," I said. "It's a horrible thing to have happened."

She nodded, fighting to compose herself.

"Poor silly woman. Always imagining she saw danger and intrigue everywhere we went. She said she was going to keep her eyes and ears open."

"Yes, she must have been prowling around and fallen. Those stairs always struck me as awfully dangerous." I didn't say what I was thinking — that she hadn't fallen at all. She had been pushed.

"Come, my Lady Middlesex." Count Dragomir took over. "There is nothing you can do here. Let me escort you back to your room and have some cognac and hot milk sent up to you."

"It's all right. I'll take her," I said. "I know you have plenty to do down here."

I had to half drag Lady Middlesex back up those horrible stairs. She staggered up like a person in a trance. But by the time we reached her room she had regained her stiff upper lip.

"So good of you," she muttered. "Bit of a shock, isn't it? Don't know what I'll do without her, actually. Grown used to having her around."

I assisted her into her room and over to her bed.

"I don't think I'll be able to sleep again," she said. "I must make arrangements some-how to have her body taken home. She wouldn't want to be buried on foreign soil. She hated it abroad, poor thing. She only came with me out of extreme devotion. I should never have expected it of her . . . it was wrong of me." And she rooted around for a handkerchief, which she pressed to her face.

"Do you want me to stay with you?" I asked.

"No, I'd rather be alone, thank you," she said stiffly.

"Send one of the servants for me if you need me, then," I said.

She nodded. As I reached the door she said in a flat voice, "She sensed it, didn't she? The moment we arrived she called it a house of death. But she never realized it was her own death that she was sensing."

I closed the door behind me and hurried back through the halls to my room. Again Darcy was nowhere to be seen. I slipped into the bed, still warm with his presence, and lay there, thinking how comfortable and secure it had felt to lie in his arms. Then an image swam into my mind of Siegfried lying in bed beside me. No! I wanted to yell. I just wanted to be away from this horrible place and to feel safe again. Because something had struck me on the way back through the hallways. If Miss Deer-Harte

392

had been killed because she had spotted the murderer and could identify him, then I was also in similar danger.

I lay awake, staring at the dark canopy of the bed over me, trying to make sense of things.

Someone creeping into my room, bending over my bed. The portrait on the wall being changed. Matty with blood around her mouth. Pirin drinking from a glass intended for Nicholas. And now Miss Deer-Harte lying dead. What did they mean? What linked them together if I was trying to be rational and not believe that I was in a place inhabited by vampires? But I couldn't come up with a rational answer. In fact I didn't like the only answer that kept coming back to me — what if the young man we had seen was a vampire who haunted this castle and now Matty, Dragomir and God knows how many of the servants were under his spell. That would account for nobody else except for Miss Deer-Harte noticing him as he stood in the archway and watched the banquet. I knew this theory sounded ridiculous, but up in Scotland you'd meet plenty of people who swore that they had seen fairies, and we had a couple of ghosts at Castle Rannoch. So who was to say that vampires didn't exist?

Eventually I suppose I must have dozed, because when I opened my eyes slanted sunlight was shining on that hideous portrait on the far wall. I was lying alone in the enormous bed and there was still no sign of Darcy. I got up, washed and dressed, then went down to breakfast. The breakfast room was full of people, chatting amiably as they ate. Nobody seemed to know or care about last night's tragedy, but then to them she was only a companion who had lost her footing and fallen. Only Lady Middlesex was not present.

Nicholas smiled at me as I poured myself some coffee. "Lovely bright sunshine for a change. Good day for hunting, I think, if the snow is not too deep."

"My bridesmaids can't come, so don't try to entice them," Matty said. "It's our final dress fitting this morning."

"I wouldn't dream of luring young ladies away from their dress fitting," Nicholas said. "I want you all to look your beautiful and radiant best on the big day."

I happened to be looking at Matty's face. I saw the briefest flash of annoyance or panic before she smiled. "Of course we will all be radiant and beautiful, my dear Nicholas. We must look our best for the big day."

I continued to watch her as she took a

nibble of toast. Something he had said had made her upset or angry. And now I studied her, I thought she looked terrible — white and drawn, with bags under her eyes. Not at all the radiant bride-to-be. She was now playing with the rest of her slice of toast, crumbling it into tiny pieces, before she pushed the plate away from her, got up and left. I got the sense that she was under a good deal of strain. So why would that be? I found an interesting train of thoughts creeping into my head. My grandfather, the former policeman, had always quoted his superior officer, an inspector he greatly admired, as saying, "Go for the obvious and then work out from there. Nine times out of ten the answer is right under your nose."

So when it came to ease of putting poison into Nicholas's glass, then Matty and Dragomir would be the two people who could have done it most easily. Until now I had dismissed Matty as the bride. Why would she want to kill her future husband? But now, as I continued to observe her, I recalled that her gaiety had seemed forced at times. She had been playing the part of the happy bride-to-be and yet she had made remarks about Nicholas being a good choice, if one had to get married. She had talked about how she would rather have stayed on in Paris. What if she had decided to take the ultimate way out of this marriage by poisoning her bridegroom?

I decided that it was about time I tackled her and got the truth out of her. I'd find an opportunity this morning during our dress fitting. After all, I'd be perfectly safe in a room full of young women and Darcy was somewhere in the castle. But just in case there was some truth to this vampire stuff, shouldn't I be prepared? I stood looking at the spread of breakfast dishes. Some of those cold meats had plenty of garlic in them, judging by the smell of them. Did that count as a defense against vampires, or did one need the actual cloves? I could hardly go down to the kitchen and ask for cloves of garlic, so I loaded up my plate with various slices of sausage. It wasn't exactly my choice of breakfast but I got through them. Afterward even I could smell the garlic on my breath — I only hoped any potential vampires could too. Now, if I could just find a small cross somewhere in the castle and slip it into my pocket . . .

As I got up to leave Nicholas was standing at the doorway, speaking with his father. His face was grim. There was a brief exchange and his father strode off down the hallway. Nicholas saw me and gave a grimace.

"The old man is making a fuss about Pirin," he said. "He wanted to know when the telephone wires will be repaired. He needs to know how Pirin is doing, whether he has reached the hospital safely and whether his physician is on his way from Sofia. He was demanding that a car be sent to find out. I kept telling him that it had snowed again and the pass would be closed, but he's not taking no for an answer. This could prove extremely tricky. I wonder where Darcy is."

I was tempted to tell him that Darcy was in the castle, but decided to leave that decision up to Darcy himself when he reappeared. I couldn't think what he might be doing, but I was sure it was important.

"Your bride is beginning to show the strain of the unfortunate events," I said.

"Yes, she's very sensitive," Nicholas said. "Another death last night. I wish to God I hadn't given in to Maria and agreed to hold the ceremony at this castle. It would have been so much more agreeable at the palace."

As I left him, I spotted Count Dragomir, hurrying ahead of me. I called his name and he turned, reluctantly.

"I was wondering if you had any news about my maid yet," I said. "I am extremely worried."

"I am sorry, Highness. I have had no news," he said. "But don't worry, my people will keep searching for her."

"She can't have disappeared," I said. "I want an out-and-out effort today to look for her, or I'll have to ask Mr. Patrascue to put his men on the job."

It was a good threat. I saw a look of alarm in his eyes. "Mr. Patrascue could not find his own nose if it were not attached to his body," he said. "I have promised we will find her and we will."

Then he hurried off, his cape flying out behind him. I wandered down the hallways, looking for a suitable cross, but could only come up with a six-foot-tall crucifix in a niche. I could hardly carry that around with me. I also spotted a cross around the neck of one of the servants, but she spoke no English and I couldn't make her understand that I only wanted to borrow it. So in the end I had no choice but to make my way to the small salon and our dress fitting. A small voice in my head whispered that I was being silly to be afraid of a school friend, but I didn't know what to believe anymore.

Some of the other bridal attendants were already in the small salon, talking together in German in a tight little group. They glanced up guiltily as I entered and I was sure they had been talking about me. Sure enough Hannelore called out to me, "We were talking of your betrothal to Prince Siegfried. We are not very happy for you. We feel perhaps you may not know the truth about him. You should find out about this Siegfried before you agree to marry him."

"Thank you," I said. "I will take your advice."

She drew me closer to her. "We hear that his interest is not in women, you understand? He will not make you satisfied in the bed."

What should I say, that I had no intention of marrying him? Her concern was genuine and touching. "Thank you," I said. "I won't rush into anything, I promise."

"And if you think it is nice to be a princess," Hannelore continued, "it is not so much fun. Always duty, duty, duty."

The other girls who understood English nodded agreement. At that moment Matty came into the room.

"So are we ready to look divine?" she asked brightly. She had made up her face with bright circles on her cheeks and red lips. The fittings started. Our dresses were almost finished and it was only a case of a final nip and tuck to make sure they hung perfectly. To go over each dress was a floor-length white fur-lined cloak — one of the most heavenly things I had ever seen. When we tried them on we looked like snow queens. My own fitting was finished but I hung around by the fire, waiting for a moment to catch Matty alone. She was certainly acting in a bright and animated way, laughing and giggling with the other girls, making me wonder if perhaps it might be drugs and not being a vampire that accounted for her mood swings.

At last she came over to the fire and held out her hands to warm them.

"It's freezing in this place, isn't it?" she said. "Reminds me of school. Remember how cold it used to be in the dormitories?"

"That was usually because Belinda had left the window open to climb out at night and visit her ski instructor," I said, smiling at the memory. I came to stand beside her and decided to take the plunge. "Matty, you and I need to talk."

She reeled a little from the amount of garlic on my breath, but she didn't collapse, run off or melt away as any good vampire should have done in the presence of garlic. "What about? Something is wrong?" The smile faded from her face.

I looked around the salon. Everyone

400

seemed to be occupied. "I know," I said in a low voice. "I know the truth."

She looked startled, then she shrugged. "Of course you do. He was silly enough to come into your room by mistake, and I was foolish enough to forget about his picture on your wall. He painted that picture for me, you know. He's a brilliant artist. He always had talent, even as a small boy."

As she talked she slipped her arm through mine and steered me away from the other girls and the clatter of sewing machines. At first I hadn't a clue what she was talking about, but gradually light began to dawn. She'd dropped enough hints that she didn't love Nicholas, that she'd wanted to stay in Paris. So she'd fallen in love with another man. But the phrase about the small boy was baffling.

"You knew him when he was a boy?"

"Of course," she said. "He grew up in this castle."

"In this castle?"

She nodded. "His father works for us. We played together when I came here in the summers. We were always such good friends as children. And then I was sent to Paris and I found he was there too, studying art. This time we fell in love — wonderful, passionate love. Then my father informed me

401

that I must marry Nicholas. I begged him to change his mind, but he wouldn't listen. A princess always puts duty first, he said. I told him I loved someone else but he forbade me to see him again." She reached out and covered my hand with her cold one. "In the end one does one's duty. Just like you and Siegfried. I'm sure you don't love him. You can't love him. But you do what the family expects of you."

I nodded. "It must be really hard for you. I'm not sure I can actually marry a man I don't love."

"Vlad wanted me to run away with him," she whispered, glancing up to make sure that the other occupants of the salon were still far away and engaged in activity. "We'd live together in Paris and be happy. But I'd been brought up with duty rammed down my throat. I couldn't do it."

"So you asked to have the wedding here because of your happy memories?"

"Vlad suggested it so that we could be together one last time," she said. "He promised he'd find a way to come and see me. He knows this castle so well. You saw him climbing up the wall, didn't you? He always was one for taking horrible risks, but how else could he get in to see me without being seen himself?"

"You left a rope for him hanging down?"

"No, I had no idea he was going to try to scale the wall. We attached the rope afterward, from my maid's room, in case he had to make a hasty retreat."

"And I am sleeping in your old bedroom," I said, understanding now. "He was expecting to find you there. No wonder he looked so surprised."

"Yes, my parents announced at the last minute that I must sleep as far as possible from my future bridegroom and close to my chaperon, Countess Von Durnstein, until the wedding. My father is very much into old-fashioned protocol, you know."

"Is Vlad still here?" I asked.

"Oh, yes. There are fortunately several secret rooms in the castle. He's been hiding out and my maid, Estelle, is so wonderfully loyal. She brings him food. And speaking of food — you also saw my other guilty secret, did you not?"

"When was that?"

"In the hallway outside the kitchen," she whispered, glancing around again. "I couldn't resist, you know."

"What exactly were you doing?" I asked cautiously, not really wanting the answer.

She leaned closer. "Cook's cherry tarts. All that wonderful gooey cherry jam. I went down to the kitchen and she'd been baking them. I stole a couple. I've had to be on this strict diet, you see, so that I fit into the wedding dress, but I've always had trouble with my weight. I like to eat. That was another thing — Vlad didn't care when I had meat on my bones. He loved me just as I was." She chewed on her lip. "Now I'm afraid that Nicolas will not like me if I put back the weight and he sees me as I was when I was eating normally."

I looked at her with compassion. I could understand how awful it must be to give up one's true love and marry someone one doesn't love at all. And to condemn oneself to not eating. But I couldn't forget the big question that still remained unanswered. "Matty, about Pirin's death. Do you know who put the poison in that glass?"

"It had to be an outsider, an assassin," she said. "Who else could it be?"

"You don't think that your Vlad might have . . ."

"Killed a foreign field marshal? Why would he do that?" she demanded angrily.

"Matty, there's something you should know," I said, realizing I was taking a risk. "The glass of wine was intended for Nicholas."

"What?"

"Pirin was a peasant," I said. "He had never learned decent table manners. And he was very drunk. He grabbed the nearest full glass of wine when he made that toast and he grabbed it with his left hand. I was sitting opposite him. I saw. It was Nicholas's wineglass, only Nicholas had switched to drinking champagne when the toasts started, remember?"

"No," she said so loudly that the other women in the room looked over at us. Then she shook her head violently and lowered her voice again. "No, that's ridiculous. Unthinkable. Vlad would never. He's sweet. He's kind. You should see how he treated me in Paris. Like a princess should be treated." She took my hand. "I can trust you as my dear old friend. Come and meet him for yourself, come and ask him yourself, then you'll see. I've told him about you, and soon you are to be my dear sister."

"All right," I said.

She led me out of the salon, then opened a door in the paneled wall that led to a narrow side staircase. "My little shortcut to the secret room," she said. "This castle is full of them. We used to have such fun playing hide-and-seek when we were children. Except for Siegfried. He was stuffy even then. Watch your step, they are very narrow and it's dark in here."

She started up the steps ahead of me. I went to follow. One second I was standing on the stone floor; the next, the slab I was standing on tilted downward and I was plunging into darkness.

CHAPTER 30

In a dungeon. Not very nice.
Saturday, November 19

I was half sliding, half tumbling down a rough stone chute, unable to stop or slow my fall, waiting for the inevitable moment when I would crash onto a hard surface below. The ridiculous image of Alice in Wonderland, falling down the rabbit hole, flashed through my mind as I struck another stone panel that swung open. Then I tumbled into nothingness, had an odd sensation of arms reaching out to me, then landing on something softer than I'd expected, before I hit the stone floor and everything went black.

I came back to consciousness to some kind of awful noise — an unearthly wailing sound. I opened my eyes. I was lying on a cold stone floor in almost total darkness. A round white thing was hovering over me — a pale moon face, staring at me with its mouth open in some kind of horrible chant. Then I made out words in the wail.

"Oh, lawks, oh, blimey, oh, miss."

"Queenie?" I murmured. I tried to sit up and the world swung around alarmingly while a pain shot through my head.

"Sorry, miss. I tried to catch you but you was coming too fast. At least I broke your fall a little."

"That was you I landed on?" I asked.

"That's right."

"Goodness. That was brave of you. Did I hurt you?"

"Not too bad. I'm well padded. But you come flying down at such a rate —"

"Well, you would too if the floor suddenly opened up beneath you," I said.

"I know. I did. Luckily I landed on me bum — pardon the expression, miss — and like I said, I'm well padded. But it weren't no worse than when my old dad used to take his belt to me when I was a kid." She helped me into a sitting position. "I ain't half glad I am to see you. You're a proper toff to come and rescue me. I knew you would, of course."

"I hate to disillusion you, Queenie," I said, "but I'm now a captive with you, not your rescuer."

"Where are we, miss? This ain't half a

408

creepy old place."

I looked around. We were in a circular chamber. A glimmer of gray light came in through a small grille near the bottom of one wall. Apart from that, every surface was stone. There was no door of any kind.

"I rather fear we're in the oubliette we were joking about earlier."

"The oobly-what?"

"It's a place where you put unwanted guests," I said. "I've heard of them in old castles but I've never actually seen one before. You step on the wrong slab, it opens and you fall into a dungeon where nobody will ever find you again."

"Ooh, don't say that, miss." She grabbed at my sleeve. "Someone's going to find us, aren't they?"

"I hope so," I said. But even as the words came out I wondered who actually knew of the presence of this place. Matty had obviously been told about it because Vlad had grown up here and knew every nook and cranny. But did others know? Servants? Dragomir? I had a horrible vision of everyone hunting for me throughout the castle and not finding me, while Queenie and I starved to death. Not the ending I would have chosen; in fact, I think I'd actually have preferred to marry Prince Siegfried if I'd had an option — which shows you how desperate I was feeling. "Don't worry," I said. "We're going to get out somehow, I promise. How did you come to be in here, by the way?"

"I don't rightly know," she said. "I saw a man taking what looked as if it would be a shortcut to the kitchen. He opened a door in the paneling and he went through, and I saw he was going down a staircase so I thought I'd follow him. Next thing I knew, I was falling down a shaft and I landed up in here."

"This man — what did he look like?"

"I can't really tell you. He was dressed in black. One of the servants, I thought."

"Did he have light blond hair?"

"Now that you mention it, he did."

"Then he thought you were following him for a reason. That's why you landed up here."

"Who is he, miss? A criminal?"

"He's the young man you saw in your room that night, and he may well be a murderer," I said. "When we get out of this place, we'll have to go carefully."

"How are we going to get out?" she asked. "There's not even a door."

"Well, we got in," I said, trying to sound more cheerful than I felt. "So we can try getting out the same way. If you're strong enough to hold me on your shoulders, I can reach the ceiling. Perhaps I can push one of those slabs open."

She crouched down and let me climb onto her back, then we inched our way around until I was directly under the high point of the arched ceiling. I found the slab that had opened to admit me all right but it was positioned so exactly that there wasn't enough room to get a grip on it. I broke my fingernails trying to drag it down, but it was no use.

"That's not going to work," I said. "You'd better let me down."

I clambered off her back and we sat panting while I examined the room.

"There's that little grille in the wall down there," I said. "I'm quite skinny, maybe I would fit through it."

"Don't try it, miss. It's bound to be dangerous," she said.

"We're not just going to sit here and hope that someone finds us," I said. "I've already had people searching for you all over the castle. If they couldn't find you I don't think there is much hope that we'll be discovered." I lay on the floor and peered out. It wasn't encouraging. All I could see was another stone wall, about ten feet away. I tugged at the grille, I pushed it, but it wouldn't budge. Truthfully I didn't think it was likely to, having been in place for several hundred years, but I had to try.

"Help me pull this thing, Queenie," I said.

We pulled together but it was hard to get our fingers through the small holes of the grille. We turned around and tried kicking it. No use.

"We need some leverage," I said. "My petticoat is silk. Are you wearing a cotton one?"

"A cotton petticoat? Yes, miss."

"Then take it off."

She obeyed, eyeing me strangely as I attempted to tear it into strips. Eventually, using teeth and nails, Queenie's hairpins and my brooch, we did manage to rip it and ended up with a couple of long strips. We tied these to the grille.

"When I say pull, you brace your feet against the wall and pull with all your might," I said.

We pulled. Suddenly there was a cracking, crumbling sound as the grille came flying out. We looked at each other and nodded with satisfaction.

"But I don't see how you're going to get out of there, miss," Queenie said. "You'll get stuck, likely as not."

I had to say that I agreed with her. The

opening couldn't have been much more than about fifteen inches high and two feet wide.

"Luckily I'm skinny and I have been told by milliners that I have a small head," I said.

"I'd go out for you if I could, miss," Queenie said, "but I don't think my big toe would fit through there, to say nothing of the rest of me."

I looked at her and smiled with real fondness. She might be the worst servant in the world, but she was trapped in a hopeless situation and she wasn't making a fuss.

"Well, here goes," I said and stuck my head out of the hole. What I saw wasn't encouraging. I was near the bottom of a long shaft of some sort. It might be a well, because there was ice below me, and there was another grille over the top, far above me. I couldn't even see any other openings in the side.

"Maybe if we shouted, someone would hear us," I said. "Try shouting 'help' with me, Queenie."

We shouted. I tried it in French. Nothing happened.

"There seem to be the remains of iron rungs on the far side," I said. "If the ice holds me, I could lower myself down and get across."

413

"What if it don't hold you, miss?"

"The worst that can happen is that I'll get really wet and cold," I said. "It's worth a try. I'm going out backward."

I lay on the floor and stuck my feet through the hole, then I inched myself backward until my feet were hanging down, then until I was bent at the waist and then until I was braced at my shoulders.

"Hold my hands and don't let go until I tell you," I said. Queenie took my hands in hers. I squeezed my shoulders together, then tilted my head to one side to take it through the hole. The ice was still about two feet below me.

"You can let go of my hands, Queenie," I said. "I'm going to try to climb down."

I hadn't bargained for the slippery rocks. I slithered down and landed hard on the ice, which groaned ominously. I immediately dropped to my knees then crawled forward. It bobbed as I moved but I reached the other wall. Then I found one of the old rungs and started to climb. They were broken and slippery and it was horrible going. One of them came out of the wall when I went to haul myself up on it and it landed on the ice with an echoing thunk.

"You can do this," I said to myself. "You've climbed mountains at home. It's no worse."

414

After what seemed an eternity I reached the top.

"I'm at the top, Queenie," I called back down. "I'm going to try to push up the grille."

As soon as I looked at it, I realized that this was going to be an impossible task. The grille was in the middle, a long stretch from where I was. I could just about reach the edge of it, but I couldn't push it with any strength at all, stretched out like that. I fought back tears of frustration. I cleared as much snow as I could from the grille and tried to look out. All I could see were blank stone walls. Not a friendly door or window in sight. Surely someone would come this way eventually. The question was how long I could hold on before my frozen hands stopped obeying me.

"Help!" I called again. *"Au secours!"* Drat. I wished I knew the word for help in German, as this area used to be part of the Hapsburg Empire and many of the peasants spoke that language.

Suddenly I heard heavy breathing above me and a face peered down at me. I looked up hopefully, only to find it was a long snout covered in gray fur. It was hard to tell, from this angle, whether it was a dog or a wolf.

"Good dog, good boy," I said.

The lip lifted in a snarl.

"That's right," I said, suddenly realizing, "go ahead and bark. Woof woof."

I flicked snow at it, making it step back. I even stuck my fingers through recklessly and waggled them. It cocked its head suspiciously but it didn't bark. Then in desperation I started to sing. I'm not the world's best singer and my singing once made the dogs at home start to howl. "Speed, bonny boat, like a bird on the wing," I sang. "The Skye Boat Song," one of my favorites.

"Are you all right, miss?" Queenie shouted.

"Just singing," I called back down. "Join in."

"I don't know it."

"Then sing something you know."

"At the same time as you?"

"It doesn't matter."

We sang. She, I believe, was singing "If you were the only girl in the world" while I continued with "The Skye Boat Song." It sounded terrible. At last the dog put his head back and howled. The song echoed up from the well and the howl echoed from those walls.

Then I heard a human voice, cursing the dog.

"Help!" I called. "Get me out."

A face appeared on the limits of my vision. The woman gasped, crossed herself and went to back away.

"Get help!" I shouted after her in English and French. "English princess."

She went. The dog went. I hung there, fighting back disappointment. She thought I was some kind of evil spirit or something. She had run away. They'd probably avoid this place for years after this. Then I heard the most blessed of sounds: several raised voices. And men stood over me, one of them carrying an ancient shotgun, the others with sticks, their faces taut with fear.

"Help me, please," I said. "Fetch Count Dragomir. I English princess." This was a slight exaggeration but I knew the word was the same in all the languages.

They were talking furiously among themselves, then suddenly one of them came back with a crowbar, the grille was pried open and hands pulled me free. At that moment Count Dragomir came striding into the courtyard. His face registered horror and shock as he recognized me.

"*Mon Dieu.* Lady Georgiana. What has happened to you?"

"I was tipped into your famous oubliette," I said. "My servant is still down there."

"But the oubliette, it was just a legend,"

he said. "Nobody ever discovered it."

"It exists, trust me. My servant is in it and the opening is too small to get her out. Send down some hot tea or soup or something to her and then we'll try to find the opening in the castle."

Dragomir was already barking commands. "We'll soon get you out, Queenie," I shouted. "Help is on the way. Don't worry."

The sound echoed so strangely down the shaft that I wasn't quite sure she understood me. "My dear Lady Georgiana, come inside and let us warm you up," Dragomir said, opening a door into some kind of outbuilding. "Some hot coffee and blankets."

"We have to get my maid out first," I said. "Take me back to the castle immediately, please."

"Very well. As you wish." Dragomir escorted me across a couple of courtyards, through a door in a wall and up some steps and we were back in the castle proper.

"How did you happen to fall into this oubliette, Highness?" he asked.

"I was following Princess Maria Theresa," I said. "She went ahead of me and . . ." I couldn't bring myself to say to him that she had taken me that way deliberately so that I would step on the wrong slab and fall. I was now quite sure that she and Vlad had planned the murder of Prince Nicholas together. I didn't know which of them administered the poison, but one of them did. The problem was that we were all assembled for her wedding — two royal families, plenty of important personages and plenty of opportunities for a diplomatic incident. If only I could locate Darcy, he'd know what to do. But my first task was to rescue Queenie.

"I'll show you the oubliette," I said and led Dragomir through the halls until we reached the right spot. I was just searching for the door in the paneled wall when I heard the sound of feet behind me. I turned to see two of Patrascue's men bearing down on me.

"Please to come with us," one said in atrocious French. He grabbed my arm.

"Wait," I said trying to shake myself free. "Where are you taking me? We must save my friend first."

But another man grabbed my other arm and I was swept along the corridor at a great pace.

"Wait a minute. Slow down and listen to me," I shouted but to no avail. The third man went ahead and flung open a door. I was borne inside and came upon a tableau. The king of Romania and Siegfried were sitting in high-backed chairs on one side of the fireplace. The king of Bulgaria, Nicholas and Anton sat on the other. In front of them stood Darcy, his arms being held by two policemen. And beside him stood Patrascue.

CHAPTER 31

Bran Castle
Saturday, November 19

As I was thrust into the room, the tableau moved and they all turned to stare at me in horror.

"What is the meaning of this?" the king demanded, rising to his feet. "My dear, what has happened to you?"

"She was obviously attempting to flee and she was caught by my men," Patrascue said before I could answer. "Now we have apprehended both the suspects. The case is complete. You can proceed with your wedding with confidence and serenity."

"What are you talking about?" I demanded.

Darcy gave me a long look that warned me not to say too much. "This idiot has told Their Majesties that Pirin was poisoned, and what's more, he has got it into his head that you and I were paid to come and carry out the murder."

"It is too obvious for someone of my experience and talent," Patrascue said. "Mr. O'Mara thought he would cleverly pretend to drive away with the body before I had a chance to examine it. I expect he has tried to hide the evidence. And Lady Georgiana denies that she hid the vial of poison in the trunk in her room. But they cannot fool Patrascue. I ask myself, why are they really here? Why should she come to this wedding instead of a member of the British royal family?"

"I am a member," I said. "The king is my cousin."

"But why send a mere cousin to represent the English people, when the king could send one of his own children?"

"Because I asked my daughter to invite her," the king said in a voice taut with annoyance. "My son let it be known that he had selected her as his future bride and we wanted her to have a chance to know us better. So you will please treat her with the same respect you accord to us. Is that clear?"

Patrascue gave the merest hint of a bow. "Of course, Majesty. But if she is involved in the cold-blooded murder of an important man, surely your son would wish to know the truth about this before he entered into marriage with such a woman."

"Of course I'm not involved," I said.

Siegfried came over to me. "Georgiana, did these men hurt you? You look terrible. You are bleeding."

"Not these men," I said. "I fell into a dungeon. Count Dragomir did not believe me but there really is an oubliette in this castle. My maid is still down there."

"An oubliette in this castle? Surely it is just a legend."

"I assure you it's very real," I said.

"How did you come to stumble upon this oubliette?" the king asked.

I hesitated. I was in a foreign country about to implicate its princess. What if nobody believed me? It would be easy enough for the king to agree with Patrascue that Darcy and I were the guilty ones. But if I were her father, I'd want to know the truth, wouldn't I? Maybe I could make her confess somehow.

"Would you ask your daughter to join us, Your Majesty?" I said. "I believe she can help prove my innocence."

"Of course. Please tell the princess her presence is required in my private sitting room." One of Patrascue's men bowed and departed.

"Perhaps you are innocent, Lady Georgiana," Patrascue said. "Perhaps it is this Mr. O'Mara who hid the poison in your room to implicate you while he fled with the body. We have heard rumors about Mr. O'Mara. He is a ruthless man and very interested in making money, is this not correct? A certain scandal at a casino?"

Darcy actually laughed. "The scandal was that I was chucked out because I kept winning. They thought I was cheating. Actually I was just damned lucky. The luck of the Irish, don't you know? But let me assure you that I'm the son of a respected Irish lord. Killing people for money is not something I'd do. Killing people because they annoy me, on the other hand . . ." He stared hard at Patrascue. If the matter hadn't been so serious I would have laughed. Darcy didn't seem to be particularly worried.

"Then why are you here, Mr. O'Mara? I understand from interviewing the other young men that you are not a particular friend of Prince Nicholas."

"We were good friends at school," Nicholas said angrily. "The rest doesn't concern you."

Suddenly it struck me that Nicholas might have anticipated some kind of trouble at this wedding and Darcy had been invited to protect him.

"But understand that he is here at my invitation and I have absolute confidence that he has nothing to do with the death of Field Marshal Pirin. The whole suggestion is ludicrous. You should be looking for —"

He broke off as Matty came in, looking puzzled and concerned. When she saw me, a relieved smile crossed her face.

"There you are, Georgie," she said. "I wondered where you had disappeared to. We were all looking for you."

I smiled back. "Oh, I think you know very well where I went to, since you sent me there."

"What do you mean? One minute you were following me up the stairs, but when I reached the top, I turned around and you weren't there."

"Maybe that was because I was in the process of falling down the oubliette," I said.

She gave a tight, nervous laugh. "Oubliette? There's no such thing. Believe me, we hunted for it when we were children, didn't we, Siegfried?"

"Then allow me to show you," I said. "My maid is still trapped in the dungeon below and it's about time someone rescued her."

I marched them back through the halls until I recognized the place where the door had to be.

"Would you please show us the door in the paneling, Your Highness?" I asked Matty.

She shrugged, stepped forward and pushed open a section of the wall.

"You'll see a staircase leads up from here," I said, "and one of these flagstones tips an unsuspecting victim down into a dungeon. I'm not sure which."

"But I go up and down this way all the time," Matty said. "It is a shortcut from my room to the main floor."

"Then, Your Highness, would you like to try them out for us?" I asked.

"Of course." She walked confidently to the staircase and ascended the first couple of steps.

"You see?" She turned and smiled. "There is nothing here but an ordinary passageway."

"There must be a knob or a lever or something that triggers the mechanism," I said. "Look on the walls. Princess Maria was ahead of me, and —"

Matty looked up sharply. "One minute. You don't think that I sent you into this dungeon? That I brought you here to trick you?"

"I'm afraid that's exactly what I think," I said. "I'm sorry, Matty, but you didn't really want to introduce me to Vlad, did you? You

426

wanted him to stay hidden."

"What?" Matty's father roared. "Vladimir? That boy is here, in the castle? When I forbade you to see him again?"

"No, Father. Of course not," Matty said. "Here's not here. I don't know what Georgiana is talking about."

"Come down here, young woman," the king commanded. "Come out into the light where I can see your face. I always know if you are lying to me."

"Father, please, not in front of these people." Matty came back down the stairs. Patrascue's men, who had crammed themselves into the narrow hallway, stepped aside for her. There was a lot of jostling and moving and as she stepped down from the bottom step the floor suddenly tilted beneath her. Matty screamed as she started to fall. Hands reached out to grab her and she was dragged back to safety. We stood staring at the black cavity below us.

"Now do you believe me?" I asked. "Queenie?" I shouted. "Can you hear me?"

"Is that you, miss?" a voice echoed up, sounding distant and hollow. "I'm still here."

"We'll have you out in a jiffy," I shouted back.

"Your Majesty, what is happening?" Count

427

Dragomir appeared behind us. "Is there really an oubliette? After all these years! I thought it was just a legend."

"My maid is still down there," I said.

"I apologize, Lady Georgiana. We will have her brought out instantly."

The king turned to him. "And I ask you, Dragomir — did you know that Vlad was in the castle?"

"I did not, Majesty," Dragomir said angrily. "I made it clear to him that he should stay away."

"I want the castle searched in case he is hiding out," the king said. "You will set every available man to this task, is that clear?"

"Yes, Majesty," Dragomir said in a flat voice, "but Vlad gave me his word and —"

"He's not here, Father," Matty shouted.

"Every available man!" the king thundered. "And as for you, madam" — he turned to glare at his daughter — "I want to know the truth from you. Return to my study this instant. We can't have matters like this shouted up and down the halls for everyone to hear."

He marched his daughter back to the study. The rest of us followed. When the door was shut behind us the king spoke coldly.

"The truth, Maria. Is that boy in the castle? Have you dared to see him again?"

"No, Father," Matty said. "Georgiana misunderstood."

"I saw him," I said. "I'm sorry, Matty, if it weren't a question of murder I wouldn't have betrayed your secret, but it is. And your bridegroom has a right to know that you tried to kill him."

"What?" Matty shrieked. "No, that's quite wrong. I told you Vlad is sweet. He'd never kill anyone."

"And what about you?" I said. "You dropped enough hints that you didn't want to marry Nicholas, that you were being forced into it when you loved someone else."

"You think that I put poison in Nicholas's glass?"

"One moment, if you please." Patrascue stepped between us. "I do not understand. It was a Bulgarian field marshal who was poisoned. This I was told. Is it not true?"

"The poison was intended for me," Nicholas said. He was staring at Matty with horror and disbelief on his face. "Pirin was a peasant. He had no table manners. He grabbed the nearest full glass and it was mine." He shook his head. "I can't believe this of you, Maria. If the idea of marrying me was so abhorrent to you, why didn't you

429

tell me? I would never have expected you to subject yourself to a life of unhappiness."

"No, Nicholas." She went over to him and put her hand gently on his arm. "You are not abhorrent to me. You are a kind, decent person and I should not object to spending my life with you. I just happened to fall in love with someone else. Someone beneath me whom I could not marry. But I swear that I didn't try to kill you. Neither did Vlad."

"Then you admit he was here?" Patrascue threw himself into the fray. It was almost like watching a play.

"All right. I admit it. But he just came to say good-bye to me, that's all."

"Where is he now?" Patrascue asked.

"Gone. Long gone."

"How could he leave the castle when we are snowed in?"

"He had skis with him," Matty said. "He left before that man was poisoned."

I didn't believe her for a minute and neither did Patrascue.

"You say that you saw him, Lady Georgiana?" he asked, spinning sharply to address me. "When was this?"

"On my first night here he came into my room by mistake. He thought that it was Princess Maria's room. And someone else spotted him, observing the banquet — Miss Deer-Harte, the English lady who is now also dead, whom we can conclude was pushed from a staircase as she was snooping at night."

"So, it is a question of two murders, not just one?" Patrascue asked.

"The English lady could have fallen," Siegfried pointed out.

"She would not have been going down those stairs if she had not been following somebody," I said. "She was determined to catch the man she had seen."

"I can prove to you that Vlad had nothing to do with this second death," Matty said. "All right, he is not long gone. He was with me all night. He didn't leave my side once." And she tossed her head defiantly.

"Maria!" The king opened his mouth in horror. "You do not announce this shameful conduct to the world. Do you think your bridegroom would want you now that you have told the world you are no longer a virgin?"

Matty looked across at Nicholas. "I'm sorry, Nicholas. I never wanted to embarrass you or put you in this awkward position, but I can't let the man I love be accused of a crime I know he didn't commit."

Nicholas nodded. "I applaud your bravery,

Maria," he said.

"Then how do we know that the man this English lady saw was not Mr. O'Mara?" Patrascue asked. "I am still not satisfied that we have not all been barking up the wrong tree, since Lady Georgiana made these accusations against the princess. I think she was trying to throw us off the scent."

"As to that, I'm afraid I have the same alibi as Princess Maria," Darcy said. "At the time the poor woman was being pushed down the stairs, I was in bed with Lady Georgiana."

Of course I turned scarlet as I felt all those eyes on me.

"Then this is true?" Siegfried asked me. "You do not deny it?"

"I'm afraid it is true," I said. "Darcy was with me when we heard the screams from down below."

"But if these people have an alibi for the second murder, what then?" Patrascue said. "I would like to discount one of these alibis but I see from the guilty looks on the faces of these young highnesses that their stories are true. Is the murderer someone quite different? Someone we haven't considered until now?"

Someone behind me cleared his throat and Dragomir stepped forward. I hadn't noticed him in the room until that moment. His cloak swirled rather impressively around him. "Your Majesty, this has gone on long enough. I do not wish to put your daughter through any more pain. I should like to plead guilty to the murders."

The king stepped toward him. "You, old friend? You tried to kill Prince Nicholas? But why? Why would you do this?"

"I have my reasons," Dragomir replied. "Let us just say that this is my ancestral home and I am avenging the ghosts of my ancestors for the wrongs done to them."

The door behind us was thrown open, letting in a great gust of cold wind. "Don't be ridiculous, Father," said a voice and the elusive Vlad stepped into the room. By daylight he was even more handsome than his portrait, but there was something wild about his eyes and in his right hand he held a gun.

"Father? He called you Father?" the king stammered.

"That's right," Dragomir said. "He is my son. I couldn't marry his mother because of her lowly rank but I have done my duty by him. I paid for his schooling and sent him off to study in Paris. And I love him as any father loves his only child."

"And now he's trying to show his nobility

433

and take the blame for something he didn't do," Vlad said. "I attempted to poison Prince Nicholas. I put a gelatin capsule containing cyanide into his red wine at the start of the meal. I planned to be well away by the time it acted. I was not about to let him have the woman I love. I am just angry that I failed. I shall not fail a second time."

"Vlad!" Matty ran toward him. "How could you? I trusted you. I loved you. I never thought for an instant . . ."

"For you, Maria," Vlad said. "I did it for you. I didn't want you to be condemned to marrying someone you didn't love, when you loved me."

"We went through that before," Matty said. "I told you that my duty to my family came first and always will come first. Now put that gun down. You're not going to shoot anyone."

"Stand aside, Maria." Vlad prodded her with the barrel of the pistol.

"You'll have to shoot me first," she said, eyeing him calmly and defiantly.

"Of course I don't want to shoot you." His voice had risen dangerously.

"I'm not going to let you shoot Nicholas," Matty said, "or anybody else."

"Why do you always have to be so bloody noble?" Vlad demanded.

"Because I was born to it," Matty said.

"Damn you," Vlad shouted. "Damn all of you to hell."

Without warning he grabbed Matty around the throat and pulled her in front of him. "She's coming with me," he said. "Did you think I was going to give you up that easily?"

"You're mad. Let go of me," she gasped as the arm tightened around her throat.

Nicholas took a step toward them.

"Stay back," Vlad warned. "I won't hesitate to shoot her, you know. I have nothing to lose now. In fact, why not? Shoot her and then myself. At least we'll be together in death."

He was dragging her back to the door, which had now swung shut again. He was reaching behind him with the hand that held the gun when suddenly the door came flying open, catching him in the side of the head and knocking him off balance. As he staggered, Nicholas and Anton fell on him and overpowered him, while Patrascue dragged Matty clear. Vlad cried out in pain as he was pinned to the floor and Nicholas wrenched his arms up behind him.

In the doorway stood a grimy, disheveled and bewildered-looking Queenie.

"Sorry, miss, I didn't mean to hit nobody,

but they said you was in here," she said. "He's going to be all right, ain't he?"

"Princess Maria is going to be all right, which is all that matters," I said.

CHAPTER 32

November 24
Finally going home. Can't wait.

After that only one strange thing happened, or possibly two. Vlad was locked in one of the old dungeons until the pass was cleared. When the snow melted sufficiently, two days later, the cell was found to be empty. Matty and Dragomir both swore that they had not helped him to escape, and indeed the only way out of that cell block was past a door that was guarded at all times. As far as I have heard he has never been found. And I was awoken one of those nights by what sounded like the flapping of large wings outside my window. By the time I got up and managed to open the shutters, there was nothing to be seen.

Lady Middlesex departed, accompanying Miss Deer-Harte's body home to England. She was a changed woman, subdued and grateful for any little kindness, the bullying and bluster gone out of her like a pricked balloon.

Matty and Nicholas were married as planned a few days later. Nicholas's father decided not to postpone the wedding, decreeing that the period of mourning for the field marshal would begin after his state funeral, which would be conducted with all the pomp and ceremony and, hopefully, appease the Macedonians. I thought Nicholas was being jolly understanding, considering everything, but he seemed to be genuinely fond of Matty and she of him. As we dressed for the wedding Matty drew me aside.

"We're friends again, I hope."

"Of course," I said.

"You don't still think that I sent you down that oubliette?"

"Since you almost fell down it yourself, I have to believe that you didn't," I said. "Vlad must have been hiding and pushed the button after you'd gone past."

"How awful if you hadn't managed to get out."

"It's all right. I'd have eaten Queenie," I said, laughing.

"Poor thing. She was frightfully brave, and she did save you, even if she didn't mean to."

We fell silent.

438

"I couldn't really vouch that Vlad was in bed with me all night," she said. "He could well have slipped out and pushed that English woman down the stairs."

"Or his father did it to protect him. I don't suppose we'll ever know now."

"I don't know what I was thinking," she said at last.

"I do," I said. "Vlad was awfully good-looking."

She smiled sadly. "Yes, he was, wasn't he? And I was alone in Paris and ripe for romance, and he appeared, my childhood playmate now turned into a gorgeous man. And what's more he was no longer a servant's son but a confident man-about-town. I was innocent and self-conscious and no man had ever looked at me that way before. It's no wonder I fell madly in love." She looked at me, pleading for understanding. I nodded. "But I should have seen," she said. "He took too many risks. He courted danger. He has the heritage of his terrible ancestor, after all."

"I think you'll find happiness with Nicholas," I said.

"He has been very understanding and kind," she said. "It could have been far worse. Speaking of which, I'm sorry that you are not going to be my sister-in-law."

439

I haven't yet mentioned that Siegfried and I had a little talk. He told me that after he heard about my wanton behavior with Darcy there was no way he could consider marrying me. I tried to keep a straight face when I said I quite understood and wished him well.

"You realize you have ruined my reputation forever, don't you?" I said to Darcy afterward.

Darcy grinned. "Which would you rather have — a sullied reputation or a lifetime of marriage to Siegfried?"

"So that's why you said it, wasn't it? You didn't really think either of us would be considered suspects in the murder of Miss Deer-Harte. You thought Siegfried would never marry me if he knew I'd spent the night with another man."

"Something like that," Darcy agreed. "My only regret is that we spent that night sleeping."

"I liked it," I said. "It felt so comforting having you beside me."

He slipped an arm around my waist. "I liked it too," he said. "But that doesn't mean I'm not open to other nocturnal pursuits with you, at a more suitable time and place."

"There will be other opportunities," I said.

And so the wedding took place with all

the pomp and ceremony one expects at royal weddings. I wore my tiara and the smashing fur-lined cloak over my Parisian dress. I looked so good that even Mummy was impressed.

"If you weren't so tall you could go to Hollywood and try a career in films, darling," she said. "You have inherited my bone structure. The camera loves us."

Trumpeters heralded our procession down the aisle of the castle chapel. The organ thundered. A choir sang from the gallery and the congregation was resplendent with crowns and dashing uniforms. Nicholas and Matty made a handsome couple. There was only one small thing — she wore a thick collar of pearls, so I never did have a chance to see her neck up close. So I suppose I'll never really know, one hundred percent, whether Vlad really was a vampire or not. But I'll tell you one thing — I was really glad for once to be going home.

Queenie echoed those sentiments as we stood on the deck of the Channel steamer as it docked in Dover. "I ain't half glad to see the coast of good old England again, ain't you, me lady?"

"Yes, I am, actually, Queenie."

Belinda had got wind of a house party at

a villa in the south of France and was headed to Nice. She was going to try the car-breaking-down-outside-the-gates trick again and begged me to come with her. "Think of it: sun, good food, gorgeous men," she had said. It was tempting, but I had turned her down because I wasn't the party-crashing type; also I sensed that Queenie had had enough of being abroad, and I felt it was my duty to get her home safely. Besides, I too longed for the familiarity of life in London, even if it would include Binky and Fig at close quarters. At least I knew where I was with them. At least they didn't grow fangs in the middle of the night. And Darcy had promised he'd be back in London shortly, after a little matter he had to look into in Belgrade.

I glanced at Queenie's vacant moon face. I was actually coming home with a nice amount of money in my pocket, thanks to those roulette winnings. I could afford to pay a maid for a while, especially now that Binky and Fig would be buying the food. I took a deep breath, feeling that I might well regret what I was about to say.

"Queenie," I said, "I'm willing to keep you on as my maid, if you are prepared to learn how a lady's maid behaves properly."

"You are, miss?" She looked thrilled. "I

did all right then, did I?"

"No, you were an utter disaster from start to finish, but you were brave and you didn't complain, and I've somehow grown fond of you. I can offer you fifty pounds a year, all found. I know it's not much, but . . ."

"I'll take it, miss," she said. "Me, going to be a toff's lady's maid. Just wait till I tell her down the Three Bells, what gives herself airs just because she went on that day trip to France and brought back a frilly garter."

"Queenie," I said. "It's not 'miss,' it's 'my lady.' "

"Bob's yer uncle, miss," she said.

ABOUT THE AUTHOR

Rhys Bowen has been nominated for every major award in mystery writing, including the Edgar®, and has won eight, including both the Agatha and Anthony awards. She is also the author of the Molly Murphy Mysteries, set in turn-of-the-century New York, and the Constable Evans Mysteries, set in Wales. She was born in England and lives in northern California. Visit her Web site at www.rhysbowen.com.